Through The Embers - Volume One

Adriana Sargent

SPECTRUM BOOKS

Contents

Trigger Warnings

violence, sexual assault (off page), drinking, on page sex, abuse, war, death, blood and gore, death, sex working, murder, death of an unborn child, loss of a parent/parents.

CHAPTER I

AIFE

Of the four hours I perched on the branch high in the trees, the last thirty minutes were the worst. My legs had finally cramped with the crouch, my back stiff with the hunch, and my calves and feet threatened to jerk me right out of this tree.

But I continued to wait. Even as it snowed; cold, sticky, wet snow that coated my lashes and weighed down the hood of my cloak that did little to stop the angled flakes from assaulting my face.

Slow and controlled breathing, with subtle adjustments, kept my balance and the remaining parts of my sanity. While it hurt, it was the most calming part of my job, even while I sat on the edge of freezing.

Snow that was probably older than I had surrounded me. The terrain in Forgum Woodlands was utterly dead, as it had been for the last three decades. Stuck in a constant state of winter, the woods had to adapt to living without vegetation, though the trees found a way to thrive and continue to grow. Animals and creatures that dwell within survived off bark and the remains of whatever traveled through that had not been prepared for the perpetual cold.

By the time the footsteps reached my ears, I had almost thrown myself to the ground from boredom. The steps were thunderous in the otherwise silent tundra as two males and a female appeared just within my line of sight. Sitting this high up had given me the best vantage point of the ground.

I pulled the bow from around my shoulders and notched two arrows, leveling my sight to where they pounded through the trees like a herd of ornery cattle. The voices carried through the air and broken sentences met my ears.

"...Damita."

"Fight."

"Child."

Angling my torso down, I lined up my sights, took a deep breath, and released the string with the twin arrows. Snow stirred into a cloud as two bodies dropped. The man left alive whirled as I dropped soundlessly onto the forest floor and leaned against the tree I had just inhabited for four miserable hours. He whipped around, un-sheathing his sword, the taste of his anxiety coating my tongue.

"Hello there Cassius," I drawled, picking at my thumbnail with the blade of my dagger.

The sword flipped in his hand as he raised it. Light brown eyes took in my long cloak and the dagger. "Assassin," he sneered, his voice gruff and irritated.

"Glad to see introductions are unnecessary." I pushed off the tree and walked towards him. He shifted back slightly tensing, not dropping the defensive stance. "So, you know why I am here."

"Can't say I do," he grunted, passing his sword between hands and twirled it with a grace that only years of wielding could give. His body towering over mine even with the distance I kept between us, keeping just out of the reach of his strike. He trembled slightly, his eyes looking around for a potential escape.

"Come now, Cassius. Dig through that thick skull of yours and think, otherwise I will have to peel the answers out myself." I angled my head as if the thought intrigued me.

He shifted. "I hear you don't like to play with your food." His voice was hard as he tried to keep the fear out of it. But it was there, right beneath the thick accent, that made him sound as if he were chewing a meaty piece of steak.

"Nasty things rumors," I smirked.

"What you want?" He took another step back, angling his body.

"The Emperor seems to think that you and your cohorts," I motion to the bodies being covered in a thin layer of snow, "are in support of something very naughty." I clicked my tongue and tapped the blade of my knife on my index finger. "I'm just here to see who it was you escorted to Pearl City a few weeks ago."

His already pale face paled even more, fading to match the scars that littered his cheeks. Much like the ones that graced mine, they were old and healed but forever marring the once smooth skin.

"Rumors have you killing the wrong people, assassin."

I threw the dagger at his knee and with a scream he dropped to the ground, blood painting the snow. He kept a hold of his sword with one hand and grabbed the hilt of the dagger with the other as he tried to pull it out. I kicked his hand, loosening his grip on the sword before kicking it out of his grasp completely. Using the toe of my boot, I pushed his hand away from the dagger and pinned his wrist to the ground. Yanking the blade out, I used it to slice up his arm from wrist to bicep. He screamed and tried to grab his arm, but I kneeled and pushed the dagger under his chin.

"Don't lie to me again, Cassius."

"I haven't done..."

I flipped the dagger and slammed it into his already injured leg, through his thigh cutting off his words with another scream that shook snow from the tree branches above. Exhilaration pumped through my veins as the pain and blood loss took their toll on whatever adrenaline he had previously built up. His face was slick with sweat and his hair matted to his forehead as he panted and cried. I reached behind me and pulled the sword from its sheath, and pushed it to his throat.

"I do enjoy a good torture session, Cassius, but I am in a bit of a hurry." I angled the sword tip into his skin until a bead of red colored the tip. "I can take your life quickly, allowing you to join your friends in the afterlife. Or I can do this slowly, making sure that even when you greet death, you remember my name," he screamed as my knee dropped into his freshly cut forearm.

"Marcellus," Cassius yelled, and I pulled the blade back, allowing him to swallow.

"Who is he?"

"Stupid bitch..." he sobbed, his voice carrying over the light breeze and the trees groaned.

"Shhh," I whispered, yanking the dagger from his thigh wiping the blade on his fur covered chest, "do not want to wake the trees. I have the impression you are not telling me the whole truth." I sheathed the dagger at my thigh and lifted the sword to his ear.

"I swear, I don't..."

"Swear to who?" I tried to bite down the frenzy that threatened to pour out of me, that part of me that called for blood and pain, the part of me that thrived in the anger. I knew he was lying. There is always a tell. Something General Zelu had taught me when I first started. No one is a perfect liar, the tells can be minuscule, but the trained eye will always be able to see it regardless of what it was. Cassius's happened to be a little vein right at his jawline that seemed to pop with each fabrication.

His brow furrowed. "What?"

"You said you swear. Who do you swear to? The old Gods? New Gods? The Revolution? The King? The Emperor?"

Cassius hesitated, "I, I..."

"You should swear to me." I angled the tip of the blade to his eye, setting it at the corner. "Because I am the one who holds your life in their hands. No Gods can save you now. I decide how you die. Your life rests with me."

He whimpered, "He's one...one of the Revolution's top!" I lifted my knee from his arm and his face relaxed slightly.

"I think you're being honest with me right now." Moving the blade to his throat, angling it to serve him a quick death. "Thank you, Cassius."

The air buzzed with a nervous energy that bounced around the room. Ripples of magic and fear searing the tip of my tongue as a soft white light illuminated a dozen tributes that stood in the center of the grand hall.

Most of them could not have been older than sixteen, the oldest appearing to be around twenty. The tributes were females collected from cities, towns, and farms within Fursomerra to serve the Emperor. Their lower station was obvious in the hemming and re-hemming of their dresses. Their eyes shifted around the lavishly decorated Ceremony Chamber, passing blindly over the stone pillar that I rested comfortably against. Clean and bathed from my escapades a few hours ago.

Six elder females were positioned at the corners of the hexagon shaped room, at the center of which was a dais. On the dais was a large bronze throne forged from the melted blades of swords and encrusted with jewels that were removed from the hilts of the same. The elder females in the room were all frowning. This was not their first Welcoming Ceremony; and it would not be their last. They anticipated the events as much as the children who had been surrendered by their families.

A loud thud in the back of the room drew my eye. The over-sized oak doors swung open, the guards bowed, deep gold armor reflecting in the light. Emperor Gregorovich sauntered in, his crown a halo of gold, green, and red. His gray eyes slither across the room watching as the tributes bowed, their heads low and dresses bunched in their fists. His answering smile slid down my spine and spread goosebumps on my flesh. Behind the Emperor was his first in command, General Zelu and his advisor, Priestess Josephine.

They made their way down the aisle, the tributes standing as he passed, keeping their eyes trained on the floor. Gregorovich ascended the stairs and twisted to sit on his bronze throne and running fingers along the twin golden eagles on the arms of the chair, each eagle had a black gleaming snake in its talons. The symbol of the Empire. He leaned against the cushioned back of the chair sprawling his legs, completely relaxed as the young females trembled before him.

Zelu and Josephine flanked the throne, Zelu taking the position closest to me, arms crossed and legs spread, a solid wall of terror. His tan skin always seemed to always ripple with the hidden form beneath it, the minotaur that begged to shift. It added to the imposing form that was General Zelu.

I stepped out of the shadows ascending the dais to stand beside Zelu.

"And?" Zelu clipped, not looking away from Gregorovich, who was grabbing a wine goblet from a servant.

"His name is Marcellus," I whispered, his head angling towards me. "As of this morning, he was in Pearl City." He gave me a brief nod, and I stepped back off the dais, perching on the pillar.

Josephine stepped forward, her red dress almost sheer in the candlelight, the very thin panels that draped in a v down her chest connecting just below her belly button and draping to the floor, doing little to hide her body. "Welcome tributes." She lifted her arms in an invisible embrace before clasping her hands in front of her. "Your abilities have honored you to be selected to serve the Parnitus Empire and the Emperor." She glanced at an older girl in front who caught the Emperor's attention. "Most of you anyway," the girl said as she flushed, and a green light flashed at the base of the girl's throat.

Siren.

A laugh boomed from Gregorovich, causing the youngest tribute to yelp in surprise. The siren looked up and gave him a smile that curled my stomach.

I could admit he is an attractive male. Tall, with a strong jaw holding a permanent barely there beard, tanned skin that complimented his short, fluffed dirty blond hair and steely gray eyes with freckles spattering his cheeks. There was a draw to him, pulling people in and making them want to serve, to just be around him. That same draw repelled every instinct within me. Being on the receiving end of his unhappiness could do that to someone. Gregorovich was ambitious. His yearning for power was contagious to all of those who served him.

"I'll have her tonight," Gregorovich said to Zelu, not taking his eyes off the siren, the stubble casting shadows on his jaw.

The porcelain skin of Josephine's hands reddened as she tightened her grip before continuing, "Each of you have been assigned an Elder, who holds the same magic in their veins as you. They will train you to control your powers, emotions, and teach you how to best service the Emperor. Whatever that may entail," an air of discomfort shifted through the tributes.

Over the last ten years since The Great Übernehmen, the great war, Emperor Gregorovich had exercised his power in taking gifted female tributes from throughout the Realm every six months.

"This as an honor," Josephine continued, "being allowed to learn and tutor beneath some of the greatest of your kind. Not learning to control this could hold you back and possibly get you killed in the future," her white eyes flashed beneath the black lace tulle.

Josephine was all sharp lines and angles, red hair curling, stopping just below the slope of her backside. Her body, like her face, was all edges with limited curves. Attractive in a severe way, pointy and angled enough to cut diamonds. "You are misunderstood and must know that once you leave these safe walls, you are no longer protected."

I had to look away from it and instead started to take in the room. I had not been here since the last Welcoming Ceremony, six months ago. New emerald and black tarps covered the walls, the window murals depicting the battles from The Great Übernehmen had been refreshed. The one that always caught my eye was of Gregorovich standing over a pile of burning bodies, holding a detached head wearing a bright silver helmet. A painting of the second battle of the war, the battle of my home, Matrador.

The Emperor made me sit there as it was painted, telling me how he slaughtered my elvish brethren and slit my mother's throat. The head within the helmet belonged to my father. Zelu held my head up as it was being painted, making sure I saw every brush stroke, every detail of my father's death.

I was nine. Young enough to be shaped and molded, and with the gift of elvish blood in my veins, Zelu knew I would make a valuable assassin. So Gregorovich had me thank Zelu for being alive.

The high ceiling held more paintings with beautifully ornate bodies. Naked men and women wrapped in sheer white cloth sprawled on chaises and pressed against trees.

Draped along the ceiling were long chandeliers that sparkled, reflecting rainbows across the ceilings and walls. Striking and extremely deadly. Chains made from Ignis Esuriens, the land of the Dwarves. If someone were to resist and try fighting against the chains, they would tighten enough to cut muscle. If resisted enough, they would sever whatever they are holding onto.

Dirchar Chains.

The false God sat on a throne of thousands of souls.

My palm twitched, my attention snagging to the vein pounding at the curve of his sleek neck. I could easily grab the dagger at my thigh and shove it right beneath his Adam's apple. Gregorovich would bleed out and die so quickly. Well, he would be easy to kill if he were just a mortal. He was a dichotomy if I had ever seen one. Handsome, with a disgusting heart; a kind face hiding the monster underneath and charismatic, hiding the cunning jealousy that simmered beneath his tanned skin.

He was not immortal, but a Siphon, one of the most dangerous gifts someone could possess. One touch and he could take all the magic from someone, take their very being into himself. While it never lasted long, it was a horrible way to die, since magic is tied to the life essence, taking it away forces someone to take their last breath. There was no way to survive it.

His ability tied directly into what I believe his reason for taking the tributes was. While he held such a dangerous power, there was no permanence to it. He would Siphon the powers and use them once, twice if he was lucky, then they were gone. Dozens of tributes have disappeared over the years and while Zelu stood firm that they had been given titles and married off to wealthy nobility as the Emperor had promised, I was offended. For Zelu to think that I was naïve enough to not see right through the lie, to not know that she would have never left without saying goodbye.

Rose, my friend since we both arrived at the castle almost twenty years ago. Whom, along with Joyce, saved me from completely surrendering to the shadows that engulfed my soul. Rose 'left' last year without saying goodbye or even hinting to me that she was leaving. She was more than just my friend.

Josephine's voice cut through my thoughts; the ceremony was about to begin. Tying the tributes to the Emperor meant they would die a terribly slow, suffocating death. Barbaric but genius.

"Seers, step forward." Four girls did as commanded, the youngest of the entire group between them.

"Repeat after me," Joyce said, opening a vial of silver powder. "The power, strength, and mind forever tied to the ruler of these lands. Forever in debt and forever repaying, I will never disobey or conspire against. Emperor Gregorovich has my full obedience as a seer." As the girls repeated, Joyce tipped the vial of powder into her hand, her fingers curling slightly as she blew it over the tributes. A glow emitted from the tributes as they finished the words and Joyce dropped her hands, her mouth set into a firm line as she retreated to her place.

Witches, Nymphs, Sirens, Wraiths, Fairies followed in the ceremony respectively and once again I remained the only one of my kind within this castle.

"Welcome to all of you." Gregorovich stood, straightening his jacket. "I am aware that we have pulled you from your families, from the only homes that you have known, and that you probably hate me! Wish to slit my throat and watch me bleed all over the floor." Silence filled the room as he smiled, his white teeth flashing. "I want you to know that nothing will be done here with ill intent. You will be fed better than you have ever been at home, have a warm bed every night and any comfort you could imagine.

"Your families are cared for during your service here. I do not ask you to follow blindly, nor without compensation. Another war is coming, from the Revolucija. The Visreala who conspired against everything we have worked so hard for! They will not care about anything but killing and destroying what we have worked so hard for. I seek your assistance with this and while you serve me and long after you depart this castle, I offer you protection for your cooperation."

Always enchanting, so charismatic. Polished.

Gregorovich, once again flanked by Zelu and Josephine, stepped off the dais to leave the room. The tributes finally noticed my presence when I followed behind Gregorovich, Josephine, and Zelu.

"Assassin." The whispers followed me as I walked.

Aife, elf assassin that slaughtered families and destroyed countries in the name of the Emperor. I wondered how many of their loved ones I might have sent to the underworld. I winked to them, smirking at the answering flinch.

CHAPTER 2
TITAIA

"I'm working on it," I grumble at the stubborn creature, who was tossing her head impatiently, nipping at my ear as I cleared out the mess from her stall. Koko snorted and shifted her weight from side to side, tapping her hooves, her black mane swinging as she danced. I grabbed the spading fork, throwing some hay onto the floor of her stall, watching her shove her muzzle into it.

I swear she purred.

The barn door opened, causing me to pause. While this was the city's stables, it was typically empty and free of visitors this time of day. I pressed my back against the stall wall as Koko continued to munch happily, ignoring everything, including the potential danger. This horse would probably put me in danger if it meant that she got to eat.

"It smells like horseshit," a sing-song voice broke through the cool air, followed by the click of heels against the wooden barn floor. "And it's cold."

My shoulders dropped the tension that built, and I pushed off the wall, glancing over the door seeing a mass of curly red hair bobbing along the top of the stalls. "You work in a perfectly clean Palace that has stables right outside its gates. I can talk to Prince Brock, and we can get Koko..."

"I do not want her anywhere near that place, Katrina. And I like it down here." I patted Koko. "Closer to the people, and the horses don't talk back." I removed my gloves as she came into view around the corner of the stall, the hem of her light blue skirt peeking out of the bottom of her black jacket and kissing the floor, the dirt soiling the lining. I moved out of the stall and closed it, walking over to the water basin.

"Careful, Duchess, you might get muck on your dress."

She hissed at me, lifting her skirt, and I laughed, pumping the long brass handle twice, dousing my hands in the freezing water that erupted with a slight shiver. As much as I preferred this stable to the royal one, I do wish it shared the same luxuries. Warm water, for instance. I started to wipe my hands on my trousers when Katrina grabbed them between her gloved ones, and I melted into the warmth.

"You are going to get your gloves all dirty," I protested, trying to pull away from her vice-like grip.

"Nonsense, you're going to catch a cold!" She scoffed and dug into her wool coat and pulled out a pair of mahogany brown gloves from her pocket.

"Take these and let's go before the smell ruins my jacket." Of the many things I love about my best friend Katrina, at the top of my list right now is how prepared she always is. The gloves I had been wearing were soaked through and dirty from my work in the stable and with Koko.

"Might be too late for that one." I shoved my hands into the gloves, savoring the warmth. Katrina groaned as we stepped into the chilled winter air. I closed and locked the stable door. Pulling my jacket tighter we started down the cobble path headed towards the beautiful Palace that felt like being locked in a large cage with dozens of rooms and hundreds of other detainees. Giving the twisted illusion of freedom while binding your hands and legs to keep you from ever leaving.

Tall, muted buildings surrounded the cobblestone roads, fit together in a pattern of beauty and individuality. A deception of equality and happiness that brings so many people to the city. The door colors reflecting the ranking of each member that lived there or owned the shops. Red was the highest of nobility, followed by yellow, orange, green, blue, and purple. Creating Aurora Row. A festival of color and livelihood.

We pushed past the Row and into the square where a market was in full swing. Thick crowds bustled around to the small stalls set up. Each stall is lit with a mixture of candles and fairy lights.

Beautiful rugs, handmade jewelry, paintings, dresses, everything one could ever want lined the streets. Each shop owner brought out their finest to gain the business of travelers and new residents. The smell of chocolate and ice cream filled my senses and my mouth watered. I worked too long with Koko and had not eaten in a few hours.

I was starving.

"I love you dearly, Elle, but you never listen!" Katrina pinched my arm, and I yanked away from her.

"For someone so dainty, you have some pretty strong fingers." I pulled up my sleeve to reveal the small red mark that had started forming.

"As I was saying before you rudely ignored me, King Heptus called court for tonight." My heart stuttered. When the King called court without weeks of preparation it meant either great news for the Kingdom and terrible for the realm, or great news for the realm and terrible news for the Kingdom. Which usually leads to bad news for everyone, anyway. Whenever the King, Emperor, Queen, Priestess, and General, or Quinque as they affectionately like to call themselves, got together there was danger on the horizon.

Katrina wrapped her arm through mine as she pulled me to a stop in front of a stall of dresses. Pink, lilac, white amongst many other fabrics lined the hangers. "We do not know what this is about yet," she whispered reassuringly, "but something I know is that we need to get you out of those horrible pants. How about this one?" She held up a stunning lilac dress, a scalloped lacy neckline dropping into a long satin skirt with a high slit.

I glanced down at my green pleated pants, comfortable and practical, and complained, "But they are so stretchy!"

She rolled her eyes before handing the dress to the merchant and before I could protest, said, "We will take this one, add it to my account."

He wrapped it up and handed it back to Katrina, who gestured towards me. I bit my lip and grabbed the bag.

"Thank you!" she said cheerfully to the merchant before threading her arm through mine. We passed through the rest of the market and turned the last corner towards the white stone archway of the Palace.

As impressive as it was foreboding.

Solid white limestone with black pillars forming an archway, leading to a long stone pathway that was suspended over fast-moving water with crushing rocks.

Small black winged Sphinx's lined the path up to the palace, on the other side of which was another archway with gold and iron rod gates flanked with two giant gold dipped Sphinx's.

Awe and terror, the same feelings I had over ten years ago when I first set eyes on it, when Katrina had saved my life and brought me right into enemy territory, flooded my veins. Under the nose of the man who committed genocide to my people and who thinks that I am still alive and wants to crush the rebellion that threatens his power. King Heptus, ruler of the Kingdom of Austiria and the Fursomerra Realm.

It is one thing to know who killed your entire family; it is quite another to live with them. The guards at the front of the archway opened the gates and bowed as we moved between the guarding sphinxes.

"Emperor Gregorovich is supposed to be here as well. He arrived with General Zelu and Priestess Josephine this morning." Katrina squealed in my ear.

I shivered. "That female scares me."

Katrina grunted, "She is but a ghost, a shell of a female. Do you remember the last time she was here? I thought her bones were going to fold in on themselves and turn to dust." She giggled. "But Emperor Gregorovich is a very handsome male."

"Well, you can get in line with the thousands of other girls who grace his bedchamber," I said, disgusted.

"He is a very desirable man, Elle. One night with him...."

"Do not, under any circumstances, finish that sentence."

"Such a prude," she scolded, as we approached the main doors of the castle. "Although I remember a few people passing through your door."

"Katrina," I growled.

She giggled.

"I am just saying." She waved her hands. "I'm just surprised at your judgment when you clearly have some amazing charisma yourself."

"Duchess Katrina, Maiden Elle," the guards at the gate said, and I held back a groan. I hate being called a maiden; it makes me feel like a virgin waiting to be bedded.

"I was hoping this place would have burned down while we were gone," I muttered, looking at the overly white walls, embellished with gold details. The inside of the Palace was just as grand as the outside. Ornamental arched ceilings trimmed in red and gold, intricate gold statues and sculptures lining the entrance hall the majority of which was Sphinx's.

A giant crystal and chain chandelier fell between the two staircases connected by a landing. The floors were covered in a smooth stone, much like marble white with black and gold veining, covered by gold rugs and colorful designs.

Two arches led beyond the staircase on our current level leading further into the palace, double doors stood to the right and smaller ones directly to our right and left. Four smaller statues concealed servants' entrances on either side of the hall, two up and two down.

"We have about four hours before court, go get ready and then I will need your help to change into something more…" she leaned into my ear, her hand circling my bicep, "alluring."

I pried my arm out of her grip and turned on my heel. "You disgust me, Duchess." Her laughter followed me around the curve of the stairwell as I sprinted up the stairs.

Katrina had been a Duchess all her life yet the pressure to maintain that status had become even more important after the Great Ubernehmen, even though she had been engaged since before we were out of diapers.

I stepped into my room. It had enough space for a large bed, dresser, dainty table with two chairs, and a small bathing room. I shed my clothes and washed quickly before putting on the dress Katrina had purchased for me and braiding my hair from one side of my head to the other draping it over my shoulder.

Once done, I headed back to the grand hall and up the staircase to the left. The Palace had many hidden passageways, but I found sometimes the best way to move undetected is to move in the open. The passageways had become an intimate place for the servants to have a break between chores and a favorite patrol for the Kings and Emperor's soldiers, Caeruleus Knights, to take advantage.

My first run in with the Caeruleus Knights had been when I first arrived to Austiria. I had been exploring the city and found myself cornered in an alley by a group of men. The sting of their fists still aches.

I first arrived in Austiria and was walking around and found my way into an alley. A group of men had cornered me. I can still feel their fists on my body, the side of my head, my stomach. It was going to get much worse before someone stepped in. That was Sigurd, one of the Captains in the Caeruleus Knights. He saved, then he trained me, so I would never go through that again. Trained me to fight with swords, knives, arrows, and my fists.

My second run in with the Knights was not as pleasant. They caught me in one of the Palace passageways and I froze. It was as if I had never trained a day in my life, given it had only been a few months since we started. Luckily, another maid stepped into the hall, and I was able to run. Once Katrina heard about the encounter, she had the Knights dismissed, but I still refused to go near them and that was years ago. At this point I found it best to just avoid the Knights all together. Dismissing a few for a single incident is one thing, but I doubt the King and Emperor would be willing to do it again.

I wove in and out of maids and cooks that filled the halls as they rushed to complete last-minute preparations for court. I made it up to the wing that Katrina's room was in, in the same corridor as the rest of the royal family since she was soon to wed Prince Brock. I slowed my run to a walk, my head angled down as I passed a few Duchesses and Dukes that were visiting the Palace. I turned the corner and reached towards Katrina's door when the hair on my arms prickled.

The King rounded the corner before I could open the door and I found myself caught in the hallway with King Heptus, Queen Alhma, and their youngest children; Prince William and Princess Mathilda.

Clenching my jaw, I slid my left leg back, dropping into a courtesy. "Your Highness," I said with gritted teeth. The Queen's gown pushed against my foot, nearly knocking me to the ground as they passed, ignoring my existence. Every inch of my body was on fire with emotions. Even after ten years, the feelings never went away. Hatred, fear, and anger spinning through me like a wheel.

"This is not the time for that, Alhma. We are not ready to attack Hespath. If we move now, we will lose men and the battle. It is still too early; the newest recruits are still too young to even hold a sword," Heptus said.

Alhma scoffed. "I think you are overestimating the power of the realm, Heptus. You can bring this world to its knees with just one glance."

His laugh reverberated in my spine and my foot slid further back, deepening my courtesy to a whole new level of discomfort.

Sigurd had been right. I needed to stretch more. Two small feet stepped into my vision, and someone tapped the hand that was holding my skirt.

"Give it time, my Queen. I promise nothing will keep us from taking what belongs to us."

I looked up to meet the bright green eyes and smiling face of the youngest princess, Mathilda. Her dark blonde hair tied in an elegant wrap around her blue tiara.

"Hi, Elle!" she said happily. I smiled back, my leg cramping as I continued holding the courtesy. Who knew that legs could cramp so quickly? Was I drinking enough water?

"Hello Princess Mathilda, you look very pretty." She grabbed the side of her pink dress, swinging it back and forth. Her innocent green eyes were wide with delight.

I felt Alhma's glare before she spoke. "Mathilda, get away from that filth. You do not know where it has been."

I cast my eyes downward as Mathilda flinched. I watched the pink dress disappear from my line of sight as she moved away.

"Mommy, can I wear a purple dress instead..." her voice echoed down the hall, and I pushed back to my feet, groaning. How could such horrible people create such beautiful, innocent children? I limped past the cramp in my left calf and pushed open the door, only to be met with Katrina's shriek of impatience.

"Well, it is about time! I have been struggling with this damn zipper for two hours!" I blinked and took in the mess she had made in the room. Dozens of dresses lobbed across the bed and floor, shoes pulled haphazardly from the closet and jewelry, expensive jewelry, spread across her vanity and one hung from her bed curtains. I glanced at her reflection in the mirror, where she stood with a glass of wine and her hair disheveled.

"I got caught in the hall with the royal family." Her gaze met mine in the mirror.

"I swear, sometimes they move in slow motion." I grabbed the back of her dress, fastening it into place. Katrina sat at the plush vanity chair, sighing at the look of her hair. We were quiet as she finished her makeup, and I pinned her hair up into an elegant bun. I had always been jealous of her hair, the bright red color, the silky and full curly strands that held whatever style they were put in. I quickly glanced at my reflection in the mirror at my own dull brown hair. Some people are just born with it.

"Perfect," I said.

She looked up, her mossy green eyes darker with the smoky makeup.

"Good, have to make sure the Emperor does not miss me," she said with a wink, adjusting the bust of her deep red dress as if she could make the already ample cleavage show any more without flashing the world her nipples.

"I do not know how you live with yourself and your terrible taste in men."

CHAPTER 3
AIFE

When the Emperor, General, and Priestess had departed for their trip to Austiria, I allowed the hope that I would have a quiet fortnight without an assignment.

I should have known better.

I walked Zelu to his horse while he muttered those damned words, "I have a job for you."

He told me my next mission, mounted his horse, and rode off like the messenger of doom he was. I stood there for a while, even after the horses and carriages disappeared beyond the horizon. The wind nipped at my cheeks while I stared at the frozen stream. Winter was ending. Snow was melting and small bits of powder fell off the trees in clumps. I rested my hand on the hilt of my sword, the metal biting into my skin. It had been a long, frosty winter and the old ladies here loved to say how it was cleansing the realm for change.

I moved down a small corridor and descended a set of stairs into the belly of the castle, into a large circular room. In the center was a red carpet with an eagle and a black snake in its talon embroidered on it, the walls were lined with doors and overhead in the center of the room was another chandelier made of Dirchar Chains, a grotesque reminder to every female within this castle the power Gregorovich had.

This is where the elders and their tributes stayed. Behind each door were lounge rooms with bedrooms rooms paired off. I went for the eye with a half-moon pupil on it.

Seers.

I cracked the door and slid through the opening into the small antechamber. Slow, dragging footsteps reached my ears, and I pressed myself further into the wall.

"Hello, Aife," an aged croaky voice said.

My shoulders dropped. "That is not fair." I stepped away from the wall into the sitting room just beyond. She was hobbling past me, her small body hunched. The room was unsurprisingly empty. Every time the Quinque leave the castle it clears out, everyone taking advantage of the quiet.

"What's not fair is a leaf licker like you trying to scare a vulnerable old lady."

"Feeling a little bit spicy today, Joyce?"

She huffed before hobbling to a pair of emerald chairs that sat in a corner, separated by an ornate table holding a teapot and two cups.

"Don't try to butter me up with tea." The smell of mint drifting in the air, my weakness.

"Who is it?" Joyce dropped herself into the chair with a grunt and grabbed the pot, her black fingers shaking.

"I wish you would see a healer..." she interrupted me with a wave of her hand.

"Leave me and my infinite wisdom alone." She filled the two cups and leaned against the armrest, facing me.

I got comfortable stretching my legs, the chair sucking in my weight. "His name is Angus. Zelu thinks he has been using trade routes through Galvidore to get information about the Kingdom of Austiria and Parnitus Empire. He will be traveling toward Hespath and Zelu wants me to intercept...." I trailed off, noting the pinch in Joyce's face.

I wrapped my fingers around the cup, basking in the warmth. "You know who he is," I stated. Joyce knew everything and everyone, not because she is a seer, but because she has been alive so long she probably remembers the Old Gods disappearing 1,000 years ago.

"Angus is not just any merchant," Joyce confirmed with a tight nod. "He is within the top tier of Revolucija."

Some of my past targets told me about the Revolucija. A group of revolutionists established when Heptus and Gregorovich conquered Doumland, right before my home was destroyed and I was taken. For being in some large revolution, they were easy to break. I was hardly an hour in when they gave me names, names that Joyce asked me to keep from the Quinque. Only for Joyce would I keep information from Zelu to the potential detriment of my own life.

"Their rebellion has grown significantly over the last ten years. New leadership, you know how that goes. Angus works as a merchant to carry information between Austiria and Parnitus, but I doubt that he would go to Hespath with it. Especially since they have finally infiltrated Heptus' court."

I lurched, almost spilling the hot tea on myself. "What do you mean, infiltrated the court?"

"When was the last time you cleaned those large ears, child? Exactly as I said my sisters have someone who King Heptus believes is completely loyal to the cause and holds a position of power."

I considered her. The female who kept me from completely turning over to the darkness. Joyce took me in as her own, always asked too much and never enough of me. She never put up with my, as she called it, 'broody shit.'

"Who?"

"It is not just humans. From what my sisters have told me, they have garnered support all the way from Harenae to Liladon." She met my eyes, "even the Island of Isaldore."

I froze. "Elves?"

Rumors, that is all they had ever been. Rumors that after Matrador was destroyed, the surviving elves settled in Isaldore. I had been taken, and they never came for me; I am not sure they even know I am still alive.

"Yes." Joyce took another sip of her tea, her brown eyes dilated. "It is unfortunate that Zelu has found out about Angus. They cannot afford to lose him. Did he mention how he found out about this?"

"Yes actually. He told me all about his sources and how he finds out all his information, right after he invited me in for whiskey and crumpets and fashioned me a teddy bear from his favorite tunic," I said, deadpan.

"Point taken," Joyce snorted, putting her cup down and grasping my hand from the edge of the chair arm. "I need you to help him. I need another Roman."

"Of course you do. Because that went so well last time. Oh, wait. It did not! I almost died!"

Joyce waved her hand as if my life were of little consequence. "But that means you're an expert now!"

"I got stabbed, old bat!" Her laugh was deep and tinged with evil. "Why exactly can he not know that I am coming?"

Joyce gave my hand a quick squeeze before dropping it and picking up her mug again. "He is a huge fan of yours. If he knew you were coming after him, he would have a challenging time keeping it together. He might actually brag about it."

"Is he a child?"

"He's actually a little older than you."

"Who brags that an assassin has been sent to kill them? He must be unhinged, right? Are you sure you need someone like that in the rebellion? Should I be worried that he is going to try to wear my skin?" I draped my ankle over my knee. "I will stab him, you know, if he tries to peel my skin off. I will stab him a lot."

"I have no doubt of that. Though please try not to, even if he provokes you to."

"Provoke me to stab him?"

"He would wear it like a badge of honor. Stabbed by the famed assassin and surviving to tell the tale."

What a deranged male. I shook my head. "Do you know why they left?"

Her lips thinned. "Whatever the reason, it's not good."

A shuffle outside my door roused me the next morning. Pink light peaked through the small window in my room, sending every signal to me that it was too early to be awake. I turned on my stomach and flipped the pillow to the blessed cool side before dropping back on it. My mind had whirled half the night, taking me that long to fall asleep as I thought about what Joyce had asked me to do. I could not count on one hand how many people I had spared at her behest. Putting my own life on the line consistently. However, it never proved to be an issue. There was always a plan to get them out and have them remain unseen.

The first person whose life Joyce asked me to spare, I had trailed for two days, reconsidering my decision after I dropped them off at the checkpoint. At some point, I decided to let them live, and when I got home, I avoided Zelu for days. Claiming an injury, going as far as to pay a healer to lie about broken ribs for fear that I would crack and tell him everything.

Low voices came from beyond my door, and I shoved my face further into the pillow, flattening it to my ears. I growled, and the voices hesitated before footsteps scurried away. I tried to relax again, to clear my mind and let the peaceful quiet float away all thoughts on white, fluffy clouds. My thoughts crossed to Rose; I was a mess for weeks after she disappeared. Joyce had to keep me away from Gregorovich and Josephine. All I saw was red. I wanted to bleed them dry until they told me where she was and what happened. It took two years to fully accept she was gone.

With a groan, I rolled out of bed and stretched my arms over my head, nails digging into the ceiling before folding over and pressing my palms to the floor. I walked into the tiny bathroom attached to the room, washing the sleep from my eyes and wiping them with a coarse black towel.

I drenched my fingers in my black coal and dragged four fingers down my face. I stopped at the top of my lips, then covered my forehead, pulling the color up into my hairline. A ritual that I had adopted over a decade ago from one of the witches I met after saving her from an incredibly angry Dwarf. She had cursed him so that every gem he touched turned into coal. One thing I know about dwarves is they are profoundly serious about their gems: rubies, emeralds, sapphires. I learned that during one of my torture sessions of them; they are grimy little bastards that have dulled pain points, so finding how to cause actual pain took some finagling. But find it I did.

I walked over to my dresser and grabbed a black travel bag that had been blessed by an expansion spell that gave me endless space and was relatively weightless. It was a gift from Zelu, since my assignments kept me traveling for days. I shoved random items into it and wrapped a black cloak around my shoulders.

Joyce leaned against the wall opposite my room, digging her nails into the worn stones as I closed and locked my door.

"Well, it's about time." She grunted as I donned my hood, taking in her hunched back, thin gray hair, and black wrinkled skin. She handed me a piece of rolled parchment that was tied in a dark red bow. "Give it to him once you find him. Come."

I dragged my feet, following her towards the main hall, shoving the paper into my pack. "I was hoping to stop at..."

"The kitchen I know. Good thing you have elvish blood, otherwise I would have to roll you out of the doors." I scowled; it is not my fault that I liked food. We reached a landing and took a sharp left towards the kitchen until she stopped, opened a door, and signaled for me to enter.

Arching a brow, I said, "Um, Joyce. That is a broom closet."

She stood there staring at me and, with a sigh, I stepped in. The ceiling was so low I had to hunch to fit. Joyce slammed the door shut, facing me.

"Now, since Angus does not know you are coming, there is a phrase the Revolucija uses to recognize each other. I am not sure how quickly he will catch on once you say it. Keep that in mind."

"Reassuring."

"Say, 'I am a traveler in search of a merchant who is selling goods worthy of the King.'"

"Well, that's a mouthful," I murmured.

"Hush, foolish elf. He will say, 'I have no goods worthy of a King, less he would like fresh spirits.'"

"Fresh... spirits?"

"Give him the parchment and escort him to Pearl City. Once there, you are to meet seer Tegan at the Village Inn."

I dropped my eyebrows.

"What is with this revolution and Pearl City?" She stared at me. "Fine, I got it. Can we get out of this closet now? I am catching a cramp." I was not lying. The hunch I had forced my neck into was starting to ache down my shoulder.

Joyce opened the door and stalked her way to the kitchen. Her limp was more evident today and concerned dread filled my stomach, causing my steps to slow. I have tried countless times to ask her how old she was. All it earned me was a smack on the back of the head with a stick that came from Goddess knows where. She had to be a century or two at least, from what I know about how Seers age. The stone floors echoed as we crossed beneath the archway to the kitchen and the delicious smell of food drifted towards me. Fresh baked bread, eggs, bacon, steak.

My mouth watered.

"Joyce." A beautiful blonde female flashed a bright smile as she walked over to the pair of us. The look she gave me tickled down to the bottom of my stomach. "Hello, Assassin." Her accent was a heavy, high-pitched lilt.

"Emily," I responded. From the corner of my eye, I saw Joyce's eyes ping-pong between us, a sly smile on her face before she cleared her throat. Emily was a siren who had been vying for me. Her short blonde hair, beautiful bright blue eyes and sculpted jawline caught my attention, but something had kept me from pursuing her advances.

"I got what ya asked for." She finally looked away from me. I nodded at Joyce in gratitude. While she had a knack for taking care of me, she was always extra attentive when she put my life in additional danger.

How nice of her.

Emily slid a basket wrapped in a white cloth across the counter to me. "Enough food to last at least four days." She rolled her four in an unnecessarily sexual manner and I glanced at Joyce, who had found a sudden interest in a flour bag that sat nearby.

I reached for the basket and Emily's fingers lingered on mine as she smiled shyly at me and said, "Thank you."

"Anytime," she purred before turning and strutting away. I placed the basket on the counter and used the white cloth to wrap the food and placed it in my bag.

"Someone has a crush," Joyce declared as we walked out of the kitchen, stalking our way out of the warmth of the castle into the chilly winter day. She clasped my hands as we passed the threshold, her brown eyes twinkling.

"I won't forget." I squeezed her hand and leaned down, placing a kiss on top of her head. I walked into the stables and called, "Rain."

There was a ticking sound from the furthest stall and hooves tapped the ground. I walked towards his stall and was greeted by a chocolate brown stallion. "There he is." I rubbed on his muzzle, smiling when he nipped at me affectionately. "We have a long journey ahead of us. I hope you are ready to stretch your legs." I brought him to the water trough and laid the blanked over his back as he drank. Joyce gave me this blanket and said it was from my home, Matrador. It was black with a golden border and designs twisting and wrapping around each other in different geometric shapes that she said were Yantra's. Whatever the hell those were. I threw the saddle over Rain's body, and he grunted in displeasure.

"As much as I would like to," I said, and tightened the straps under his belly, "I am not riding bareback for two days straight." I steered him out of the stable and towards the forest at the back of the castle. I climbed on his back, and we took off. The wind bit against my face. Rain's breath sent a fog out, his legs loosening the further we went. I guided him towards the hidden trail and moved easily through the foliage. His ears were twitching as the frozen trees were amplifying the sounds around us.

What the Parnitus Empire lacks in overall goodness, it makes up for in forests and water. Unfortunately, for the people of Parnitus, the forest vegetation has long been polluted. It's unsafe to eat, drink, dig or replant anything within the surrounding areas of the forest. Even in the spring and summer. While Austiria had some good farm grounds, the most fruitful places were those that had not been taken; that did not have innocent blood spilled.

It gave them reason to want to keep taking the lands, and why their eyes were set so firmly on the Land of Hespath. Rumor had it they have the most sustainable lands throughout Fursomerra.

After The Great Übernehmen large sections of Fursomerra were divided between two major rules. The Kingdom of Austiria with King Heptus ruling, and the Parnitus Empire with Emperor Gregorovich as its ward. The entirety of the Realm belonged to Heptus including Parnitus, but he never ventured without Gregorovich's approval or knowledge. A deep bond between the males kept them loyal to each other. Even though Heptus treated Gregorovich as an equal, the King's power far outweighed the Emperor's.

Some of the Kingdom's boarders married Parnitus but there were many lands left unclaimed. Lands they had not been bothered yet to conquer and those that prove to be too difficult to encroach just yet. Like the Hidden Isle, thought to be the original home to the Old Gods. Harenae, Land of Hespath, Isaldore, Foedo were just a few that had yet to be conquered.

My home, Matrador had once been a place of wealth. Elves had a knack for gardening, building, and forging. The Quinque had not known, at the time, that spilling all that elvish blood would taint the land. I guided Rain east, toward Landreasken, a city within Parnitus.

CHAPTER 4
TITAIA

I could practically feel the nerves of the hundreds of people in the room that waited for the arrival of the King and Emperor. The feeling making my blood boil like a hot pot of water. The two males loved to make an entrance and remind everyone who held the true power.

The radiant form in the front of the room was both enticing and repealing the crowd as I worked studiously to avoid Priestess Josephine's wandering gaze. I stood behind Katrina, who was currently giggling into Prince Brock's shoulder like he had told the best story in the entire world. His monotonous voice bored me to tears while Josephine's presence kept me on high alert. It was an exhausting conflict of feelings.

Josephine's narrowed eyes traveled to the other side of the room, and I glanced up with the safety of her distracted gaze. We were close to the platform where Brock would be expected to be, being next in line for the throne. Next in line to a male who is unlikely to ever give up the power of being King, I do not know if even death would take that crown from his thick skull.

Priestess Josephine seemed to have gotten younger and more beautiful since the last time I had seen her more than a month ago. Her skin rosier and the lines on her face smoothed to almost nonexistence.

Josephine's face was so severe in its beauty she was doll like. Her hair swept up into ringlets that trailed down her back, her thin lips painted a deep red like dried blood. It was hard not to compare Josephine to Queen Alhma, who stood beside her. They had the same sharp features, hooked noses, and penetrating stares. A stare that could see right through your soul and burn it alive. My spine prickled at the thought. If either had the opportunity, they probably would burn anyone and everyone alive.

Josephine's eyes were completely white and Alhma's were purple and hazy. The purple being the signature of a druid, and the haziness signifying that she had been disowned from her clan. I did not know what the white of Josephine's eyes meant; I had never found anything written in our texts or seen anyone with similar eyes.

Standing on Josephine's other side was the haughty General Zelu, his armor shining with the Eagle emblazoned on his chest as he held it out proud. His blond hair cut short to his head made him seem almost bald, but he was still unnervingly handsome.

And very intimidating, as most shapeshifters are.

Guard Nikolas's voice echoed throughout the room. "King Heptus and Emperor Gregorovich." Everyone shifted towards the door, bodies lowered into bows and curtsies as two sets of footsteps tramped into the room. The intensity in their strides was similar, even with the difference in power.

"Heptus, these celebrations get bigger by the hundreds every time I visit!" Gregorovich's voice caressed every bone in my body. Inviting, sexy, and charismatic. Katrina inhaled sharply as we held our bows, waiting for them to move past. She is a female obsessed; I would prefer her to be obsessed with Zelu. At least he keeps his conquests secret.

"Look at you, Brock," Gregorovich said as he approached. We rose, but I kept my head low. The hair that fell from my braid cast my face in a broken shadow. Through my lashes, I watched Gregorovich throw his arm around Brock, embracing him in a way that had Katrina nearly bouncing in hopes of being on the receiving end of that soon.

"It has been a month, Greg," Brock responded with pink cheese as he returned the hug. "I trust you remember my fiancée, Duchess Katrina." The corner of his lips tugged down as Gregorovich turned towards his betrothed. No need to wonder why with how Gregorovich's eyes raked over her body, intimately and hungrily.

"She is still too beautiful for you, young man." Gregorovich's voice was velvet as he grabbed her hand and pressed his full lips to her fingers.

"She definitely is." Brock's smile did not reach his eyes as he pulled her firmly to his side.

"You are too kind, Emperor." Goddess bless Katrina and her ability to move through any interaction. Her hand was still in Gregorovich's. He caressed her knuckles, and I watched Brock's eyes narrow in on the touch. His fingers dug into her side; the boning of her corset bit into her skin. I wonder if Gregorovich knew what trouble he had just brought Katrina. Brock was no fool, knew exactly how desirable Katrina was and was very jealous of anyone, male or female, who showed her attention.

I felt Gregorovich's gaze hit me like a thousand weights as he asked, "And who is this stunning creature?" I flinched against his cold hand as he ran it down my cheek and I dropped my eyes to the floor, focusing on a gold swirl of my shoe that disappeared beneath the hem of my dress.

Katrina tensed and said, "She is my lady-in-waiting, Emperor. You have met her plenty of times before." Her fingers twitched, trying to signal me away, but my body had suctioned to the floor, my breathing coming in short bursts.

"I'm sure I would remember someone like you." His fingers traced down my cheek to my chin and he forced my face up to meet his gray eyes. I was frozen for a few seconds, shocked by the strength of his eyes, before I flicked my eyes back down to the tip of his boots. He growled in approval of the subservience and heavy iron fell into my gut.

"Enough of this, Gregorovich, let the little whore go on without fear of your advances." Heptus grunted, continuing towards the dais. Gregorovich ran a finger across my lips before grabbing my hand and placing a light kiss to it and following Heptus.

My breathing was ragged as I tried to regain control of my body, fighting the urge to wipe my hand on my skirt to rid the feeling of his lips. It felt like my blood had been replaced with ice, the feeling leaving me chilled and uncomfortable. Gregorovich had never shown an interest in me before, never glanced in my direction or noticed when I was in the room.

I felt the hostility of Josephine's attention and every cell in my body was fighting against meeting her eyes. While Gregorovich had never shown Josephine, she seemed to be infatuated with him, and I wanted to distance myself from anything and everything. Not just for the fact that I had absolutely no interest in him, but for the extra danger it would bring me.

"I know you are all wondering why we have brought you here, especially on such short notice," Heptus started.

As he spoke, I looked over at the Quinque, the most powerful people in the realm of Fursomerra.

Heptus sat in the grandest of the four thrones. Made of black Rhodium, the back was tall with five points shaped into arrows, the tallest in the middle and getting smaller the further away it went. The seat was the softest black velvet with gold and silver stitching and two sphinx bodies for arm rests with the faces pointing out to the crowd.

Gregorovich's throne was also made of Rhodium but much less grand. Alhma's was noticeably smaller, Zelu stood, and Josephine might as well have been sitting on a bench.

There is no doubt in my mind that Queen Alhma is responsible for that. Both Alhma and Heptus find different beds to occupy most nights, but Alhma is a very jealous female. She had to show who held true power to anyone attractive who caught her husband's attention for too long. The first time I saw her exercise was when someone made their way to Heptus' chambers without her knowledge. The female, Helen, had been level-headed and sweet before she went to his bed. When I saw her the next day, she was being dragged out by Palace guards while she screamed and ripped her hair out at its roots.

Heptus only took Alhma to his bed for a month after, and that is when the middle child, Princess Erin, was conceived. I had been here for a year at that point, and I am still convinced there is some twisted foreplay between them.

Regardless, I made sure to keep my distance. She may have been disowned by her druid family, but they had taught her how to hone her magic in the most dreadful ways.

"We are one step closer to the destruction of the biggest threat to the crown, the threat that is Hespath," Heptus said, the smile that lifted his face portraying a promise of danger and pain. His green eyes, so stark against his deep brown skin, sparkled with triumph and excitement.

Gregorovich stood and looked towards the back of the room. "Bring him in," he ordered. Nikolas snapped to attention and walked out the door, whilst saying, "The Parnitus Empire has been working diligently to find a way to conquer those who try to disrupt the peaceful existence that we have grown accustomed to these last ten years."

"We have been fighting opposition from those who do not see the importance of what we are doing. Peace and unity throughout Fursomerra, giving land and money to those who deserve it. Putting the weak humans and lesser beings in their places, keeping them from taking what is ours." Gregorovich's hands flourished as he spoke. There were shouts of agreement around the room. "To find healthy land to cultivate and better the world, to make it to the other realms. Realms where those who have been made to serve do just that. Serve the true born leaders."

"This revolution being led by the seers from Hespath must be stomped out before they disrupt our lives even more!" Heptus added.

The sound of chains being dragged pulled my attention to the back of the room and I sucked my cheek between my teeth. Two guards led a prisoner through the center of the room to the platform where the Quinque stood together.

The male's head hung low, his shaggy brown hair covered his face and his bare feet dragged behind him. His tunic was drenched in blood and blue pants were tattered. A whimper escaped his mouth as he was thrown on the ground before the dais.

"Pathetic," Josephine growled, crossing her legs. The split of her dress exposed the top of her thigh. Alhma threw her a look before turning her attention back to the prisoner.

"This child," Gregorovich said as he squatted, his red cloak spreading around like a pool of blood, "has some unbelievably valuable information about how to infiltrate the Land of Hespath. Go on, tell the court how you betrayed your King and Fursomerra. Tell them what you know about the seers."

The male lifted his head, his brown eyes wide and surprisingly gentle as he looked around at the crowd.

Gregorovich snapped his fingers in the prisoner's face. "Look at me, boy."

The male's lips twisted, and he spit on Gregorovich's robes. Blood and saliva splattering.

Gasps spread across the crowd.

The King was on his feet; a violent pulse of his fury emanated through the room as his full seven-foot figure appeared to grow before us, in height and muscle. His face changed as he stomped down the dais stairs. His black hair faded into a deep gray, his nose lengthened and sharpened, ears grew and pointed straight up, rising to peek over his head. Heptus' body shook with pain and rage as he morphed from man to Sphinx.

The prisoner whimpered and slid backwards, trying to move away from the monster that stood only feet away. It had been a long time since Heptus had shown his true form. The form that proved why so many fell to his feet in his struggle for complete control.

The power and strength that radiated from him was staggering, leaving a feeling of suppression and a desire to bow to him.

The power that was unmatched and unyielding.

Gregorovich had a silky smile aimed at the shocked faces in the room until his steely gaze met mine. His pupils expanded before he sent a wink that made my stomach roll and forced me to look away.

"It is quite alright, old friend," Gregorovich said, placing a hand on Heptus' shoulder.

Heptus' face reverted to the otherworldly beauty that hid a monster. His face was a balance between beautiful and hideous. The truth beneath his strength hid under a thin layer of camouflage. The real reason Gregorovich would never make a move against Heptus. He may be powerful in his own right, but he would never stand a chance against the most powerful Sphinx to ever live. Anyone who fought against Heptus died, and he enjoyed every bone he broke from their bodies.

Where Gregorovich was grace and hidden ferocity, Heptus was all brutality. He had not earned his crown from politics. No, he spilled blood across the realm to ensure that glittering crown sat atop his head.

Heptus had always been in line for a throne, just not the throne he wanted. He came from one of the royal families holding one of the most powerful bloodlines. It was no surprise his callous father sired such a male. Although, Heptus' father ruled with the fear of the Gods and Goddesses, Heptus fancied himself one. And why would a God only rule some of the land when he could rule it all?

Alhma watched her husband, her face etched with concern, while Josephine's pale features glowed with happiness.

"You should speak truth before you anger the King beyond how you already have. I am not sure he would entertain my request a second time." Gregorovich said through a chuckle, as flippantly as if they had shared a joke.

Heptus returned to his seat, his fingers digging into the Rhodium Sphinx as the metal warped beneath his grip.

"I am not a traitor," the boy whispered. "I am Marcellus, from the Land of Hespath."

A mocking laughter blew across the room.

"There are no children in Hespath, it is a dirty land full of filthy barren woman. Barren because they turned their backs on the one true god," Brock shouted from beside me, and I imagined Katrina slapping the back of his head.

Heptus's dark laugh filled the room, his regality barely covering the still festering anger. "Well said dear Prince, but do continue with your gripping tale boy."

"It is true," the boy confessed. "The seers of Hespath are barren. My mother dropped me when I was young. I am from Doumland."

I shivered at the name. Doumland was one of the most destructive and bloody conquests during the war. Not because of the fight they put up, but because it was the first to be conquered. Everyone, including Heptus and Gregorovich, had something to prove and no limits to their anger and twisted belief of honor. The people of Doumland were human and, having no real defense system, were destroyed quickly and brutally.

There were no survivors from that fight. The human race was almost eradicated. Aside from Matrador, Doumland remained the most tyrannical wins of Heptus.

Before The Great Übernehmen our realm had found peace between humans and us, the Visreala, those who have magic. There were five Kingdoms: Engrich, Doumland, Zane Republic, Island of Isaldore, and Galvidore. The overarching rule was Galvidore. After taking the rest of Fursomerra, the Quinque turned their sights on Galvidore. Killing or turning all the allies that would have ridden to Galvidore's aid and murdering the last of the true rulers of the realm.

"So, you're from Doumland." Gregorovich chuckled, glancing at Heptus. "That had to be my favorite battle from the war. What do you think, Heptus?"

"It is where I got my first battle wound." With a serpentine grin, Heptus patted his knee where a deep scar ran from the side of his thigh across to the bottom of his knee. Courtesy of an enchanted blade from one of Doumland's human princesses, one of the most fearsome warriors in Fursomerra. Or she was until Heptus gutted her and spiked her head to his battle flag.

"Why don't we give him a taste of what he missed while he cowered with the seers, Gregorovich?" Heptus said and I felt the Emperor's magic spear into the room, groping and taking whatever power he could. There was a ghost of objection from the crowd, but before it could be voiced, Marcellus was screaming. Bile swelled in my throat as Marcellus' arm was separated from his body. His blood began to seep from him in earnest, and a few people fainted from the sight. I was unable to look away from the horror that filled his face as he tried to grasp his missing limb.

Most in this room are beneficiaries from the power the King and Emperor granted them. I could probably count on one hand how many participated in the war. Preferring to send their soldiers while they hid beneath the ground in chambers. Thinking the dirt could protect them from the wrath that would have come. That should have come.

That is true power though, isn't it? Sending others to fight the wars you agreed to participate in? Seeking the benefits while your people return home, if they have one anymore, weak, and unable to recover because of the hunger and living conditions you leave them in. Marcellus' screams reverberated through my skull, bringing forth memories and images of the destruction of my home. His screams echoed out by those from another time.

Fire stretched through my limbs, a weak flame pushing into my palms. It felt like coming home, like waking up after a long nap. It was invigorating until fingers wrapped around my arm and jerked me back.

"Stand behind me," Katrina whispered harshly in my ear, her voice tight and I could barely hear her over the screams. "Remember who you are." She pushed me behind her and repeated, "Remember where you are."

Katrina stepped forward next to Brock, who looked hungrily at Marcellus. I took deep breaths, in my nose, out my mouth as I tried to place my thoughts together.

One. I am Elle.

Two. I am lady-in-waiting to Katrina.

Three. I am in the Kingdom of Austiria.

I glanced down at my fingers; the tips were red, and I balled them into fists, pushing them into my dress pockets.

Four. I am with the enemy.

Five. They do not know who I am.

I repeated it; *one. I am Elle. Two, I am maid to Katrina. Three, I am in the Kingdom of Austiria. Four, I am with the enemy. Five, they do not know who I am.* I repeated it again, silencing the screams in my head and extinguishing the flames in my blood.

There was pandemonium in the room as I returned to the present. Heptus and Gregorovich appeared to be reveling in it, smiling, and laughing as Josephine stood over Marcellus, her mouth moving fast. The wound from his missing arm stopped bleeding and angry new skin formed over it. Alhma stared at Josephine as she worked, her eyes sparkled with jealousy and envy.

"That's enough," Heptus said. Josephine stopped and turned. Her dress glittered in the light as she inclined her head to Alhma and sat back in her tiny throne. Heptus walked to Marcellus, flanked by Gregorovich.

"There is a part of me that hopes you are not ready to talk yet. I am feeling blood hungry tonight," Heptus snarled.

Marcellus was pale and flinched as they approached. He had lost so much blood I was surprised to see him still conscious.

I put my fingertips together and brought them to my lips. "Viribus," I whispered and blew gently, granting him strength. His body straightened and with wide eyes he looked around the room for the source, for the magick.

With a cough, Marcellus turned back to the King and Emperor who stood before him. "It takes a blood sacrifice to get through the gate."

"Did you hear that, good friends?" Gregorovich's voice lifted with excitement. "Why would such a friendly land require a blood sacrifice to seek solace and freedom?" The court shouted in agreement. The brutality forgotten, even some servants nodded in agreement.

I tasted a hint of copper and realized I had bitten through my lip. I had hoped he would not share any information, that he would rather die than give up the secrets of the seers. Katrina glanced back at me and wrapped her icy hand around mine and I returned her hold, greedily seeking solace in my friend.

"A land that claims to be peaceful and worked in the best interest of Fursomerra requires a deadly burden for entry. Land that is rich in fertile ground and healthy food, yet they keep it from those most in need. What kind of creatures would do that? Allow Fursomerra to starve because they refuse to bow to the rightful King and Emperor. To the true Gods."

Marcellus went to object; Gregorovich noticed and signaled to Zelu. In a blink, Zelu was behind Marcellus, a dagger in hand and embedded into the males' neck.

Marcellus fell. Dead.

Katrina had turned and pushed her head into Brock's shoulder, who did not comfort her. His arms were crossed, a bright, satisfied smile on his face. In his eyes, justice had been served. Many females and males averted their gazes from the scene.

Mine, however, was glued to Marcellus, his eyes that had been so aware stared vacantly at me.

In his death, he had finally found an ally.

CHAPTER 5
AIFE

Landreasken, one of the biggest cities within Lorngastein, contained four noble houses, some of the oldest in the realm. House of Bathengal, House of Lathargden, House of Xander, and House of Jagdane; given their titles by Gregorovich after their assistance with the Great Übernehmen. Lorngastein is one of the biggest trading routes, given its centralized location to both the Empire and Kingdom. It took me the entire day to travel to Landreasken since I avoided the main roads. It is best not to let anyone know my travel plans until it is too late for anyone to hide.

Go in unseen, get out unseen. It gives the Emperor a degree of deny-ability, if no one sees me it cannot be traced back to him. If it cannot be traced back to him, he can maintain his self-proclaimed 'hero' status. Pointing the finger at me also meant acknowledging the dirty side of Zelu and Gregorovich, which in turn meant Heptus. And at least right now, no one was that stupid.

Snow gave way to green and lush grass. Lorngastein was in a constant state of summer and sat in a valley between the base of two mountains, surrounded by a vast woodside. Impeccably designed buildings and concrete roads containing shops filled with clothing, armor, and food.

Sunflowers surrounded an elaborate gazebo within the Central Square, the Kingdom and Empire's flag flying beside each other in a symbol of unity. The sun hit the surrounding building's windows, sending rainbow lights all over, giving the center an ethereal glow of happiness and beauty. While covering up the poverty and brothels that lay just around the corner where buildings were made from what was available; leftover wood and branches with roofs made from hay and straw.

I guided Rain toward the stable, my cloak shadowing my face from the lights. A boy ran out of the stable, grabbing the reins before addressing me as I dismounted. "Evenin' Miss! Stall fo' the nigh'?"

"A few nights, thank you." I covered my snort and flipped a coin to his outstretched hand, grabbed my bag, and gave Rain a goodbye pat. He grunted at me, ready for the saddle to be removed and to rest.

"What are you? Some kind of assassin or something?" the boy asked, his large eyes spying the knives belted at my waist.

I leaned down, shifting so the sword on my other side flashed in the light, grinning as his jaw dropped. "Now would not that be something? Make sure you take care of Rain."

The Abyglatory's Tavern sign swung crooked, the black wood barely hanging on as I faced the tattered red door. The familiar sounds of drunken laughter and mugs slamming on tables drifted through as I entered.

Immediately greeted with cigarette smoke and musk that clung to the air. Card games ending in fights with fists being thrown and money exchanged. Half-dressed bodies dragged drooling fares up the stairs, their counterparts draped over other males, faking giggles.

I forgot how much fun these places were.

"I need a room," I said to the burly, mustached man behind the counter.

"How many nights, love?" He wiped a dirty mug with an equally dirty rag, his eyes twinkling as they looked at me.

"One."

"Just you?" I raised a brow and noted the smirk beneath his graying mustache. He reached under the bar, setting a key with the number seven engraved on it.

"What's on for tonight?"

His tongue darted across his lips before he responded, "Meat stew."

"I'll take it and an ale." I took the empty stool and watched as he poured the drink into one of the relatively cleaner glasses. I took a long sip, basking in the cold liquid as it slid down my throat. While I am normally a whiskey drinker, something about an ale in little shitty taverns in little shitty towns is perfect. Malty and delicious.

"Here for some fun, darling?" a beautiful black woman asked as she leaned into me; bright pink wings peaked over her shoulders as she pressed her chest against me. I wrapped an arm around her waist and her scent filled my nose; beer and smoke as she gave me a knowing smile, her hand clenching my thigh.

"As enticing as that sounds, I am unavailable tonight," I replied and ran a hand up her arm, replacing the strap of her dress back on her smooth, dark shoulder.

Her head dropped on my chest in a pout. "Pity," she murmured before using my shoulder to push herself up and striding, or rather, stumbling away, giggling, as she was yanked into the lap of another female patron.

The barkeep placed the food before me and nodded towards the woman. "No company for you tonight?" he asked in a gruff voice.

I ignored him and grabbed the drink and food, offering a cursory, "Thank you."

The wood creaked beneath my weight as I walked up the narrow staircase. A mixture of real and forced moans followed me up as patrons and workers trailed off into empty rooms while I made my way to the third floor. The number seven was etched into the wood and painted a bright yellow. The room was small and damp and smelled of smoke, mold, and a questionable underlying stench that I decided was best not to decipher.

A single bed sat in the corner of the room covered in a pink and white patched quilt, mismatched pillows, a ripped headboard, a heavy white curtain covered the single window, and a blue table with a chair sat in the opposite corner. The sound of laughter seeped through the window as I set the food on the table and bag on the bed. I closed the door, twisting the lock, which was pathetically loose. Pulling off my hood, I rested my hand on the tarnished surface.

"Tamoliv ramore utopa ta." My palm warmed on the knob, a glow emitting from it. After close calls with males who tried to take advantage of a female traveling alone, Joyce taught me a few spells to keep myself and others safe. Those close calls let me know that the look the barkeep gave me meant I needed to protect myself. And while I could take that barbaric male with minimal effort, I needed sleep.

The chair felt like it was going to collapse beneath me as I sat and started eating the stew. In my years of staying in establishments like this, I learned to never ask what the meat was, how the food was made, or who made it. When I first started doing these tasks, I was too young to fully appreciate any food was good food if you were truly hungry. I did learn early enough that the drinks were always good, though.

I thought back to my conversation with Joyce as I ate; that the Revolucija had become an organized threat. The Quinque had always downplayed potential threats, making it seem minimal and working to discredit anything led by the seers. Throughout my travels, I had heard the whispers of how they were recruiting, stealing, and spreading their word, creating dissent. Words to shame the Kingdom and Empire and everything they stood for, which is surprisingly easy given the number of people within the realm that have been suffering in the twenty years since the start of the war; even more-so in the ten years since the war when the pledges proved false. The promise that their lives would improve showing as false as the male who sat upon the throne.

The Quinque claimed that they were working to improve the existing living standard, which never guaranteed improved living conditions for those who actually needed it, only bettering those who were already succeeding, making them wealthier. Those who were deemed lesser Visreala, and humans were lower than they had ever been. Witches, nymphs, and even goblins treated as slaves subjected to the back breaking farming and substandard spell work and apothecaries, being forced to serve in the guard. All in fear of the one who now called himself God, the idea that his power could be considered anywhere near where the Gods is laughable.

But the stories of the true Goddesses and God's powers faded from history, erased by the very male who claims himself one. If he truly had been on that level, why did he feel the need to eradicate an entire race of Rulers? Phoenixes were the rightful heirs over all of Fursomerra, their abilities reaching as close to the Gods and Goddesses as possible.

When I was younger, I read that the Ancient Ones tied their powers together. Thousands of years ago, when the first Phoenix rose from the ashes of a fallen Deity and Goddess who died after being betrayed by their lovers. He became the first and only Visreala born fortuitously. The Great Goddess took him in and raised him. When he was old enough, she allowed him to rule the realm. However, with the pushback from her siblings and children, she decided to divide the world into three; Holuranda, Fursomerra, and Pomulola.

Separated by thousands of miles of water with impassible weather and monsters, there had never been contamination between the realms in the thousands of years since their creation. Though Heptus has eluded a few times that he wants to; needs to. His war destroyed the very foundation we stand on. Blood seeped too far into the dirt, it made farming impossible. Survival falling into the possibility of crossing that ocean.

Gregorovich and his charming lies helped convince a majority of Fursomerra that the pain and loss of their families and the land was because of the Phoenix bloodline, the Normaran's. Nothing was bad before Heptus. Somehow in the four years before his war, Fursomerra fell into a horrendous amount of debt. People were starving, and the Realm was in disarray.

Regardless of whatever the Normarans did, they could not fix it.

When it came time to take Galvidore, they were also fighting in anger that their lands had been destroyed. Galvidore was attacked without anyone to come to their aid because all of their allies had been turned against them. The entire royal family should have been killed, effectively ending their entire bloodline...rumor had it, though, one survived. One that had been hunted ever since.

I dropped onto the poorly cushioned bed, the springs pressing sharply against my body, and I stared up at the torn ceiling. A shuffle in the hallway and the sound of the lock releasing reached my ears. A body pushed against it, but the door did not budge. A frustrated grunt and wood creaking beneath the weight of the body. I chucked the dagger into the center of the door, embedding it halfway. There was a yelp followed by the sound of a hasty retreat, and my door stood silent once again.

Predictable.

Pathetic.

Infuriating.

I sat up. This was not the first time I had experienced the disgusting traits of some males. In the past, I would let these instances pass and find another time to come back and settle the score. But I wondered how many other females had gone through this and did not get away? How many before me, and how many would face the stench of unwanted advances after me? I teetered on the cliff of indecision with my lip between my teeth before I donned my cloak, grabbing the handle of the door, and uttered, "Guiere."

I yanked the dagger from the door and paused. I had never been one for impulse. Simple tasks often took me hours to plan. When I was younger, I made one mistake. One mistake that caused my face and body to get carved up like a holiday pig. I am sure Heptus would have loved to stuff me with cotton and mount me on a wall.

It took months to recover, and I had not acted on impulse ever since, tracking the way in and out of every room I was in.

This dwelling had three exits. The front door that I had entered, one through the back for the unsavory creatures to escape for emergencies, and the one through the kitchen cellar.

The noise rose from the bar as I crept down the stairs. Since he was unable to get me, there was every possibility the barkeep would force himself on someone else. Half of the two dozen tables were full; the barmaid sang, and the entire room was focused on her, including the very male I was after. I moved to the bar, shrouded by darkness in the corner. I sat down and slammed the tip of my blade into the counter.

The bar keep jumped, his eyes flicking to the dagger before looking at me. Unease clouded his brown eyes as he asked, "Wha' can I do for ya?"

"That's a great question." My voice was as cold as the hilt of my dagger as I curled my fingers around it. The cool metal comforted me as anticipation tickled my nerves. "Safety, security, a restful night's sleep without fear of being assaulted."

His eyes darkened, and he tilted a shoulder in indifference. "I'm not sure what you mean..."

"Do not lie to me." Pulling my dagger out, I hopped on the bar and kicked the center of his chest, making him stagger back. Before he caught his balance, I pushed one foot from under him and he dropped to a knee. Stepping on his thigh, I shoved my forearm into his throat and tilted his head with my blade, forcing him to meet my eyes. A sharp thrill shot through me as blood dribbled down the serrated edge.

"No one would save you even if they noticed." My blood thrummed with power and anticipation. The room's attention had been dragged to the barmaid; her beautiful voice an octave higher than it had been.

"Do you have any idea who I am?"

"Some crazy bitch," he spat.

I barked a laugh. "I could have killed you with the blade I threw at my door earlier if I had wanted to."

"Is tha' supposed to scare me?"

My eyebrow lifted and I shook my head, my hood falling off. His bushy black brows furrowed, but recognition flared when I tilted my head, parting my hair over the long-pointed ears.

"Assassin," he whispered, genuine fear filling the word.

I grinned, all teeth.

"Yes, but I prefer Aife so make sure you tell whoever you greet in death who sent you." I palmed the hilt and shoved the blade into his throat. There was little resistance as I anchored my body against his, shoving it until I felt wood splinter behind him. Blood seeped across my hand and floated up my arm as I watched life leave his eyes, satisfaction filling my blood.

CHAPTER 6
AIFE

I left the inn early the next morning partially to situate myself for the chase ahead, partially to see the aftermath of taking the life of the barkeep. No one said anything about it, and when I left, the body was gone and blood wiped away, no traces of someone being murdered. He would hardly be missed. I picked at my nails with my dagger and scanned the busy market from my place against the stone wall.

It was too early for people to start shopping, but the square was still bustling as merchants set up. Visreala and humans alike preparing to sell their goods to whatever customers would show. Bracelets, crystals, clothes, and food brighten the otherwise blandly colored yard.

I knew the market would not be anywhere near as busy as it had been on my last visit a few months ago. The Quinque had been steadily raising taxes over the years and it seemed to have finally hit the wealthier classes.

Prices are higher and goods are not of the quality they used to be. The merchants also looked worse for wear. Their best clothing for a day on the market was not what it used to be. Littered with holes that they attempted to repair and worn shoes with loosened soles. Heptus and Gregorovich were aware of the suffering their people were going through, but somehow, found a way to keep them satisfied with their promises. It was a fluctuation of good and miserable, the good keeping the people well enough to not rebel, the miserable lasting just long enough to keep them jaded but too weak to do anything threatening. At least not yet.

Directly next to me, an older woman threw a deep red linen on the table she set up. Smoothed the creases before she walked back to her small wagon and pulled out a multicolored bag. Nutmeg, sage, and lavender wafted around to me.

I glanced at the table and watched her set out jars of Star Anise, Wolfsbane, Mugwurt, and Jasmine, among many other spices. Bowls of crystals were lined up, sending rainbow light around her. She hobbled toward me, and I straightened, sheathing my dagger. With a grunt, she reached out and dropped a cool black stone into my palm.

Obsidian.

I met her eye and even though my face was shrouded in darkness beneath my hood; I knew she could see my raised eyebrow.

She winked and said, "You look like you could use one of those." She was back at her table before I could respond. I put the stone in the hidden pocket inside of my cloak, smoothing it, so it melded into the fabric.

The sun had peaked over the highest building in Landreasken by the time shoppers emerged and started working their way through the market. I joined them, taking in what the merchants had to offer. This was once the best market within Parnitus. This city used to be one of the richest. But there was no silk, gold, or the finer luxuries anymore. It seemed the most essential were being brought and bartered. Faces were flushed with anger and hunger. Some were muttering curses beneath their breath and bartering in languages I barely knew. I stopped in front of a particularly enthusiastic wheat merchant when I caught sight of him.

He blended in well with the crowd, perusing as he edged around unnoticed. Anyone who knew what they were looking for would be able to see the trained bulk of his muscle. Angus was very tall, maybe slightly taller than I was. He carried a thick black leather bag that was slung over his shoulder, but he held against his side with a casually draped arm. I backed into the shadows along the wall and watched. The sun caught his white, blond hair as he looked around, weaving his way through people to the table I just abandoned and handed the man a few coins before grabbing a loaf of bread.

He approached a human man, shook the merchant's hand, and I watched a piece of paper pass between them. The merchant shoved it into his pocket before tossing Angus an apple. Lifting his hand in cheers, he took a bite. With a grin, he strolled out of the market into the alleyway that led to the forest. His body was moving in a pompous feline way. I wonder how upset Joyce would be if I just killed him.

On accident, of course.

Blowing out a deep breath, I tightened my cloak and stalked behind him, the shadows curling around me keeping prying eyes away.

He practically ran through the alley, emerging into the open-air heading to the forest. I waited until he

breached the tree line before following, approaching at an angle slightly away from where he entered
and scaled a low tree, and using a thick branch,
pulling myself into the canopy. His hair shined like
a godsdammed beacon, making it easy to find him
in the lightly shaded forest. He all but skipped mer-
rily, munching on his apple. His footsteps were sure
enough to let me know he had taken this path many
times in his life. Shadowing his movements above, I
kept behind him, passing birds and squirrels who remained unaware or apathetic of my presence. Tossing
the apple core, he dug into a side pocket of his bag,
ripped away a piece of bread, and ate as he walked.

After about two hours, the dense wood cleared into
a small opening, and I slowed as he stopped close to a
stump and flopped on the ground. There was always a
certain rush to hunting, being able to watch someone
at their most vulnerable and most honest without them
knowing. True colors always show when people think
they are alone. Everyone has secrets and while my job
has never been to necessarily know those secrets, it is
hard not to listen to the whispers, the moments, and
the actions of them. Sure, I extracted what I could from
some; it was not the main goal of my job.

There were some people that had a heightened
awareness, the tingle that sent of sensors into their
brains to alert them of danger, or the feeling of being
watched. Seeing their paranoia rise, they try to figure
out the cause of the sensation, or if their mind was
playing tricks on them.

I will never understand how someone can be so
oblivious to danger, especially when it is breathing
down their neck.

Sometimes I wonder if I would have grown into this
even if I was not taken from my family. I was a child

when I was forced into training, but some things from that were natural. The feel of the blade in my hand, my skill with extracting information.

Taking a life. That was hard the first time, but became almost second nature after that.

Angus had laid back with a sandwich in his hand, his back propped against the tree stump as he hummed. His relaxation unnerved me, as well as his never-ending supply of food and hunger. Either he was very stupid and did not know he was being tracked, or he knew I was watching and did not care.

I trekked around the branches, stopping once I was behind him, the grass barely rustling beneath my weight as I dropped down onto the forest floor. Dagger in hand I approached him waiting for the surprise attack, for something worthy of holding a high seat in Revolucija, worthy of being a leader trying to bring Fursomerra into salvation.

Nothing. Joyce said he was a shapeshifter. An ability that should make him almost impossible to sneak upon since they keep the abilities of their shifters in their natural form. And yet.

Disappointment was lead in my stomach, and irrational anger bubbled beneath my flesh like acid. I moved and dropped my boot in his chest, the tip of my blade pressing into his Adam's apple.

Hazel eyes flashed to mine. "Not very smart to come out here alone, unarmed, when you're a very wanted man, Angus."

He smirked. "I do not know who would have ever told you I was smart, assassin."

"Some old bat."

Angus's laugh was croaked, like he had been smoking since he was a child. "Those seem to be in abundance around here."

I kneeled, pressing my blade further into his throat, "give me one good reason why I shouldn't carve your throat out and send it to your beloved revolution."

"Poor form for one."

The blade bit deeper into his neck. A thin red line bloomed to my delight. "But it would be funny."

"You have the wrong guy."

"Do. Not. Insult. Me." His throat bobbed through his swallow, smearing the blood from the small nick. I pressed more weight into the boot that pushed against his sternum.

"I don't mean to disrespect you," Angus rasped, his chest heaving. A flash of light caught my eye, and I twisted, crouching on the trunk as the force of his attempted blow rotated him sideways.

Angus jumped, his fingers curving into wicked black talons. He wiped his neck. "I really hate when people make me bleed my own blood."

I cocked my head with a smirk. "Would it be more acceptable if I had brought someone else to bleed out in front of you instead?"

"Depends on the person."

"As much as I would love to continue this witty banter we have going, I am in a hurry..."

"Off to kill more innocent souls?" I pursed my lips; I wonder how badly they actually need this dimwit. Joyce would not be too upset, right?

"Actually," I said as I lowered my hand, "I am in search of a merchant who is selling goods worthy of the King." His face was blank as he stared at me, his hands falling to his sides like stones.

"You're joking."

I *tsked* and jumped off the stump. "I don't think that's right." I crossed my arms. "And with that insult you just threw at me, I would really love for you to know the correct response."

His claws retracted. "Um, something about fresh spirits..."

"Pretty sure that's not it."

"No goods for the false king, something fresh spirits."

I smirked. If he was not a jackass, I might have been able to like him. "I am supposed to provide you escort to Pearl City to meet Tegan." I pulled the wrapped parchment from my pocket, holding it out to him. "This is from the seers." His mouth hung open and what looked like glee filled his eyes.

"You really need to stop looking at me like you had sex for the first time in your life or I will stab you."

His mouth snapped shut as he grabbed the parchment from me, not taking his eyes from mine. "I never would have thought it possible."

"Me neither," I mumbled.

"I never thought that you would be one of us."

"I am not one of you."

"If you were one of them, I would be dead right now. Along with whatever seer it is you are working with. That makes it clear that you do not serve the King."

A hiss escaped before I could stanch it. "I serve no one."

"I didn't mean to offend you."

I did not say anything. He was right, but also wrong. I served the Emperor and the rest of the Quinque. I lived my whole life working through whatever tasks Zelu gave me that continued to taint my already suffering soul. But I spared those at Joyce's request, and I was playing a dangerous game.

There was no part of me that wanted to join something as pure as Revolucija, I am not good enough for that nor would I ever be. Not after taking so many of their lives, killing those sitting high within their ranks who had families and loved ones.

Here I am, stuck in this perpetual limbo where the only loyalty I feel is to Joyce.

When I did not respond, he extended a hand and uttered, "Regardless. Thank you."

I grasped his forearm. "Aife."

The gleam in his eye told me that he would be wearing the small cut on his neck like a badge of honor, and my lip curled in disgust. He grinned, as if he knew exactly where my mind went.

"The sun is setting; we are moving further into the woods. We leave at first light."

"Whatever you say, boss." We found a little area with enough space to lay our sleeping mats down and trees high enough that we could have a fire. We gathered some branches and started a small fire between us. I suspended a pot over the flames, filling it with beans.

As it warmed, Angus asked, "Who sent you for me?"

I eyed him over the fire, the red and orange light danced on his pale skin. He had a young face, freshly shaved, and free of scars. I wonder if he had ever fought anyone.

"Joyce."

He nodded. "I have heard a lot about Joyce. Her sisters say she is the bravest of them all. If she trusts you, I have no doubt I should, too."

"If you trust me, you are even more dense than I originally believed."

He laughed whilst saying, "You would not be wrong there."

"You should not trust anyone. Especially with the dangerous games you play." I spooned the beans into the two canisters and passed one to him.

"I can't even argue with you on that one." Angus straightened; his eyes were bright with an excitement that made me groan. I do not even know why.

"I did not even hear you come up to me. I bet I would have been your easiest victim."

"Not by far, Angus. You do need to trust your instincts or get better ones."

"Well, it's a good thing I didn't trust my instincts, otherwise you would have a claw blade in your side."

I chuckled. "It is adorable you think you would have been able to."

"How long were you following me?"

"As soon as you stepped into the market. For what did you trade that merchant?"

"I had no idea."

"I'm good at what I do." I shrug.

"Why?" He asked, but I did not answer. "Why are you good at what you do? Why do you do what you do?"

I kept silent. It is a question I had mulled over most of my life. At one point, I convinced myself it was for my own survival. I am good at what I do because I had to be. If I were not good, I would be the one lying beneath a shallow grave. A grave that still awaits if I ever fail or if anyone I spared is found. But that has never been a good enough reason. Not a reason to have continued to taint my soul and submit to the darkness every day. The truth of it is hard to admit to myself and I would never admit it to anyone else.

Truth is, I am good at what I do because I want to be. Because I take pride in being the best. Because I like having control over the lives I take. Deciding when, where, and how they die. Giving over to the darkness feels good and damn, am I good at it. I didn't always feel like that, but I cannot pinpoint when I started to feel that way.

"You are from Matrador are you not?" He asked.

I placed my empty canister down and stretched my legs, glad of the change of subject, but did not say anything.

"I am a child of Saleron," he continued, even without my response, because of course he does.

Surprise rippled down my bones. The forest of the witches, one of my first battles. One that still haunted my nightmares.

"I remember you there," he said quietly. "You were a child, like me. But never in my life had I ever seen anyone cut through bodies like they were blades of grass."

"I had no limits to what I was willing to do to stay alive back then." During those years when I had been first trained to fight, I had so much anger and pain to work through. I took it out on the battlefield, cutting down whoever and whatever was in my way, often blacking out in a rage.

"That is why I fight. Not because of what you did, but because of what you were conditioned to do. Kill or be killed, forcing you to turn into something you were never supposed to be."

I blinked at him, shocked at his admission.

"Do not fight for me, Angus. I do not deserve that kindness. I might have done what I did when I was younger out of fear, but there is no fear left in me. I do not fear death anymore."

I seek it.

The unsaid words dropped like a weight between us.

He was silent for a few heartbeats as I prodded the fire, then said softly, "My entire family was slaughtered during that fight."

"Did I..." I started before the words died on my tongue.

He shrugged, and he took his shoes off, setting his blankets over his body. "I was smuggled out before it happened. It took me a long time to find out that they actually died. Even longer to stop blaming myself." Angus folded his hands behind his head staring through the tree covering overhead, moonlight sparsely illuminating the wood around us. I considered Angus in the silence that passed. Not many shifter families would be accepted into the Witches city, so it was surprising to know that he lived in Saleron.

"Even though I will have to go into hiding since I am supposed to be dead now, they will never be able to stop what we have started. They will never be able to destroy what I helped build. Cut off one head and three will grow back in its stead."

I laid down with a laugh. "Are you honestly comparing the Revolucija to a Hydra?"

"If that is what will cause the false King to shake in his over-sized kilt, then so be it."

I blanched at the image. "I have never seen that male in a kilt."

"Be glad of it."

The trees shifted as nocturnal creatures emerged from their sleep.

"I have killed a lot of people. Innocent and not, dozens within your rebellion. The only ones I regret are when I was a child, too young to fully understand the depravity. Too young to know the sickness that infests your soul with taking just one life." Words tumbled out, and I had no idea why or how to stop them. "I cannot say there are many beyond that I regret. I do not deserve the trust, loyalty or forgiveness that seems to fall within your ranks. But I can say I will do what I can to push the Revolucija to succeed." My words coated the air with an inky darkness and, as I finished, I do not know what made me make that promise.

"Do you want redemption, Aife?"

I was silent, the sounds of the forest and the crackling fire eating into my veins. I had thought about redemption when I took my first life. I cried and threw up for hours, trying to figure out how to clean the blood that seemed tattooed on my skin permanently. I lifted my hand and looked at the spirals and lines that filled them. Maybe not blood anymore, but a different kind of tribute. One that I could not wash off. But does permanently filling my skin with the memories of those who I kill constitute a desire for redemption?

"Protective spells," Angus said, his voice heavy with sleep. "Many of those merchants are selling more than just the goods they show. It has become a hot spot for exchanging anything for the Revolucija and we offer whatever help we can. We will do anything to protect our people."

CHAPTER 7
TITAIA

Marcellus' had been in the Reception Room for a week. His body swelled the repugnant smell seeped into the hallways. King Heptus had sent a clear message. By now, the news of his death would have made its way to the seers. While Heptus might not be able to make it into Hespath, or even know where it was, they were one step closer to destroying faith in the seers and potentially the Revolucija itself.

The Quinque and the royal family avoided the Reception Room and the surrounding halls, choosing instead to have the rest of their parties in the smaller rooms and formal dining rooms. I worked hard to avoid everyone with a title the whole week, which was how I ended up sitting on an overturned bucket in the supply room, my back pressed against a wall. I twisted an arrow between my fingers, too deep in thought to hear the footsteps that approached.

"Elle."

I looked up and met a pair of familiar eyes. "Indira," I said with a smile. Her black hair was wrapped in a bun at the nape of her neck her black skin enviously smooth, her eyes zoned in on my arrow. I stood and pulled her into a hug before she flipped over another bucket and sat across from me.

"Are you okay?" she asked.

I shrugged, attempting at nonchalance, before stating, "Sigurd."

"Goddess, I forgot. How long has it been?"

"Two years today," I replied, as she grasped my hand, wary of the sharp arrow of sympathy filling her face, her lips tugging down. Sigurd, the guard who saved my life, was murdered two years ago.

Murdered by the Priestess who turned and blamed it on a revolutionist. In reality, he was murdered because he offended Josephine and killed him for it. Covering it up by blaming the Revolucija was a way to keep the people's anger off them. I was not the only one he had been kind to; he had been extremely loved by everyone. The best within Heptus and Gregorovich's royal guard; the Caeruleus Knights.

"I remember you two being close." Her voice was soft. Only Katrina had known what he did for me, how he helped me gain my control back. I would trudge in to start my duties hours late, sore and covered in mud and sweat for eight long years. After he died, Katrina watched the start of my spiral and in a moment of desperation, asked me to train her. It helped me as much as it did her.

"Yeah, we were," I said, then cleared my throat and sat back. "What are you doing here?"

"I get to clean the Reception Room."

I cringed, and asked, "Why you?"

"Wrong place, wrong time." She shrugged. "Were you there?"

Marcellus's vacant eyes still played in front of me every night. The hope that he had seen me before he died, a friendly face amongst a room full of shared enemies.

"His name was Marcellus." Just saying his name tore at my heart. "He was so young, Indira."

"Twenty," was her reply. Her hands were on mine again, squeezing my fingers. "Zelu had found him hiding in a pub outside of Pearl City talking about a rebellion led by the seers."

"I had my doubts that the rebellion was a real thing," I said. I heard the whispers when I arrived in Austiria, but it was never more than that. Whispers and irritation from Heptus and Gregorovich about some of their goods being destroyed, trade routes being ambushed, and top officials being killed. Even with the evidence of the rebellion's being organized, Heptus and Gregorovich disregarded them as disgruntled lesser Visreala and humans. As the years passed though, the more their people started dying, the more whispers turned to yells for freedom and uprising.

"I think it is going to get a lot more interesting around here, dosata. The voices that surround the rebellion are getting louder." She leaned in, looking around before her brown eyes captured mine, secrets burning the edges of her pupils. "There is talk that someone infiltrated the Quinque."

If that secret had come from anyone else, I would have doubted the validity. But Indira. Indira had this way about her.

"Tell me you are not involved in this, Indira."

She grinned as she stood, flipped the bucket back over, and moved to the water sprout. "I will not lie to you, Elle. You know what was done to me, to my family."

Indira was from Liladon, which had been the most lucrative water trading front in Fursomerra. During the invasion of her home, they did not eradicate everyone. They needed to keep the trade going. The money was too important and there was a specific way to handle the water and only an Armorna, water singers, could do it. Families were separated, those who would continue to work, and those who were enslaved. Indira was too young to be useful in the water trade at the time, so she was brought here. Her eldest sister, Penelope, had been taken to the Parnitus Empire to serve Gregorovich in ways that I have long stopped considering.

"My parents may be dead, but I know my sister is alive. I can feel her." Indira paused. "I'm not the spy, but I'll do whatever I can to help them." She turned back to me with her eyebrow raised. "What about you, Elle? Would you be willing to help?"

"Great question..." I chewed my lips.

"It's a question you're going to have to answer sooner or later. The sooner the better." She tilted a shoulder and pinned me with a look that made me wonder if she could read my soul, "I know you lost your family in Galvidore, and I know you are no supporter of the Quinque."

I opened my mouth, but the protest died on my lips.

"Are you willing to fight to earn the world back?"

I grasped her arms. "I can say for certain that I will do whatever I can to help you see your sister again, Indira."

She smiled and kissed my cheek. "What can a little lady-in-waiting like you do for me?"

A few hours later, I was in Katrina's chambers drawing her a bath. I leaned over the back of my chair, chin on one hand and the other swirled through the hot water. Every time I talked to Indira; she always gave me so much to think about. Her relentless need to avenge her family and regain her power is part of why I idolize her. She had a family to fight for, to reunite with, and it makes my heart hurt with jealousy. My mother, father, and brother all died the night my home was invaded.

Murdered by Heptus. They were all that stood between him and legitimate power over Fursomerra. The Quinque knew that my parents had two children and they had the idea that one survived—me. But they had no idea who I was, or that I was living, quite literally, beneath their eyes. In their very own home. What is that silly saying? The safest place to hide is in plain sight.

Indira was fighting for her family; I do not do that anymore. So, for whom do I have to fight? *Oh, you know, just the entire world.* The last of my family, the last of my name, the last true heir to Galvidore to Fursomerra. I was the only one with a true claim to the throne, and I could not even find the strength to join the Revolucija.

I was a coward.

Sometimes the urge to fight, to stab Heptus in his throat when I stood close to him, was so strong it left me breathless. When I felt the desire to leave this place and join the rebellion, I swear I could hear my parents cheer me on. That is who they were, righteous to the end.

Even when it led to their downfall.

My parents had tried to reunite the unconquered Kingdoms and even the remnants of the conquered together to fight. It might have worked. If our allies had not already turned on us. They were betrayed by one of the eldest noble families who sought to earn Heptus' favor. Gregorovich had him killed immediately and hung his decapitated corpse off the tallest tower of Galvidore once they had won. Katrina's father.

The door flew open, and Katrina swept in, slammed it behind her before bolting and turning to face me. I sat up; eyebrows raised in alarm.

She murmured, "It's fine."

I stood and helped her undress for her bath. Her movements were slow and stiff and concern wormed its way through my body.

"Calor," I whispered, holding my hand over the water. Steam billowed. I returned to my seated position, both hands on the tall back of the chair, my chin rested on my fingers.

Katrina lowered herself into the tub and I noted fingertip bruises on her thighs and waist.

"You're getting better at that," she groaned, her eyes closed. I glared at the new bruises that peppered her collarbone.

"You are getting better at it as well. Lying to me."

Katrina's jaw tightened. "Everything is fine. Brock is just...."

"Sadistic?"

She leaned her head back against the tub, her mossy eyes pinned on me. My lips were pinched as I met and held her gaze.

Katrina had sacrificed a lot since we had been here. When we were younger, she would always fight every single boy who tried to talk to her. Which was a lot. She was part Siren, and that made her desired above all others. Her reason was that she wanted to hurt them before they could hurt her. Akin to her father, who was as cruel a man I had ever met. Her mother was a gentle soul but never fought against him. Never once stood up for Katrina. Her mother was always covered in bruises, even being well placed, she could always detect them.

Try as she might, my mother could not convince her to leave the sadistic asshole. She once told my mother and father to keep their royal nosy asses out of her business, respectfully, of course.

We never understood why her mother stayed. Katrina would spend days with us to escape him when he went on a drinking bender. Eventually, my father intervened. That did not end well.

"He doesn't take criticism from his father well..." she trailed off, her eyes rimmed with red, blinking away the unshed tears.

As much as I wanted to push, she would not tell me anything she did not want to. Not yet.

"Indira said Marcellus was twenty."

"How the hell does that female find stuff out?"

I shrugged. "She is everywhere and nowhere all the time."

"A damn ghost?" she snorted.

I cracked a smile. "She said someone from the r..."

"I know," she interrupted.

Brock and the others think that Katrina is a vapid beauty, completely oblivious to the world around her. Her father raised her that way, to be obedient, stupid, and pliable. Her mother taught her how to be clever and powerful. Katrina did not make it this far based on her pretty looks and ability to sing a room into submission. Her survival skills saved both her life and mine.

She always played the doting fiancée and diligent duchess in public and had played it for so long that she found it hard to separate the game from reality. But sometimes I got my best friend back. The ditsy, intelligent, brave friend that I grew up with.

"I don't think you know wha...."

"I know."

"You know?"

"Elle." Her voice was strong but there was a tightness. "I may not have been completely honest with you."

CHAPTER 8
TITAIA

I was silent as Katrina dried off with a fluffy white towel before she wrapped her bruised body in a pink robe. She sat in one of the twin red paisley chairs situated side by side in front of the burning fireplace. I sat in the chair and watched her as she watched the flames dance.

"Are you the spy?"

Her gaze was serious, her pupils dilated. I inhaled deeply and watched her.

Then Katrina burst into laughter. The sound danced beautifully around the room. I tried to keep my lip from tugging up.

"In what world would I be able to be a spy on anything?" she gasped, crossing her legs, the pink silk parting at her knee.

"Well, you don't have to be so rude about it."

She shrugged and wiped a tear from her eye with another giggle.

"It is you."

After a few minutes' silence, she responded, "Yeah, it is."

My heart fell to my ass, the beating as uncomfortable as it was annoying.

"I am sorry I did not tell you. You, of all people, deserve to know what is going on."

I waved my hand to tell her to carry on.

Katrina shook her head. "Let us go for a picnic tomorrow. I could use some fresh air and Brock will be occupied trying to convince Zelu to train him like his assassins. Well, the one assassin he seems to admire. We will go to Price Point, and you can ask me anything."

"He admires an assassin?" I asked, temporarily distracted. She stared back at me. "Ah, yes. Sadist. You better have a good story for me, Katrina, because I am pissed. Goodnight."

"Goodnight." Her voice reached me right before I closed the door.

Katrina saved me from death, smuggled me out of Galvidore before the King and Emperor could add my body next to my families. Everything I knew about Katrina married to her standing up against the Quinque but working for the Revolucija? That was something I did not predict. Her family was murdered by Heptus, he called them, necessary collateral. She showed the utmost diplomacy and sided with the King successfully averting his gaze from us. We have walked side by side our entire lives. Her parents had been Duke and Duchess in our home of Galvidore, with their death she succeeded to Duchess. When we made it to Austiria we found out that after they burned my family alive, they killed her parents as well.

My back was on fire as I walked back to my room, and I dug my nails into my palms, trying to calm my heart. I know this might be my way to bring myself into the fight and win back my crown, but Goddess if I am not hurt that she did not tell me.

My cheeks stung with the slap of wind as we rode. My hair down, the brown strands whipped in the cool air. The snow was melting and spring was on the horizon, but it did not stop the cold. Puddles splashed around our horses' hooves as we pushed further into the woods, towards the mountains and away from the Palace. Katrina's laugh was exhilarated next to me as she leaned down on her horse, Joe, trying to keep up with Koko's stride. The Point was about an hour away and relatively clear enough for our horses to ride as fast as they wanted.

Joe had been the horse she escaped on when we ran from Galvidore. His snow-white coat and sleek black eyes had caught Koko's attention long ago. He always ran at Koko's hip, never ahead of her. Not that she had let him, she was terrifyingly alpha and asserted dominance over all the other animals she had contact with, species be damned. We called her the Queen of horses. The air was warmer the closer we got to the mountains, no clouds in the sky allowing the sun to beat against my back. Birds chattered and flew around us as our breath heated the air. The trees were tall and endless, large roots winding in and out of the dirt floor and piles of snow.

Finally, the trees broke apart and there she was. A beautiful twenty-foot goddess made of marble in a small clearing surrounded by trees. The white stone was untarnished even in the many years since her creation. Her legs were bent with a femininity that I had never seen captured on canvas, stone, or painting before, that had been hardly replicated in life. The Goddess's dress exposed her hip, where it dripped gracefully across her form. Her arms were raised, one hand pointed in front of her and the other varnished a sword that gleamed as if it had been made from metal. There were carved designs on the hilt that faded with time. Her lips were drawn back in a sneer, but her eyes were soft and focused. The perfect balance of elegance and wrath. Around her waist was a rotted rope that had had been scorched up to the knot that kept it secured. It looked as if someone had tried to remove her from her dais.

The ground around the status was a deep green, the grass blooming in earnest caressing the marble pedestal that she stood on. I glanced around and realized the entire area was full of patches of the same grass. The small clearing where we normally left Koko and Joe somehow already clear of snow. There should at least be the signs of winter, not fully bloomed flowers and leaves that graced the should-be-dead trees.

"Is this real?" I asked Katrina and saw the same awed face that mirrored mine.

"It has been months since I've been able to enjoy the sun without being assaulted by snow." The sun reflected brightly against Katrina's red hair as she spread her arms out, smiling to the sky. I grabbed my satchel and went to the gentle stream that had made its way around the statue. We moved towards a hidden tower that looked as old as Goddess, but the crumbled stones said it had not been made to the same standard. The stones had fallen over to expose stairways and landings throughout the tower. We climbed through one of the openings and started up the ridiculous amount of stairs. I had tried to count, but lost it around 173 or 174.

The walls were painted with the Goddess in different situations. Killing a large creature that could only be a Titan, facing an army of hundreds if not thousands alone, flying over a fire engulfed Kingdom with large bat-like wings, men bowed and prayed as she sat on a giant throne. In every picture, her lip always curled in the same sneer. Our breath was labored by the time we pushed the broken wooden door open to the crumbling balcony. The view was breathtaking, snow-covered trees, and life seemed to stretch on forever. It was the middle of nowhere. No one had claimed the land. No buildings, homes, farms, or castles.

We laid out a blanket and pulled wine and food before wrapping ourselves in a second set of blankets. I sat and enjoyed the feeling of the sun on my face as we drank. Katrina filled our glasses a second time before she started to talk.

"About two years ago, I was approached by a Caeruleus Knight. I had seen him before, around the castle whenever Gregorovich was here. You know him, he is not one to have the same guards twice. I am convinced that he kills them between visits," she huffed. "I had seen this guy on every single visit for the last year." She took a sip of her wine, staring at the winter landscape before us.

"You weren't with me that night. It was right after the Queen's birthday celebration and after." She paused as if gearing me up for her next words. "After Sigurd was murdered."

I flinched. I had been inconsolable after that and did not leave my room until Josephine was out of the castle; I knew I would have tried to kill her the moment I saw her. It took me months to stop crying; it hit hardest when I woke up to prepare for our training sessions only to remember that he was gone.

"I had felt someone there. Watching and listening and I could not figure out where they had come from or why they were there. I told him to stop hiding like a coward and he walked right through the stone wall and straight to me."

Wall walking was difficult. Apparently, it was common to get stuck. "He told me he was working with the Revolucija, and the seers were interested in having me as an ally. I thought the same thing! It took some balls to come to the fiancée of the Prince and proposition me. Then he started talking about a prophecy."

I rolled my eyes. "Seriously, Katrina, a prophecy? Are you going to inherit some wicked cool ability? Like mind reading? Oh, or killing an entire army with the snap of your fingers? Or! Or! Mind control!"

"Very funny. No, my current ability is one of the reasons they chose me." Gaznios, being able to quite literally know when they were being spied on. Something I bet the Quinque wished they possessed and something Katrina had kept secret. It was an exceedingly rare and oddly convenient ability.

"How did they know that?"

Katrina shrugged, undaunted. "You know, seers. Anyway, after I got over the initial shock of someone so damn attractive in my room alone with me."

"Dammit, Katrina."

She giggled and my lip tugged up. "He opened a line of communication with the fireplace, of all things. I talked to the seers, some wrinkly old ladies, and I agreed. Since then, I have been passing information to them and giving them movements of the army and whatever else I overhear that might be useful. They knew that Zelu was going to be in Galvidore, and they knew that Marcellus was going to be captured."

My body felt like it had been dropped into ice. "They sent him anyways? That is real grand coming from some old witches that do not ever leave their land. What makes them better than the Quinque?"

"He wanted to, Titaia. They told him not to go and that there would be other opportunities. He refused and went anyways, said this was their best shot, which is the difference, Titaia. The sacrifices the people make are based on their own desires."

"Opportunities for what?

"To merge the two rebellions."

"Katrina, what the hell are you talking about?" I said it with more anger than was necessary. It was hard not to. There had never been any mention of two rebellions in the years I have been in Austiria. There had only ever been one, the one led by the Seers who called themselves Revolucija.

"There is another group of people leading a revolution. They are responsible for killing major military officers and leading attacks on land controlled by the Quinque."

I could not fathom who would be brave, or stupid, enough to challenge the King but the Seers. I thought the Revolucija had been raging into a war. "Who?" I asked.

"The druids."

I reared back like I had been slapped, the imaginary sting making my eyes water.

"Marcellus was successful. The druids have contacted the leader of the Revolucija."

I raised a brow. Questions bounced around my head so quickly I had no idea how to even start asking. What did it mean? Why had I never heard of a second rebellion? Who was this leader? What acts of 'terrorism' were led by the Revolucija and which by the druids? But one question fought its way to the front, demanding to be heard to quell the sense of betrayal I felt.

"Why haven't you told me any of this?" I asked, then watched as birds scattered from a tree before taking to the skies, their caws echoing at us.

"When it first happened, you were so distraught over Sigurd I did not think it would be the right time. After that, I just... I knew you were toeing a precarious line with the rebellion." She shrugged, her mossy eyes rimmed with tears as she looked at me imploringly. "I do not know why I did not tell you, Ti. I was scared of how you would react for putting you at risk. You only recently became yourself again, and I know how you feel about the rebellion. I wanted you to make your own decision."

I scoffed. The last thing I cared about was the risk of my life when it came to her; she held up a hand and silenced me as my mouth opened to say just that.

"I know you would have been more upset about the risk I was putting myself in. But after a few months, I was scared at how upset you would be with me not telling you. So, not telling you, as cowardice as it sounds, became the clearest option for me."

Truthfully, if she had told me two years ago, I would have lost my mind. Just losing Sigurd and Katrina doing something so dangerous, I would not have been able to handle it.

"What exactly did you think I would do if you told me? I would not cut your head off." I grumbled, irritation peeling at my insides as I squirmed. While I may not be the calmest out there, there was no reason I would have overreacted. I was not even upset when she initially told me she had been working for the Revolucija. It was because she kept it a secret.

Katrina's face was pinched in shame. "There is no real reason. I could have told you a few months after Sigurd's passing, but I did not. It was something I wanted to keep to myself, something that I could do for you and not because of you."

My anger softened at her confession.

"Damn you and your bleeding heart," I said, pulling her into a hug. Big parts of our conversations throughout these past ten years had been when to leave, or if we even should leave. Something my parents had never prepared me for before their death was how to think and act like a Queen, and an adult. I was only seventeen when they died and while others in the surrounding Kingdoms had been trained from young ages to sit on the throne, my mother found ways to keep me away from it. She had never met her mother, her having died during her birth and she seemed to want to give me the experiences she never got when she married my father and took the throne so young. We never could have imagined that it would lead to me being so ill prepared for a situation like this.

Katrina took it upon herself to protect me, to be the one person in the world that I could trust. The sacrifices she made for me never hit as hard as it did at that moment. I had already put her at such risk with her knowing my identity, but now, because of me, she was spying for the Revolucija. For a bunch of seers who did not seem to care if she lived or died. She held me tight, and every inch of appreciation I had for her burrowed itself into a chasm of guilt.

"I'm sorry I didn't tell you," she said as we pulled away and I shook my head.

"I understand." We sat in silence for a bit, sipping on the remnants of wine, and ate the bread we had brought. Another question burned within me so hot I broke the comfortable silence we formed. "Do they know about me?" I asked in trepidation.

Katrina looked over, her cheeks pink from the chilly wind breezing past us. "They know about you, as in they know you are alive. They know I brought a lady-in-waiting with me from Galvidore, but I never eluded it being you. They know I know where and who you are and luckily, the Quinque has not focused its full attention on finding you because...." she trailed off, looking at me with apprehension.

"Because what?"

"That prophecy...it's about you."

My throat closed, causing black to dot the edges of my vision, my heart going so fast I thought it was going to sprout wings and fly out of my chest. I gulped a few times and when I opened my mouth, laughter erupted. Laughter loud enough to send stones from the rickety wall behind us and birds skittering from the trees.

"I'm sorry," I choked. "That is the most ridiculous thing I have ever heard." I giggled, and continued, "What was the last prophecy that was true?"

Katrina's eyes rolled so hard I did not think that she would ever be able to see straight again before she stuck that stern stare on me. "Do you want to know what it says?" she asked.

"Oh yes, so interesting. Please bless me with the words of crazy ass old ladies. I want it word for word, please."

"It's in elvish, or Latin, or some shit." She grabbed my hands. "I don't know what it all says, and there's so much to it, but the important part is the rightful heir of Fursomerra, a Phoenix will reclaim the crown and bring down the false King." Katrina made a show of glancing around our surroundings, before she continued. "I don't see any other Phoenix's around?"

CHAPTER 9
AIFE

The Voyager Tavern was a busy, dirty inn that sat in the heart of Pearl City. Apparently, they had the best meat pies on this side of Lake Isaldore. Angus and I sat at a table in the far corner of the inn that was covered in a thick layer of dust, and I once again wondered why the Revolucija insisted on using Pearl City.

"Do you know where she is?" I asked Angus again, after another five minutes had passed. It was an hour past the set meet time and my anxiety moved slower than a troll when they woke from their evening naps. Every second we sat in the open, the closer I was to being forced to kill Angus. Whom looked irritatingly calm while he sipped his beer.

"Tegan is excessively cautious and paranoid. Probably thought she was being followed at one point and had to take a detour."

I saw the door open, and a flash of dirty blonde hair moved into the room. The person moved in such a catlike manner that had I not been watching the door so obsessively I would not have caught them. She made her way through the room, unseen by other patrons, slithered into the chair next to Angus, winked at me, and slammed her hand on the table.

"Fuck!" Angus grunted, his hand flying to his heart.

She giggled. "Got you again."

"You are late," I said. As entertained as it was to see Angus get his balls busted for lack of skill, I was exasperated from waiting so long.

"Yes." She grabbed Angus' beer and chugged the rest of it. "But here I am! There are quite a few Caeruleus Knights around, so I had to be extra sneaky."

I also noticed the extra patrol when we arrived. I knew they were not after me, but there would be no talking my way out of being caught red-handed with two obnoxiously obvious Revolucija members.

At the same time, I asked myself why they were here, and the answer ordered another round of drinks. This city had become a breeding ground for the Revolucija. Tegan and Angus were playful as if they were not involved in an uprising that could lead to the death of millions of innocent and not people.

I was intrigued and disgusted.

"We are going to the Land of Hespath." Tegan's words cut through my thoughts.

"Hespath?" I asked before I could stop.

"Of course, that's my family." On our way to the tavern, Angus had explained that Tegan is a seer and is a lot older than she looks. I do find that hard to believe. Her dirty blonde hair, blue eyes, and youthful face I would put her at around my age, thirty or so. If not younger.

"Why not tell us how this war ends or the best path to take if you are this big, bad seer?"

Tegan laughed, well, cackled. Like, she knew the world was ending but would keep the secret until the core exploded and we all were burned. "Not how visions work, darling," she said.

"Don't call me darling."

"How about pumpkin?" she joked, and I simply glared in response.

"Sweetheart," Angus supplied.

"Sugar."

"Honey."

"Duck."

"Enough," I growled. "No pet names. Especially not duck."

"Sorry to disappoint, but visions are not set in stone. They are fluid, like water. The moment intent changes, or knowledge changes, it sets off a series of events that adjusts the future."

"Come with us, assassin. There are people in Hespath that might be able to help you with that little circle in your eyes," Angus said as I blinked at his boyish grin.

"Not now," Tegan said and lifted her glass. Her eyes pierced through me. "But soon. Soon you will be with us, well. With them."

"Thank you," Angus said. "For all of this."

"Thank Joyce."

I pulled the hood over my head and leaned forward. Angus shifted as I met his eye.

"My life is now tied to yours, Angus. You are supposed to be dead. Not missing, not injured, not captured. Dead. If you are caught, I will not be questioned or given a second chance. I will be executed. After a bit of torture, of course. Gregorovich and Heptus hate elves, so nothing about my death would be kind, and I will hunt you in the afterlife."

Angus fidgeted. "I know, and I am forever grateful to you and what you have risked for me."

"I did it for Joyce. If it were up to me, you would be dead."

Angus moved and brought a gold blade to my throat, the blade a breath away from my skin. "I can take care of myself."

His face paled comically as I tapped my blade against his groin and he lowered his dagger from me.

"She's good," he murmured to Tegan, and she nodded with a bright grin.

The three-day trip back to Parnitus was uneventful. I enjoyed a few detours to visit some of my favorite farms and towns. Admiring the beautiful deserts and woodlands, even being under the rule of a tyrant, could not dull the beauty of the realm. Even as the grass gave way to wet slush and snow. It was just as hard to forget the suffering that still lay just behind the curtain, the dying and sick children, and families.

Once home, I told Joyce everything, which resulted in her door being locked in days as she worked to contact her sisters. She claimed it was for her peace of mind because she liked Angus, but I knew it was for me. It was to make sure that he went undetected, and I was not going to be hauled to my death.

There was a pond a few miles from the castle that I found myself in on a particularly warm day a week after I returned. Those were the days I lived for, being alone without a mark. Enjoying the sounds of nature, the

feeling of the sun peeking through the frozen branches and the dripping of melting snow. The death trio
would return tonight, and Zelu always expected a full
report on my tasks. I had my version of events ready.
I had burned his body and scattered the ashes. The
sound of a branch shifting made my ears and my ear
twitch.

"Here you are, foolish elf." Joyce's gruff voice sounded behind me.

"Ay, here I am, cranky old prune."

She leaned against the tree that supported my hammock and I felt it lean into the touch, lending its
strength. After a few moments, Joyce patted the tree
and pushed off, taking a seat at the large boulder next
to where I lay suspended in my hammock.

"Did you talk to your sisters?"

"Yes, Angus is in very good spirits and very impressed with you."

"He should be working to impress me. I could have
killed him with my toothbrush."

Joyce chuckled. "Tegan was impressed as well."

"Oh joy, two lunatics are enthralled with me. I can
die happy." I shifted a rock that was flung at my head.
It bounced off the fabric, pitching to the ground. "You
have to admit Joyce, they are fucking nutty!"

"They are extraordinary, Aife." Joyce tried to keep a
straight face, but the side of her mouth twitched.

"Extraordinary," I snorted. "That is one way to put
it. Tegan is barely on this side of sanity. Is that what
happens to all of you seers? You just lose touch with
reality and go mad?"

That brought a bark of laughter from Joyce, and
the woods leaned into the sound. I reached down and
brushed my fingers into the dancing grass. It gripped
at my fingers in return and soothed my aching nerves.

"I need your help again."

"Of course, you do." I sighed, lying back on the hammock. "Never 'you did well Aife, take a break Aife, I will never need anything again Aife'."

"Gregorovich returns tonight, but they will be going back soon after. We think that they have found Harenae."

My brow furrowed; the druids were in Harenae.

"With enough Druids, especially as experienced as the ones that live in Harenae, the Quinque could peek into our network. Their elder would never agree to help, but I fear that the power and strength of the Quinque could overpower him."

"Do you think they will join them?" I asked. While the power and strength have been on the Quinque's side since the war started, if the druids joined, they could eradicate the rest of the realm.

She shook her head. "No. They have been fighting against them as well. But my sisters and I fear that if they get into Harenae they will kill them all. We cannot win this war without them."

"Can't you warn them?"

"We do not have a full connection with them yet. But we need to know what they do to keep ahead of this fight. Especially how they found Harenae, because if they actually did, it means we have a mole. That is why we need you, Aife. We have to find out what they know."

"You want me to spy on the Quinque?"

Joyce did not respond; she did not need to. I knew what she was asking. I risked my life every day to find information. Yet, this this was different.

"I thought you had someone there already," I said, and turned to sit, giving Joyce space as she joined me on the hammock.

"We do, but they have not been allowed within the meetings and conferences where this is being discussed."

"How long do I have?"

She rapped my knuckles. "One month."

"This could turn the tide for the revolution, Aife. We need to know what the Quinque knows and how they found it out."

"Anything else I need to know about this trip?"

Joyce cleared her throat, her brown eyes sparkling with mischief. "Just keep your heart open, girl. The seers have everything else figured out."

"For some reason, that does not give me the sense of comfort I'm sure you thought it would."

We made it back to the castle just as the trio arrived.

The Emperor and Priestess's black and gold carriage peaked over the hill in the distance before it rolled onto the stone drive. Their laughter filled the silence when the door opened. I took a steadying breath and bowed; and was completely ignored, along with the rest of the tributes who had come out to greet them. The blonde from the Welcoming ceremony a few weeks ago cringed away from Josephine. She was not around much, and the sling holding her bandaged arm was probably the reason.

Does not take much to figure out what happened there, Josephine is very possessive and while she has no claim to Gregorovich, she still took a savage pleasure in hurting those who caught his eye.

Zelu dropped a heavy hand on my shoulder. "We have much to discuss," he said, his voice hard.

"Yes, General."

While Heptus preferred beauty and brightness, Gregorovich favored the dark and Gothic in his home. Grand towers swept into mosaic windows, grandiose

pointed arches, and vaulted ceilings. Everything pointed upwards with height and a dark grace that drew
you in. The ceilings were painted and accentuated with
ornately carved walls and pillars. While it was dark, the
castle was still inviting. I followed Zelu to one of the
arched towers that lead to his study. The walls were
lined with magically lit torches and old paintings of
people I never knew. The Knight at the door saluted
as we approached and opened the door. He glared at
me, and I smirked back at him. I flipped my cloak
back and rested my hand on the pommel of my sword,
running a finger down the leather. His eyes dropped
to the movement, with his distraction I grabbed the
dagger from my other side and rotated it in my hand
before I tapped his chin with the blade as I passed.

He flinched. Zelu walked over to his desk and
cleared it with one sweep of his arm. He grabbed a
piece of paper from his pocket and flattened it on the
table before he dropped into his seat. I settled into
the ugly brown cushioned chair across from him and
lowered my hood.

"I was glad to hear of your success in killing the
merchant." Exhaustion and anger filled his words.

I nodded my assent. "These rebellion leaders are like
Hydra."

"I have a task for you." Zelu pointed to the paper,
and I turned my head to look at it better. It was a note
written by Queen Alhma.

General,

*I fear that there is a traitor in our midst. Information
is being shared to our enemies from within the Palace.
Information that had been shared in confidence. While
Heptus has not been as selective with who he invites to
conversations, it is time we start. I have initiated my own
investigation into who the traitor could be and eliminated*

a few. I request your assistance when you return; we need to find this snake and end them.

Alhma, Queen of Fursomerra

Does not take a stretch of the imagination to know what she meant by 'eliminated'. Alhma never balked at taking a life. I remembered watching her in battle. She wielded a sword as well as any Knight and took down her enemy with a bloodied smile.

I glanced at the General and asked, "A spy?" The irony was not lost on me. There were so many spies running around, I wondered if there was such a thing as loyalty anymore.

He tilted one shoulder. "Would not surprise me. They do not have the protection we do here. It would be all too easy for anyone to get close, or anyone turned."

I raised a brow. Zelu's control over his minotaur seemed shaky at best. I just hope I am faster than he is if he does shift, I do not want to be locked in a small room with a ranging minotaur.

"How can I help?"

"You are coming with us for the Emperor's birthday. We need you to help assess who the traitor is and take them out, and you will need to stay within the Palace. We leave in a month."

I have not stepped foot in the castle in twelve years. Whenever I visited Austiria I stayed within the city. I glanced back at Zelu, who looked as if he wanted to say more.

After a world tilting hesitation, he said something that made my heart drop. "The Emperor would like to test your loyalty before we go."

CHAPTER 10
TITAIA

T he time following Katrina's confession was relatively uneventful. Spent doing what I had been
doing for the last decade, helping the people of Austiria in any way I could. Bringing food to the city
from the Palace kitchens, which the cooks had always
been generous in providing or giving them my wages
to help offset the ridiculous taxes that the King puts
out. More often than not though, I found myself at the
cities Brothel's protecting the female workers against
males or even Caeruleus Knights when they got handsy
or violent.

Being Katrina's lady gave a semblance of protection,
to that point at least. I had not been killed yet, so that
counted for something. I had not caused enough of a
stir to have been on Heptus' radar, either. Although,
I like to think the embarrassment they suffer from
getting their asses kicked by a female kept the Knight's
lips sealed.

I was avoiding it. I knew that. Avoiding the decision
of joining the Revolucija and effectively outing myself

as the most wanted Visreala to walk the realm or continue to hide and stay as safe as I could for as long as I could avoid any and all confrontation.

Fight for the crown that belonged to my family for as long as Fursomerra existed or continue to be the cowered my family would be disappointed in and stay alive.

I could not deny the urge to fight back. It was always there. To do the right thing for my people. But fear was paralyzing. Fear of failure, not being good enough, strong enough. Just not being enough. What if my joining turned into the opposite of what they desired? What if my joining is what led to the loss of the Revolucija and those who had been fighting for decades died because of me? What if I died?

Fear was a bitch to overcome.

The mere rumor of a surviving Normaran was enough to build a powerful revolution. Rumors the Quinque tried to quell until the knowledge of only three bodies being found in the fire spread over the realm. They were not even afraid of me. They were afraid of me birthing a male heir that would be the rightful ruler.

If only they knew.

Was that about what I wanted? Or was it about what the realm needed? Did I have a choice, regardless? Thousands have died. Died in my family's name, died for a better life.

How many have perished because of my failure to act? My failure to do what was right. And if I died, at least I would be with my family again.

"I have something to ask you that you're not going to like," Katrina said. I paused; the ribbon of the corset tight in my fist.

"I am on the edge of my seat with anticipation." Katrina turned when I finished the bow at the curve of her ass. "For fuck's sake, Katrina, watch where you swing those things."

She looked down and admired her chest for a moment before returning her attention to me, and saying, "The Queen needs you to fill in as her lady-in-waiting."

The sound that came from my mouth was somewhere between a choke and a strangled laugh. "Is Nora still missing?" Queen Alhma's lady-in-waiting who disappeared two nights ago.

"No, they found her. Dead. She hung herself."

My heart sunk. "Why?" I asked. Katrina sat at her vanity and started pinning her hair. Alhma was a different kind of cunning, old and calculating, but appeared warm and motherly. Her children adored her, but they did not see how she was behind closed doors. "Why does she want me?"

"Alhma mentioned last night that you were efficient, quiet, timely, and that I could stand losing you for a few weeks. That I did not need much help shoving my wide waist into narrow corsets, how I am still young enough to stand on my own two feet and how she was Queen and insulted me about twenty more times in her rant." Katrina met my gaze, and her voice continued, barely above a whisper. "I didn't have much of a choice."

I chewed my lips. There would have been no choice, even if Katrina genuinely needed me. Alhma's word was law in her eyes. Being Queen was not far from the truth.

"It would only be until Gregorovich returns; he apparently will be bringing someone to fill the position permanently. Plus, this could be good for us. Think about it, the meetings you will be invited to, the events you will attend! All the information you could get us."

"Who is this 'us'? I never said I wanted to help." The smile she gave made me wonder if she actually could read minds.

"I do not think I could stand to be around that woman more than I am already forced to. All I can imagine is wrapping my fingers around her tiny, little throat." I lifted my hands and imagined her pale throat between them.

"As much as I would love to watch that, it's probably not the best idea."

"The Goddess must truly hate me."

"Or she is giving you the opportunity to truly decide what your role will be during this war. Who you are going to be, and what you are going to do because it is going to happen, Ti. War is inevitable."

I stared at her. "Are you going to give me some inspirational speech about how I can change the world?"

She put on a pair of beautiful ruby earrings. The encrusted jewels kissed the top of her shoulders that swayed every time she moved her head. "You are the only one who can at this point...but you have to be willing to. If there is one thing I am certain of, it is the moment you paint that target on your back everything will change," Katrina said.

"Do you think that would be a bad thing?"

"No, I think it would be the best thing that could happen. Giving the Visreala and humans a fighting chance, helping the Revolucija could save the realm. You could be the one to change everything."

"You sound so sure about the role I am going to play. You must have a lot of faith in these seers and that prophecy."

"You should hurry. You have ten minutes to be in her study." Katrina stared at her reflection with a distant look when I stepped into the drafty hall.

I have lived right inside danger since arriving here, but I had never worked for any of the Quinque directly. I navigated the passageways in the most direct route to get to the Queen's lair, or study, as quickly as I could. It felt like walking into the lion's den with pieces of raw meat strapped to my body. Too soon I reached her wing. Sitting in the middle of the castle, it was the darkest and somehow driest. Lit torches lined the halls with a blood red carpet running down them. There were no pictures, no painted walls, nothing but stone that seemed to repeal warmth. Cold tendrils like fingers reached for me as I shivered my way down the hall.

Fucking creepy.

I hurried around a corner and approached a door I knew to be Alhma's study. If I had not been here before, the sickening feeling of death and fear would have alluded that I was in the right location. The heavy wooden door slammed open when I neared and two men carrying a statue that had been shattered into three pieces away exited. Alhma's enraged filled words wafted to me.

Just in time for her morning breakdown.

The whispers from the servants that worked for her, she had a few every day. I almost felt bad for her. Her husband was unfaithful to her face. Her children loved her but doted on their father more and there was not nearly as much respect for her as there was the Priestess. Before the Great Übernehmen she had been heir to one of the five Kingdoms Fursomerra once held: the Zane Republic. Although, being female, she had to marry a male to secure the line. Alhma's entire being was unfamiliar. No one really knew how her mother or father came to rule as they were both Druids without a vein of royal blood. They took the crown one day, and it was never really questioned.

When Alhma she was younger, she was sent to live with her parent's clan, to learn the skills to be a Druid.

During that time, she became infatuated with the darkest forms of magick and after six years, she was completely disowned by the clan, which was essentially unheard of. Her desire to hurt people and her ability to avoid the consequences of nature earned her the hazy purple of her eyes. It was supposed to be a curse, but she found it her best feature. It made her...unique.

When she learned of Heptus, she begged to marry him. He became infatuated with her as soon as they met, drawn to her cruelty and craving power. Heptus' was already King of Engrich his father having died a few years prior, but no one knew what happened to Alhma's parents, when the Kingdom of Austiria rose the five kingdoms crumbled. Most of the previous ruling families had been murdered, but her parents seemed to have just disappeared.

I took a deep breath and knocked. The door swung open. I barely had the chance to step back and avoid what I am sure would have been a bloody impact. A girl ran out of the room holding the side of her face. I grabbed the door to keep it from closing as a vase flew across the room. A face peered around the door, a Knight. He watched me slink into the room before closing the door. Death, fear, and anger filled the room. Queen Alhma paced the large study, her chin length black hair messy as though she ran her fingers through it a hundred of times.

The blue dressing gown billowed behind Alhma as she paced, her free hand clutched a piece of paper. Her eyes were wide and glowed in the firelight. I kept it close to the wall and moved to the bookshelf before I focused my eyes on the hem of her dress.

"That stupid woman has no idea who I am, of what I am capable. I could wave my hand and erase her from the world without blinking." She stalked to her desk and grabbed a leather-bound book, flipping through the pages. I had never been inside of the room. She kept anyone who was not absolutely necessary out. I am not even sure Heptus had been here. The walls were a deep emerald surrounded with golden trim, the furniture a beautiful mahogany, and two walls were covered in bookshelves. A desk was placed before another wall with a mahogany chair. Behind the desk sat four abstract paintings.

Beautifully chaotic; like the drowning Queen that stood at a black podium before a gold trimmed fireplace. The podium was made from a material that seemed to glow with an iridescent red light. I looked up at Alhma, who stopped muttering and was staring at me.

"Who the hell are you?"

I swallowed and dropped into a curtsy so deep my knee grazed the black carpet. "I am Elle, your Majesty, Duchess Katrina said you wished for my services." Her eyes burned into the top of my head like flames as I held my curtsy. I really need to stretch more.

"Ah yes, I remember. Stand," she ordered. I kept my face blank and followed her command. "Come here," she continued.

With slow steps, I moved to the center of the room, and she started to circle me like a hawk about to pounce on its next meal. I glanced at her hands, nails as long as talons. While not hawklike talons, they would hurt, puncture my skin at the very least. She grabbed my chin, and those talons dug into the fat on my cheeks. Katrina kept telling me that I had chubby baby cheeks, and they might get absorbed into my eyes if she kept my face this tight. She jerked my chin left and right as she studied my features. I worked to keep my face as pliable to her force as possible while praying that Katrina's spell worked well enough.

"How long have you worked for Katrina?"

"Fifteen years, your Majesty." I kept my voice even trying to enunciate through my flattened cheeks and pursed lips.

"Did you come with her from Galvidore?"

"Yes, your Majesty."

"How do I know you're not a Normaran?" She spat my last name like it was a piece of rotten fruit.

"My family hails from Engrich, Majesty. My family name is Shardon."

"And what does the Shardon family possess?"

"We are witches." Most ladies-in-waiting were what the Quinque considered "lesser Visreala" witches, nymphs, or fairies. She shoved me back, and I stumbled, my jaw raw from her grip.

"You will start every day at seven am sharp. I expect you to be in my room when I return from my morning exercise with a hot bath and three drops of eucalyptus and one lavender. You must use the drops held within the boudoir of my room. They are embedded with protective magic. Let us see the Priestess think of using something like that. I do not see her being trained by the Druids and learning how to fully protect herself. I do not see her being smart enough to do anything like that. Although the dumb witch might try to poison me, not that she would get far with my protections and charms. She probably already has.

"I do not need assistance in bathing or dressing, so you will come to this study directly after and set up my breakfast and compile my work for the morning. You will follow four steps behind me at all times. You will not be seen or heard unless I call for you. Everything you do, see, and hear will be for your ears only. You will be expected to maintain the utmost secrecy. If you betray my trust, I will peel your skin from you patch by patch while you are still alive. I will keep your face intact, though; your skin is beautiful."

I kept silent as she went through the rest of my duties, a few more threats thrown in. Tying me upside down over her fireplace and lighting the fire, watching me slowly burn to death. Breaking every one of my joints with a chisel. Cutting the sensitive skin between my fingers, ripping my eyeballs out, and stirring them in with her wine. She was highly creative.

"I want you unseen and unheard."

I dipped my head in acknowledgment.

"See Javier, this is what I need. Plain, ordinary, and obedient." The wall next to me opened. Beneath my lashes, I took in the new addition as he stepped into the room. He was handsome, with deep brown skin, cropped salt and pepper hair and sharp features. He was tall and his muscles strained beneath the tailored jacket he wore.

"I see my Queen, but everyone pales in comparison to you." The room lit up from her pleasure, and she looked even more beautiful than I had ever seen her before.

"You flatter me, Javier." He wrapped his arms around her waist, pulled her into him, and placed a seductive kiss on her fingers. I averted my eyes to the fire that danced, attempting to ignore the giggles and whispers that made the room even more stuffy than it had been moments before.

CHAPTER II
AIFE

In the years I worked for Gregorovich, I received well over a dozen Allegiance Tests.

He claimed them to be exactly that, a test to deduce if I was still loyal to the Quinque and their rule. The first happened right after I was taken from my home. He bound me to a chair and asked me questions about why I thought my family had died. Being only nine at the time, I answered incorrectly, saying that he was trying to take the crown from the rightful rulers. Since I was so young, he only hit me. Slaps to the face, elbows to the stomach, punches to any part he could reach. I eventually learned how to answer to appease his questions.

As I got older, the punishments increased in aggression.

I realized rather quickly that it did not matter how correctly I answered him. It was never good enough. The last time I had to go through one of his torturous tests was about three years ago, and it took me two months to recover. For the burns to heal enough to use my arms and hands again; I rubbed my fingers over my palm where the skin was still puckered and jagged. After that last time, Zelu talked to him about how inconvenient it was to have me out of commission because they had lost important targets. The ones they sent in my stead failed and found had learned their lesson on failure with their lives.

The halls buzzed as I descended to the dungeon's, three floors below. The air was moist and suffocating, the stairs narrow and by breath jagged and sharp. Moss covered the walls and some of the stairs making them even more treacherous. While Gregorovich's obsession with inflicting pain was no secret, he never performed it in front of others. His desire to present the charismatic, caring leader took precedence above all, which was why was in the dungeon of this Gothic castle.

I tied my hair up and opted for old clothing since it was all but guaranteed they would get ruined; I rounded the corner into the largest cell to see Gregorovich beside Zelu. They were deep in conversation and a part of me swelled with hope that Zelu had talked the beloved Emperor out of this.

The brightness of Gregorovich's eyes when he saw me let me know that my hope, as always, had been futile. I lifted my chin and dipped into a shallow bow before placing my arms behind my back. I noticed a large wooden chair sitting at the side of the room. Thick leather straps hung open at the armrests, legs, waist, and the top of the chair.

I pursed my lips and looked at Gregorovich. "Good morning, Emperor," I offered.

"It is a wonderful morning, isn't it?" He grinned as he spoke. Zelu looked as if he wanted to punch him in his eye. "Sit."

It took every ounce of willpower I had to lower myself into the unforgiving wood of the chair. These were the moments I wanted to run, to escape; only to laugh at myself the moment the thought entered my mind. I had nowhere to go. No one would take in an assassin, especially one that had probably killed someone in their family. And the price on my head if I did leave would be too great for anyone to turn down. I would be free for a week, two at the most, and then be hunted down like an animal and I would take as many of them as I could with me. Though many have not seen my face, nor know who I am, it would not take long for my likeness to be spread throughout Fursomerra.

"Strap her in," Gregorovich said to Zelu. He stepped to the other side of the room to a bucket. It was at that point that I noticed a small male standing hunched in the corner.

Zelu strapped my legs first, my boots pinched against my leg as he tightened them before moving to my left hand. I stared as he maneuvered the buckle around the strap, tightening it flush against my skin.

Gregorovich talked to the male in a voice too low for me to hear, but Zelu whispered, "Be brave, Aife." I looked up into his eyes, which were strained with pain. "And tell the truth."

I would laugh if I could. If there had been anything funny about this situation.

Honesty would mean death for not just me, but for Joyce as well. I gave him a short nod. I took a deep breath as Zelu strapped in my hips; he then pressed a wet cloth to my forehead before he guided it back to lay flush on the chair back. The cloth stayed as he wrapped the strap around my forehead. He patted my shoulder and then appeared back in my line of sight before me.

Gregorovich strutted forward with the male next to him, holding the bucket. The male threw the water on the floor that formed a puddle beneath me deep enough to cover the soles of my boots.

"Now." Gregorovich's smile still highlighted his features. "I know Zelu has informed you that we have a traitor within our ranks." He paused, and I dipped my chin as much as I could with the strap minimizing my movement. I did not trust myself to talk.

"Let's start with a warmup, so you remember how this goes."

He knew I was aware exactly how this would go. The short break I had between this one and the last was not enough to erase the knowledge from my mind.

"What are you?" he demanded.

I ground my teeth and worked to keep my face clear of the emotion for which he was hoping. He asked this question when I first arrived in Parnitus. Gregorovich had no ill will towards elves. It was Heptus who hated the blood that pumped through my veins. From what Joyce told me, Heptus' father, David, married his mother, Georgina, to gain control of her home, Saleron. Luckily enough, he was never able to take it, but he took his lack of success out on Georgina and Heptus.

In the years of his father's reign, his cruelty only grew and nothing Heptus did ever please him enough. His mother fell in love with and got pregnant by an elf. Georgina told Heptus and had a plan to escape David's clutch. Heptus, however, betrayed his mother's trust and told David in hopes of finally doing something right enough for him.

Unfortunately, it ended with his father viciously murdering Georgina in front of Heptus. That was the turn of the tides for Heptus, and he killed his father shortly after. Ever since, he blamed elves for the death of his mother.

Gregorovich was also the child of a father's rage that ended in his mother's death and because of that, they share a hatred. Me.

"I am nothing," I replied.

The smirk of Gregorovich and twitch of Zelu's head was the only response.

"Are you the spy?"

"No," I said. As easy as it would be to look at him confused, or furrow my brow, or react in any way to further my innocence. But I have done this too many times and know better. Any reaction other than answering the questions he immediately took as a lie and doled out whatever punishment he concocted.

"Do you know who the spy is?"

"I do not."

"Do you want to help the spy?"

"No," I knew my mistake as soon as it happened. My head twitched to the left in a shiver as the water seeped into the sole of my boots tickling my feet. I wore my old shoes, which apparently had lost their integrity.

Gregorovich smiled and his hand darted around the male's wrist and horror tightened my stomach as lightning burst out of his palm. White hot searing pain shot throughout me. It felt like my entire body had been set on fire and piercing sensations shot up my head, down my fingertips before the pain blinded me. I could only hear a loud crackling sound right before everything stopped and went black.

"Wake up," a voice echoed around me. I felt a hand tap against my cheek, and I blinked blearily, confused and in pain. My entire body felt like it was on fire, and I feared the smell of burning flesh would reach my nose.

"There she is!" a second voice sounded.

I blinked and Zelu's face came into focus, his lips in a tight line. Gregorovich stood with his hands on his hips, the lightening male crumpled on the floor.

"It seems I got a bit too carried away with that one," Gregorovich said through a chuckle.

I gasped for air that refused to fully inflate into my lungs. I think he might have cracked the top ten list for the most painful sessions.

"Now," he said and clapped his hands. "I will ask again, do you want to help the spy?"

"No." I replied as I tried to catch any form of breath. The pain that had disappeared when I passed out slowly built back into my body.

"Very good, get up." He kicked the crumbled form next to him, and the boy staggered up. His body was pale, his veins shone brightly through his skin. This kind of torture was not just painful for me, it was for whatever poor creature was on the other end as well. Having the very essence of life ripped from a body usually ended in their death. This may be just torture for me. It was a death sentence to the poor boy.

"Do you have plans to join the Revolucija?"

"No," I grunted, working to bite back the anger that screamed in every vessel of me.

"Very good." He nodded and grabbed the male's arm again, and he started to cry. Gregorovich extracted the boy's magic, and I watched as the poor figure paled increasingly and his eyes rolled back. When Gregorovich released him, he slumped to the ground. Dead.

"One last shock for good measure."

#

CHAPTER 12
TITAIA

Working for Alhma was hell. The Palace was hell. I had never had to endure other people having so much sex in my life. She almost never slept, which meant I never slept. I think I had received about ten hours in that last week.

Nothing could have prepared me for what it was like to work for her. I have not been able to talk to Katrina since I started and while I curse her very existence, I missed her. My best friend and the one piece of stability I have.

I had made my way to her room for the first time in twenty-two days, excited to see her and slightly dreading how I would find her. She had been making more visits to Brock's room, and it made me anxious when I considered what could be happening to her.

There were no visible bruises, but they were there, always kept unseen in the clothes she wore but still seared into her skin like a brand. Brock had anger issues that I believed stemmed from him keeping his magic contained. He lived in his father's shadow willingly, but it made him unpredictable because of the strength of his power that hummed beneath his skin. Unused and explosive.

The castle was quiet when I made my way to Katrina's room. All the snow had melted, and the castle was warming up even though winter tried to fight back at night. I paused outside her room and heard the raised voices of Katrina and someone I did not recognize. I opened the door and checked every inch of the room, only to see Katrina as she paced in front of the burning fireplace.

"I have tried, but no matter what I do, he will not budge." She stopped and stared into the fireplace. "Whatever it is, it has to be delicate for him to keep it from me." I closed the door, the fire smoldered and burned out as Katrina turned to face me.

"Titaia. You scared me!" she gasped.

I reached out and ignited the fire again. She stared into it, her face red and shoulders hunched. "What's going on Kat?"

"I am tired, Titaia. I am so tired." She flopped into one of the chairs and took a few deep breaths. "Brock has become so secretive this last week. The seers are trying to figure out what they know about Harenae and Hespath and I know there is something going on just based on how he is acting. You have been with Alhma for a while now. Any news?"

I sighed, sitting down in the twin chairs. "Well, she has had some correspondence back and forth with General Zelu. She suspects a traitor within the circle, and he will be investigating when they get here in two days."

Her shoulders tensed. "Does she have any idea..."

"If she did, we would currently be seeing how much this rebellion of yours protects its people."

"Anything else?"

"Besides her being batshit crazy and having a lot of sex with Javier? She has been doing a lot of research through the stack of assorted grimoires from all around Fursomerra that she has acquired. I do not know what she is looking for, but it is nothing good." All I wanted was rest, time to get my wits about me, especially since visitors were coming. Visitors who were looking for Katrina and wanted my head on a spike.

"The meetings are never anything useful. Alhma has been forcing Heptus to stop talking when he starts on a tangent. She is suspects everyone of being the spy and refuses to say anything around anyone, even me." I said. "I think our best chance is going to be when Gregorovich arrives. During their parties and meetings, I bet they let something important slip."

I studied Katrina. Her skin was paler than normal, her red hair frizzy, and bags beneath her tired green eyes. "Brock has been trying to set a date," she said with a sigh.

"Oh?"

"I should say, Brock has set a date; Winter Solstice."

"He expects someone like you to plan a wedding in six months?"

"Very funny," she grunted. "I pushed it off as long as I could...but if I didn't agree, it would have looked bad."

"Let's hope that we can be out of here before that happens."

"I cannot marry that male Ti. Ten years of being under control is enough."

"Why can you not get this right?" Alhma screamed in her study. The next day, the book she chucked shattered the mirror sitting over the fireplace. I bit back a sigh, which was the fifth one since I started working for her. I glanced at the Knight, who stood in the corner nodding. He leaned out the door and whispered to someone before stepping back in.

I could almost taste her anger as she grabbed her hair and pulled. "How does she do it? She has so much power, I feel it growing every time she comes."

She must be talking about Priestess Josephine, which means she noticed it too. The strange power that seemed to radiate from her now.

"I need to find a way. I have to make myself stronger than her. I have to be more valuable. I need to lead the charge to fight them. It has to be me." While Alhma was naturally frantic, it had gotten worse the closer it got to Gregorovich, Josephine, and Zelu returning. Javier placed a hand on her shoulder and she immediately relaxed into his touch. As much of a turn off their sex was, seeing them together did make me miss intimacy. I wondered if Nisha was back in the city. It had been a while since I saw her.

The thought of her ocean blue eyes made me smile. I had a weakness for dark hair and light eyes. And the way her tongue and fingers worked was fucking magic. I cleared my throat and tried to ignore the throbbing in my core and focus on the conversation. I had no desire to get aroused around those two.

"What stresses you, my Queen?" Javier's sultry voice flowed through the room and caressed my skin, making me shift uncomfortably.

"I am convinced that Josephine and Gregorovich have something going on. They are becoming more every time they visit."

"More?"

"More, Javier. I have to be the one to go into Hespath. It has to be me." She pulled away and paced the room. "It has to be me; it has to be me. If she tries to take my success, I will end her, tear out her entrails and feed them to my dogs. They would like it. The magic in her blood might make them faster."

"Why, my Queen?"

"Because it does!" Alhma grabbed a knife from her desk and sliced her thumb. "Come here," she growled at the young girl who stood next to me, who could not have been older than seventeen. Alhma grabbed her hand and used the blood from her thumb created three circles, a big one in the middle and two smaller ones that sat within the larger and a small corner of the two in the middle overlapped in the girl's palm. The blood boiled in her hand and Alhma dragged her over to the silver bowl that sat on her desk and sliced right into the center of the two overlapping circles. Alhma flipped her palm and squeezed the blood into the bowl, watching the surface. The smile Alhma gave the girl was so kind and enduring I wished I were on the receiving end of it.

"Where is your family from, child?" she asked, tucking a piece of blonde hair behind the girl's ear.

"Litladon your Majesty." Her voice was like windchimes on a summer breeze.

"Ah, Nymphs." Alhma ran the pad of her finger over the small nick in the girl's skin and the cut healed.

"Such interestingly divine creatures. What element are you connected with?"

"Plants and forests."

"Dryads…my mother used to tell me stories of nymphs when I was a babe. How the fertility and allure of the creatures could steal a male's heart, even from his fated." She grabbed the girl's chin between her forefinger and thumb and twisted her head to where Javier stood. "Do you feel inclined to pull Javier from me?"

The girl's mouth gaped, and she shook her head adamantly.

Javier smirked as Alhma said, "are you saying my love is unattractive?"

"No…no…I…" Alhma took the knife again and slid it across the pale throat of the girl.

Javier chuckled as her body slumped to the ground, blood seeping out of her throat, but did not stain the ground. The Queen flicked her fingers, and the body turned to ash. Alhma's eyes flashed to me, and she opened her mouth just as the door burst open. Brock stood there with Katrina. His lips pursed as he took in his surroundings and glared at Javier.

"Gregorovich has arrived."

CHAPTER 13
AIFE

The pillars in the room were ridiculously large, as wide as I was tall. Regardless, I situated myself against the closest to the thrones, which sat in the center of the room.

I was partially obscured by one of the pairs of banners that hung over the dais that allowed me a level of comfort in the dark.

My body still ached from the test Gregorovich had administered two weeks ago, and new scars filled my feet and legs. I must admit, they were the most interesting ones I had. They climbed up my legs like forks of lightning.

The room filled slowly with court officials in their finery, each outfit brighter than the last. Their biggest competition was to out-dress their rivals. I would kill to see their pretty dresses and tunics covered in blood. Quite literally, I would love to do it myself. The pretty pink and yellow dresses with spots of red would be picturesque.

Knights wore suit jackets with the Caeruleus crest, an eagle and a crow flying across each other. They chatted with their hands on the golden pummels of their swords. I bet they shined the gold rather than the blade; half of them had never covered that blade in blood before or had their own spilled. They found comfort in their sole escape in the still open grand doors opposite the dais. They did not realize the false wall that sat to my right or the trap door right behind the king's throne. My feelings had become especially bitter after the light show Gregorovich gave me, everything pertaining to him seemed to scorch the fire that simmered within me.

The room was different from the last time I was in here, giant banners in the back with the Kingdom and Empire crests, a pyramid with two arrows piercing the center and an eagle erupting from the center in black, white, and red. And a crow with a gleaming snake in its talons in black and white, respectively. The overly large thrones sat in the middle of the tallest dais Heptus was able to build and are still fully seen by the crowd. Five steps was just excessive for a dais in my mind. Would not want the Priestess to break her dainty neck. I smirked as that fantastic scene played out in front of me.

Sheer white and gold curtains surrounded the opened windows and draped across the mosaic ceiling. Servants walked with black trays full of wine in gold goblets. Against the right wall was an expansive table full of wrapped gifts. The table next to it held a four-tiered cake that had my mouth watering.

I do love cake. Nothing like a sweet treat to blur the smell of rust.

The roar of conversation in the room filled the corners, and all I wanted to do was set it on fire and take those too high laughs and turn them into screams. As much as I would have loved to burn my way through this room it would not be productive to anyone or anything, especially since neither Heptus nor Gregorovich were in there to burn with them.

Queen Alhma and her assortment of children walked through the door. The room quieted and dropped into a bow.

Her youngest children, twins, Mathilda, and William curtsied and bowed respectively while giggling and ran to the dais almost knocking down a servant who precariously balanced a tray full of wine goblets in her curtsy. They were the cutest and most innocent of the Queen's children. They looked like their mother, in the straight noses, tight lips, but their hair was a dark blonde like their father's. The eldest daughter, Erin, held her head high and looked down her nine-year-old nose at everyone in the room. She looked most like her mother. That unearthly beauty gave her a strong jaw, hollowed cheeks, purple eyes, and long black hair. Closely behind them was Brock, and my eyes ached as I contained their need to roll at his fiancé draped over his arm. As daft as she was beautiful.

Brock was the mirror image of his father. Cropped black hair, hauntingly handsome in a rigid way, bright green eyes.

Arriving a day early had allowed me to explore the castle relatively unseen amongst the chaos of celebration preparation. Bad for them, good for me. I am on the hunt, and it is always easier to find a slip when you are unexpected. The movement behind Brock and Katrina pulled my eyes. Someone else had walked in, choosing to slink along the wall rather than parade down the center of the room like the rest of the cattle.

I caught sight of a black glittering skirt and brown hair as the female slipped behind a horde of people. Interesting. Celebrations like this were not meant for those trying to be obscure. I kept close to the wall and made my way around the room. I caught another sight of the glittering skirt behind the two shifters with ridiculously large crowns. They were not even royalty.

I approached where she had been standing and blinked. She was gone. I froze, peering around the room. What the...

"Looking for me?" I whirled to that silvery voice. Dagger in hand, I pressed it into her chest. I know my eyes were wild. Never in my life had anyone snuck up on me before, not even before my training. Not even Zelu, I had considered it a gift. An utterly useless gift, apparently.

Her lips were pulled up in a wicked grin as her eyes dropped, long black lashes fanned across her cheeks.

Why was she smiling? I followed her gaze and saw a godsdammed dagger pressed against stomach. "You sly little minx."

Her eyes fluttered back to mine. She pulled the dagger back, parted the slit of her dress, and slid it back into the sheath at her thigh. That might be the most erotic thing I had ever seen. I pulled mine and returned it to my hip. I closed the distance between us, an intoxicating mixture of jasmine and vanilla wafted over me.

I tracked my eyes down her body. The skirt of her long black dress touched the floor. The low-cut dress hugged right above the large swell of her hips and showed the curve of her breasts between which hung a gold pendant. The sleeveless arms showed her umber skin and toned arms and broad shoulders. Her brown hair was braided in a loose plait with tendrils surrounding her oval face.

"I'm Elle," she said, holding out the same hand that grasped the blade only seconds earlier. I finally met her eyes. A weird hazel.

Unnatural.

Forced.

I looked at the graceful fingers that extended between us, the healed callous and stark black fingernails that complimented her dark skin.

The one thing I want to know is how the hell she snuck up on me, instead I found myself saying something else.

"Aife," I responded, not taking her hand, which dropped to her side.

"Aife, were you looking for me?" I watched my name float off her full lips and felt slightly embarrassed how much I loved the way her mouth formed around it. I leant against the wall beside her. She faced me, feet spread, arms loose at her sides.

Defensive stance, smart.

"What if I was?"

"Why?"

"You were creeping around here like you didn't want to be seen. Why would that be?"

The little tilt of her head was enduring. "Why?" she asked again.

"Are you six?" Her eyes trailed across my body this time, taking in the black boots, pants, and shirt that I covered with a deep purple jacket. I forewent my normal face paint and cloak today for the celebration. My skin heated as her gaze seemed to dig through every layer, cord of muscle, and bone to and burrowed into my core. I knew that I was desirable in that dangerous way, but something about her skipping over the scars littering my face set me on edge. I could not tell if I liked that she had or not.

"I don't like crowds," she finally said after a prolonged silence.

"That makes two of us."

"Why were you really following me?"

"Just doing my job, little minx." Her brows furrowed and three cute little lines appeared before them. I had a preposterous urge to smooth them with my thumb.

"Did you come with the Emperor?"

"So many questions," I purred before I pushed off the wall and walked away.

King Heptus and Emperor Gregorovich finally sauntered in right when I settled back into position. It had been a few months since I saw Heptus. His black hair cropped short to his head; his eyes glistened like clear water in the light. So stark against his dark black skin. His face still hovered between that unnatural beauty that danced between human and sphinx. He could have been a God. Well, everyone believes he is a God, the one true God.

Oh, the lies they weave.

"Happy birthday, Greg!" Heptus slurred, his hand falling heavy on the Emperor's shoulder as they stumbled into the room. Drunk off their asses.

Idiots.

The room bowed; I kept holding up the pillar.

Zelu trailed behind the pair as they approached the dais. Though he could not see me, he always knew where I would be. Irritation lined his face as he reached me in the shadows.

"Any news?" *So, no hello then?*

"Everyone in this fucking Kingdom is dodgy."

He chuckled, and said, "Keep your eyes and ears open. Especially tonight, there seems to be a lot more disgruntled courtiers than normal." He nodded towards a group of three men who were whispered, their voices low as Heptus and Gregorovich continued their slow walk up the stairs to the dais. They staggered and bumped into each other, laughing. See, five steps is asinine.

"They look especially clandestine."

"Sounds fascinating," I murmured. I saw Elle, standing next to Brock and his fiancée, as I walked to where the males were conspiring. Elle's eyes bore into Heptus and Gregorovich. It looked like a bit of flame burned behind those eyes. That is interesting.

"Welcome to the celebration of my dear friend, and death partner, your Emperor Gregorovich!" Heptus' voice stretched throughout the room, and I gritted my teeth from the sound. I guess they finally staggered their way to their seats.

"You always outdo yourself, Heptus. Always make me feel like my birthday is an extravagant affair and give the best gifts!" Their boomed laughter immediately drew a headache.

"You deserve nothing but the best, friend."

I tried to drown out their voices as I slipped closer to the group of males. I stood next to two women who were falling out of their panties at the sight of Gregorovich who had donned himself in a tight blue suit and opted for one of his smaller crowns.

"...Get into Harenae," one of the males had finished. His brown hair was long and curly and reached the middle of his back.

"Do you really think they found it?" a male with short black hair said, as Heptus raised a glass and spoke to the crowd with a bright smile and icy eyes.

"Who is to say at this point, they have been promising Hespath for at least five years," the male with curly hair responded.

"All I know is the Revolucija got into Corthia last month and killed my best officials." The male who spoke had hair as red as fire. I thought I recognized him, Lord Baron of Corthia. Where the Igniris, the fire manipulators, lived. My least favorite people were so spiteful and angry. Plus, they liked to throw fire at me. I have burn marks on my back to prove it.

"I have considered adjusting allegiance; I have a way to contact the seers. We might need to find unusual ways to protect our land and our money." The curly haired male said.

"I heard the King and Emperor have some inside information about the Revolucija." The light brown-haired male said. Baron nearly got whiplash when he snapped his head over to him.

Then he looked back at Gregorovich before asking out the side of his mouth. "What about them?"

Gregorovich and Heptus lifted their glasses in cheers, and the room copied and took long gulps before music filled the room.

The light brown-haired male shrugged. "They are keeping it pretty closely held. I believe the Queen and Priestess are even in the dark."

"I cannot say I am surprised. I do not know why they let them know anything," Baron sneered. "Fucking females."

"What did I hear about fucking females?" Brock's fiancée had approached the men, her eyes wide with innocence and intrigue.

"Duchess Katrina," Baron replied, his voice respectful and dripping with unhidden desire.

Katrina smirked. "Baron. How is your wife, Kalia's doing? Does she know you are going around fucking other females?"

He stammered and Elle peaked around behind her. I caught the shadow of a smile and she looked at me through her eyelashes.

"Duchess, Prince Brock has requested your presence." Elle's voice was still that silvery pitch that made my knees wobble.

Katrina looked over her shoulder, her lips twitching in a smirk. "Oh, but this was just getting interesting. Baron was just about to tell me about the women he is fucking. I'm interested to know how satisfied they are, Lord."

His face was red. "I have no need for females other than my wife."

Katrina giggled.

What the hell was happening?

CHAPTER 14
TITAIA

My cheek was bleeding, my teeth digging into it, trying to fight the smile as Katrina continued to berate Lord Baron. I could feel Aife's eyes on me, the cold black depths that intrigued me to the point of concern.

"This is inappropriate, Duchess," Baron bristled.

Katrina leaned in and the two men, Drakon, a curly haired male from Aurdina and Rosh, a black male from Gwendalon tilted towards her.

"Is it because you are embarrassed to talk about sex? Or because you find us..." she said, as her eyes trailed up and down his form, unimpressed, "less?"

The King and Emperor drifted around the room, and Aife shifted to stand between Rosh and me. I shot her a questioning glance, but her eyes were on the Baron whose face resembled a strawberry.

"Lord Baron." She replied in her husky voice, deep in warning, made me shiver. "I think you need to take a breath before you do something you might regret."

His red face turned towards Aife, and I watched the fear flash across his face as he met her gaze. "Assassin."

My heart dropped in surprise, and I looked over to see a cold smile fill her perfectly sculpted mouth. The scars on her face warped yet still devastatingly beautiful. "You should mind your business."

Cold radiated off her like ice, and goosebumps littered my arms. "You should take care of who you speak business in front of, Baron." She took a step forward, her arms crossed. The movement was so intimidating I was surprised Barron did not fall to the ground and beg for mercy. "You speak so carelessly about such important things. You never know who is listening."

He stammered. Again. It made me wonder how many words were in his vocabulary to be driven speechless so easily, especially by females who he had been degrading. Katrina looked at me, surprised, and I pursed my lips. She looked at Aife as if she were an afternoon snack and a snake of jealousy curled in my stomach.

"I don't know what you mean...."

"Oh Baron, you insult me."

He sneered. "Elf bitch."

Aife stilled.

She is not just an assassin, but *the* assassin. The assassin that had killed dozens, if not hundreds of people, the one they sent after the hardest to find and kill. The one they sent when they wanted answers to questions, the one that the entire Realm knew about. I had never seen her before. The people who usually saw her ended up dead. I never even knew her name, whether by design or not her identity was kept secret.

Aife was tall and lean, and I would be lying if I said she was not the most attractive person I have ever laid eyes on. I do not need dark hair and light eyes any-more. I can handle dark hair and the deepest black eyes if they are packaged up with her.

I blinked and shook my head. What the hell was I thinking? She tucked her long hair back, high-lighting her tall-pointed ears, and something trans-formed in her that had every molecule in my body screamed at me to run.

Eyes simmered with rage as Aife breathed, as if she talked to a lover, "I'll see you soon."

He sucked in a breath. "Is that a threat?"

If the words had not been, the wink she sent him was. My body churned with fear, dread, and arousal as she turned to Katrina and me.

"Ladies," she said with a bow, and walked away. Her body moved in an unnatural leisurely way for someone who killed people on the regular. I jumped as Katrina threw her head back and laughed. The room was startled at her outburst and turned to-wards us.

"What's so funny, beautiful?" Gregorovich asked as he sauntered up. His eyes raked Katrina and found me. His gaze, like heated steel, lingered at the bare skin between my breasts. He licked his lips, and I instantly regretted every decision I made to wear this dress. Well, not every decision. Not after Aife looked at me how she did. Her attention was like a drug and when her eyes met mine, it felt like so much more than electricity.

"Baron tells the best jokes," Katrina giggled, giv-ing Gregorovich a look that soured my stomach.

All I wanted was a piece of cake.

Baron's shoulders sagged, and he smiled at Gre-gorovich before bowing deeply. "Happy birthday, Em-peror. It is a marvelous celebration, and we are honored to have been invited." Drakon and Rosh were enthusiastic in their agreement.

"Of course, Lord Baron. You are one of our favorite traders in the North. Fursomerra would be nothing without you fire bastards." Gregorovich had not taken his eyes off me as he talked, a promise deep within his irises.

He reached out and twirled a strand of my hair between his fingers before Katrina's giggle pulled his attention as she placed a hand on his arm. Gregorovich looked away and dropped his hand, giving me time to retreat to a corner of the room, planting myself there for the rest of the party. Without my cake.

Heptus and Gregorovich continued to stumble around the room drunk, Alhma catered to her younger children's every whim until it was time for them to go to bed, then she signaled to Javier and left the room. All the while, Josephine sat on her throne monitoring Gregorovich's every move. I was glad Alhma allowed me to attend this party with Katrina, claiming that I would hinder her ability to care for her children.

I felt Aife's attention for the rest of the night. The intense feeling of her attention was debilitating, and I mentally slapped myself for not realizing who she was. I bit my cheek to stop the smile as I thought back to her surprise when I caught her unaware and then bested her with the dagger. Given she would have killed me before I had the chance to do anything, but I would have at least given her a nick, it was an accomplishment. And then the smirk that made every part of my body inside and out clench in response. Nothing like the smile she had given Baron and nothing like smile I got from Gregorovich.

While she was covered in scars both outside and undoubtedly inside, a smile like that would drop any and all panties.

I tried to keep track of her throughout the night, but aside from the flashes of her suit jacket and the tall silhouette that was embedded in my memory she moved to quickly and carefully for me to catch sight of her again.

Phoebe.

That was Queen Alhma's new lady-in-waiting that I had been introduced to after the party, and had been shadowing me for the last five hours. And who was currently breathing directly into my ear as we stood in the dining room waiting for Heptus and Gregorovich.

In. Out. Inhale. Exhale.

My hair tickled my cheek as her hot breath fanned across my face, and I considered grabbing a fork and sticking it to the side of her face. She had done...fine in her duties to that point; she proved to be clumsy with her own limbs. When she held trays or ran a bath, she was able to keep herself together, but the moment the tray was on a table, or walked away, she ended up sprawled on the ground with the tray tipped over and bath overflowing. A part of me felt guilty for leaving her with Alhma, knowing how unhinged she was. But when she went into her study and rampaged, throwing ancient binders in the fire and blowing holes into the ceiling, I shoved that guilt down deep into a metal lined chest and closed it with an iron lock.

The dining room was inviting, with white walls and natural wood accents. An eight-seat table filled up the center of the room with a roaring fireplace against the back wall and plush chairs lining the rest. A hutch holding assortments of liquor and crystal glasses sat along the far side of the wall. Nothing like what was in the throne room or the celebration room.

The table was already laden with food that made my mouth water. Chicken, lamb, rice, potatoes, vegetables, pies, cakes, and cookies and it was all I could do to not climb on the damn table. My self-control had been severely tested, and that was not helping.

Phoebe and I were the first ones in the room since Alhma required us to be in any room, at least thirty minutes before she arrived. Phoebe almost had a panic attack when I told her to sit in Alhma's seat to warm it up. We poured her water, placed a cover over it, and wrapped it in a cold towel. Even adjusted the food on the table to have the fruits and vegetables closest to her seat. After all of that, she stood behind me, breathing in my ear.

I turned to tell her to step the fuck away when Katrina strolled in with Brock on her arm like a trophy husband. She was bedecked in a beautiful gold dress that sparkled when the light caught it, a compliment to Brock's gold threaded black suit.

"Look at this Brock, everything looks and smells delicious," Katrina crooned. "I wish every day was the Emperor's birthday if we continue getting this spoiled." Katrina took a seat towards the middle of the table and Brock sat next to her, his face bright with excitement. She twisted to me. "Hello, Elle. I cannot wait to have you back with me. These proxies hardly know how to warm a bath or even help me dress. Not to mention they can barely handle a proper plait."

Indeed, her braid was at an awkward angle, the natural frizz of her hair something that took me months to learn. I smiled. "I should be with you in the morning, Duchess. Phoebe here is the new lady for the Queen." I gestured to Phoebe, and she shifted from behind me, tripped over the hem of her skirt and flew headfirst to the stone floor.

I went to grab her, only to find someone else's hands already there. Long, tattooed fingers wrapped around Phoebe's upper arm and stopped her from face planting and breaking a nose or tooth. My eyes jumped to meet the impenetrably black ones of Aife. Her hood was down, long black hair pulled back into a bun that displayed her pointed ears. She had drawn black lines across her face, one from ear to ear with dots below it, down the center of her forehead to the bridge of her nose and from her lip to chin was another thick black line with smaller lines surrounding both. She yanked Phoebe back up with a brow raised.

"Watch your step." Aife's voice was a delicious contradiction of cold and alluring. "I doubt the servants would like to clean blood off the floor."

Phoebe's eyes were wide as she straightened and stepped out of Aife's grasp to my side. "Th...thank you." She stammered before she curtsied. Her brow furrowed, and she turned to me and curtsied again before her eyes darted around. She turned to Katrina and bowed. "I'm Phoebe, Katri...Du...Duchess Katrina."

I stared at her.

Katrina's eyebrows were to her hairline, and she bit her lips between her teeth as she met Phoebe's eyes.

"Pleasure to meet you, Phoebe."

I looked at Aife to see her watching me. I tilted my head to Phoebe and tipped my eyebrows up. A ghost of a smile graced her ridiculously attractive mouth. Heat coursed through my cheeks, and I looked towards the door just as the rest of the party walked in.

Heptus, Gregorovich, Alhma, Josephine, and Zelu filtered into the room together. Heptus and Gregorovich sat at either end of the table, Alhma to Heptus' right, Brock across from her, Josephine to Gregorovich's right and Zelu to his left. One empty chair sat between Alhma and Josephine. That was for the best, though it might have been safer to have them in separate rooms. Phoebe stood as stiff as if she had been taped flush with a pole.

"You have to breathe or you're going to pass out," I whispered. "This is going to be a long lunch." Her dress shifted. "Go remove the cloth."

Taking slow steps like I instructed, she moved towards Alhma.

"How long are you here Greg?" Katrina asked.

"How many times has she fallen today?" a husky voice whispered in my ear, and I leaned into the heat of her body and voice. Treacherous body.

"I lost count after seven." I peered at the tall elf beside me. She leaned against the mantle of the fireplace, a silver goblet gripped between her fingers. Fingers that she probably knew how to use well. Her chuckle spread goosebumps down my spine, and I blushed, wondering if she could read minds. That would be just my luck. "Thank you for catching her."

"I would have rather had you falling into my arms, but I suppose we will have to wait for that." My face flamed, and I opened my mouth to retort when a crash cut off my words.

"I told her to pull up, not out." I toed around the room and filled another goblet of water. I grabbed Phoebe's arm and passed her the new glass, took the towel, and swept up the shards of the shattered one as she placed the new glass down.

I laced my fingers with hers and pulled her around the table past Josephine and Gregorovich. His eyes were concentrated beams on me; unease spread through my body like water.

"You have to stop crying." I sandwiched Phoebe between the wall and me beside the fireplace, attempting to block her shaking body.

"She called me a stupid, ignorant bitch," she cried.

"You have to pull it together, Phoebe. She knows it affects you and it will only get worse if she sees you crying."

"I know, I'm sorry." Phoebe gasped and sniffled once more before going quiet.

I knew exactly how she felt, but for varied reasons. When I first came to the Palace, I found it difficult to change my life from being served as a royal to serving royalty. I never considered myself someone who clung to the life of being waited on. I hated the dresses, boring dinners, and the constant supervision that came with being a Princess. Hated it enough that I had a habit of escaping my guards. Yet, I never truly realized how different it was being on the other side of the stage. The residents of this Palace had no trouble breaking me of that.

When phoebe stepped beside me; she was a mask of calm. "Very good. Now all we have to do is wait."

"Julaera has failed to pay again," Josephine said as she cut a piece of chicken into tiny pieces. "Portia claimed there is nothing left for her people to give."

Heptus chuckled. "The cost of freedom isn't free."

"They are now three months behind; how would you like for us to handle it your Majesty?" My jaw clenched but tried to keep my face neutral, the nobles hardly cared enough to consider the safety of their people. The people who were too poor and hungry to take up arms to fight against the very ones who take their livelihood. They barely had money to eat, yet were expected to give everything they had to the crown.

Brock smirked. "I would love to go have a chat with Portia."

Gregorovich said, "I would love to be with you for that. While you are at it, stop by Sravah and talk to those pixie harlots. If they want to sell themselves, that is fine, but we do get a portion of those earnings as well."

"I didn't realize Pixies were involved in that kind of work." Katrina said her face was pink.

"There's a lot more than just sex work those females do," Heptus huffed. "They are involved in the skin trade now. Speaking of which, how would you feel about a trip to Aurdina tomorrow?"

Aurdina was a beautiful city a few hours outside of Austiria. A sprawling countryside holding the farms within the Kingdom. A city that had been tainted with the Duke Learman and his trade of females and males.

"Is there something wrong?" Josephine's satin voice caused Alhma to sneer.

Heptus spoke. "Of course not, dear Priestess. We have not visited the countryside in quite a while. I think a trip to the estate for Greg's birthday would be perfect."

"Ah, the estate." Gregorovich's mouth pulled up in a smile behind his goblet. "I would love to visit."

My stomach twisted. Dark. Disgusting debauchery. Willing and unwilling participants and always lots of blood. I had never been to the estate in Aurdina, but Katrina's first visit had left her pale and shaking for days. Torture and sex were the main attractions there. Apparently, of the many things Heptus and Gregorovich had in common, the biggest of their bonding came from their love of inflicting pain.

"Who will be joining us?" Gregorovich asked.

"She's scary." Phoebe leaned into me and nodded her head towards where the assassin leaned against the wall by General Zelu.

She watched the table, her eyes darted around as if she could see the words that spilled from their mouths. Aife's arms were folded across her body; sleeves rolled up as one of her fingers idly tapped her bicep, the other still held a goblet. Her arms covered in black ink of abstruse lines, like a labyrinth and puckered skin from scars. She was toned, tall, and had a general *fuck off* aura about her. Danger and anger rolled from her like waves on a beach.

Or maybe it was the scars that lined her face. A long one dragged from her right hairline across her eyebrow and nose, stopping at the top of her lip. A short one crossed the other right above her eyebrow and just missed her eye. Another set sliced across her other cheek from the bridge of her nose to ear. The last one down her right lip from below the nose to her chin. They faded with age, but the flesh was slightly pinker than the rest even with the black coal that lined her face.

"What about her?" Gregorovich asked as he turned towards me. Katrina's goblet froze halfway to her mouth as the table kept eating. My lips trembled as he stared at me. "You are a stunningly delicious vixen."

"Those are kind words, Emperor," Josephine said, and my heart thundered at the threat I felt in those words.

Gregorovich's gaze moved to her, and I cut mine to Aife whose face was frozen with rage as she stared at him.

"No," Heptus said. "The female will stay here. I told you to leave her alone to her duties, Gregorovich. We cannot lose anymore servants to you."

Katrina said, "I'm rather fond of her as well."

"Mmm," Gregorovich licked his lips and looked back at me. "I am as well, Duchess. Keep a close eye on her and do not look at me if she goes missing."

CHAPTER 15
AIFE

O bviously, I had not been invited to enjoy the exquisiteness of Aurdina. Aside from the less desirable offenses, it was a beautiful place to visit. If one kept on the main road at all times, avoiding Sinners Alley, where the name is exactly what it means and is Heptus and Gregorovich's favorite place.

After the lunch that turned into dinner, Zelu let me know that I, in fact, did not get time off. I not only was still tasked with finding the spy but also got to make my way to a store called Threadbare and wreak havoc on someone named Norro.

That was all Zelu told me, the name and where he worked. Not what he did, not why he had to die, nothing.

Blowing on the hot, black coffee, I took a sip, welcoming the bitter earthy taste burning down my throat. A pastry covered in some unknown white frosting sat untouched in front of me as I watched the store across the street. The street was busy, all patrons ignorant of who I was, what I was doing.

I had opted for cream pants and a long sleeve black tunic to blend in as much as possible, if it was possible for a six-foot elf to blend in anywhere. Heptus' hatred of elves made them exceedingly rare in the city. I left my hair down to conceal my ears, and with my sleeves rolled up.

The sun was on its slow descent and the bodies that filled the streets thinned as people made their way home or into the stores they aimed to visit before they closed. It seemed that while other cities suffered from the loss of income, those within Austiria and Parnitus thrived. The coffee seemed to be freshly ground, and the food was clear of mold.

"Come on Hera, sit right here. Let me help." The chair at the table before me was pulled out and a little girl was placed into it. Hera jumped to her knees and started sticking her fingers through the grated metal of the table. A female, potentially her mother, sat next to her, smoothed out the child's tight blonde curls and pulled her finger out of the table. "What would you like to eat?"

"I want that!" she replied loudly, pointing at the untouched pastry on my table.

"Let's save the sweets for after dinner," her mother cooed. The server came out and took her order and filled up my coffee again. The nutty aroma smelled more alluring than the taste of it. She winked at me, her brown eyes glittering as she walked away.

Norro and his wife Molly were visible through the window, straightening up fabric and assisting customers. The old male had cropped gray hair and a mustache that he kept twisting into a tight curl. He was tall but hunched from age and work. Molly had continued to dye her hair brown, and she stood a good foot and a half shorter than Norro, even with his hunched form. Their shop was small, Threadbare spelled out with gold foil lettering in the window with strips of fabric hanging just behind it. Dark blue with light blue embossed leaves; white with swirls of yellow, green, blue, and red; and silver with black lines.

Within the store were rows and rows of rolls of different fabric lining shelves. Their pair were in their late sixties, having owned the shop since Austiria was established. They had flourished in the aftermath of the war, with the nobles wealthier than they had ever been and willing to spend money on the most extravagant items to look the part. The couple never had any children or pets and lived in a modest house right outside of the city. An itch on the side of my face pulled my eyes back over to the table next to me, where the little girl stared at me. I raised an eyebrow, and she grinned; her mother focused on an open book before her. The server dropped two plates at their table and some drinks.

"Need anything, darlin'?" she asked.

"No, thank you." I responded, lifting my still full coffee.

She placed her hand over mine and slid a piece of paper into my palm. "Jus' let me know."

I looked back up at the little girl, who was still staring at me, and lifted my mouth in a sneer. Her lips quivered and her eyes watered. Good.

I really hate children. They are sticky, snotty, annoying, and touch everything. And quite rude, staring at people. I dropped the paper in the coffee, placed some money on the table, and walked down the street. The city was huge. Stores, museums, restaurants, it was endless. It was the richest city within Fursomerra, Parnitus fell in a close second. Large statues sat in all major squares and districts, paintings, smaller statues, and more were held within museums within the Art district.

I headed to the Art district and did my best to ignore the eyes that followed my stroll.

Murals painted every visible surface. Painted females and males, flowers, the sky at night and during the day, landscapes, and so much more. Sculptures made of metal, clay, marble, flowers, and even animal skins filled the district. It was beautiful and tragic. This censored version of life, nothing here predated the war.

Another positive of the Art district was it held the best taverns in the city, I slipped behind a staircase hidden in alley, climbing to a hidden balcony that allowed me to see Threadbare.

The balcony was an unofficial bar. Magic made it look as if it was part of the brick building and kept the noise within. During one of my visits here I found this place. The music and art within should have been destroyed after the war, portraits showing original Goddesses and Gods and music speaking of freedom and loyalty. I took a seat at one of the cushioned chairs that overlooked the city and leaned back. Threadbare closed in a few hours. I knew that Molly would head home before they closed to prepare dinner, so I had time. I got a drink and crossed my ankle over my knee and watched the sunset.

Hours later, I was crouched on the roof of Threadbare. Molly had departed home a little while ago. I dropped into an abandoned alley in the back of the store and maneuvered to the back door carefully. The butcher that sat just behind my target had tossed some meat into the trash just before I arrived, and the smell burned my nose. I opened the door in the store and slid through it into a small supply room. Voices drifted to the back as I settled into a chair that sat just to the side of the open door that separated the rooms.

"You still have the best, Norro."

Norro's chuckle was forced. "Yes, well, I think the Mrs. and I will be retiring soon. We are ready to settle down with the money we saved and live a quiet life."

"Is it possible for you to live a quiet life?"

"You know, a decade of success and all. We are ready to just live the good life out." I spied a small, squat man at the counter. His hair and mustache are gray and wrinkles abundant.

"Just last week you were saying that you'd love to keep going for another few years."

"Things change quickly around here Gary, you know that." Norro wrapped up the purchased items and handed them to Gary, "give Beth our best."

"She will come by to show Molly the dress she's making with this."

"Request of the Duchess you know!" said Gary, a jolly male who was about as wide as he was tall.

Norro escorted him out, said his goodbyes, and locked the door and windows. His movements were jumpy and agitated, as if he were expecting someone. As if he knew there was a target on his head.

He shuffled around the room, shutting down for the night. I sat back against the cold metal chair and grabbed the blade from my boot. After a few minutes, the lights in the front clicked off. His steps had a drag on them, either age or an injury that had not healed properly.

Norro walked into the storage room and closed the door behind him, I pressed myself further against the back of the chair and caressed the long black hilt of my favorite dagger. Finally, beady brown eyes met mine, and he jumped with a yell, hand on his heart.

"Who, who are you?" His voice wobbled as he grabbed the handle of the door he had just closed.

"Norro, release the door." His Adam's apple bobbed and knuckles turned white. "You can run if you wish. You already locked up and cast the blinds and I bet I can get this knife in your back before you can make it to the front door." His eyes were wide as he looked around, the wrinkles on his face prominent in his fear. "Please run. I do love a good chase."

"Who are you?"

I clicked my tongue. "You know exactly who I am."

"Assassin."

I admired the sleek black hilt and the carved runes of the blade in my hand. "Very good."

"What... what do you want?"

"There is only one reason I would be darkening your doorstep, old man. You know that."

His fingers had not yet released the knob as he watched me. "I have done nothing."

"Such ugly lies you tell."

His mouth floundered. "Molly and I will disappear. We will go far away and never pose any threat ever again."

"I have no intention of harming your wife, Mr. Norro. She will not die by my hand." I raised a brow; the rest of his words raised a question. "Do tell me, to whom do you pose a threat to?"

His laugh was a bark that reminded me of my grandfather. "You don't know why you're here?"

I ground my teeth and felt a vein in my jaw pop. Zelu rarely found it in his interest to give me certain information. There are times when my lack of knowledge turns into embarrassment for me. "The more you tell, the less painful I will make this for you."

"You do not care how much pain I am in assassin. From what I hear, you enjoy torturing your kills as much as possible."

"Funny, just a few months ago, someone told me I didn't like to play with my food. So now I'm wondering who you heard that from because I'm sure the only ones who know what pain I've dealt or withheld are dead."

His mouth was tight, and I tipped his shoulder. With a short breath I chucked the blade into the meat of his thigh, right above his knee. He screamed and dropped to the floor. I moved a hand beneath his head to keep his skull from cracking and grabbed the hilt of the blade.

I twisted and smiled at his scream. If I had any inclination, I could make beautiful music with the screams I pull. "Come now Mr. Norro. You can tell me your secrets."

"We are a safehouse for people who choose to leave the Kingdom," he gasped out, his bleeding leg tight in his grip.

"Leave the Kingdom?"

His laugh was manic. "There's another war coming assassin."

The Revolucija recruited and influenced those who had been faithful to the King and Emperor in the previous war. In their ten years of what they called peaceful reign, the people had come to know what it truly meant to be within the Quinque's allegiance. None of this was news to me, and neither would it be to Zelu.

"How many have you helped?"

"Dozens. We would not make the same mistake we did during the last war."

"Thank you," I said, before I drove my blade into his Adam's apple, shoving up and sideways, giving him a quick death.

CHAPTER 16
TITAIA

Katrina left me. The King, Emperor, Queen, Prince, Priestess, General, and Katrina. All gone. Part of me was worried about what she would witness in that city and part was glad for the silence. The castle was quiet, without the constant screams and stomping of the royal family.

Since Aurdina was so close to Austiria, Heptus never found it imperative to name a proxy in his stead. He would rule from Aurdina if there was any time for him to do so between the drugs, sex, and torture.

I found myself outside the day after they left, having spent the previous day before preparing Katrina for her trip and ensuring Phoebe was taken care of, unfortunately she was going with them. Which had made me even more thankful for not being the Queen's lady-in-waiting anymore. I do not know why Gregorovich had a sudden interest, but I had no desire to find out.

My legs hung off the small lip of the pond outside of the Palace, my toes dangled in the cool water. Summer had finally arrived and cleared the last chill of spring. The bright moon illuminated the statue in the center of the pond. The smooth white marble depicted an unknown woman. Whoever she was, she had been beautiful with long hair curled down over her breasts, a wrap tied around her waist that trailed down the water. Her head was angled down, one hand holding some of the toga out of the water and the other elegantly pointing to the sky above. She was not a Goddess, since Heptus destroyed any portrayals of any Goddess or God that was not him or his self-proclaimed ancestor Linx, the God of War.

The grass was as plush as a freshly stuffed pillow. The pounds of snow that had melted giving the ground much needed moisture. The trees bloomed with leaves and the world was full of life again. I closed my eyes and inhaled the smell of summer and the feel of the moonlight on my skin. I should be on my way to the city right now. I had promised some of the girls that I would be there. They had been having trouble with visiting males and Guards. Especially the few that had attended Gregorovich's party. It seemed that when his Guards visited our city they lost all sensibility. The full moon tonight usually promised violence, so the girls asked me for some protection.

It was good practice. Since Sigurd died, I did not have regular instruction and training. I spent a lot of time training with Katrina, but I did not want my skills to rust with contained sparring and real targets always taught me something new. And protecting those who did not harness the skills to protect themselves let me feel as if I was helping in some way. I was pathetic, pathetic enough to let basic courtesy tide me over while the rest of the people within the realm died at the hands of tyranny. People that were supposed to belong to me. I sighed and looked up at the moon.

"It's beautiful," a voice reached my ear. I yelped, threw my head back and curled my legs in an attempt to roll back in a maneuver Sigurd taught me years ago. Unfortunately, it was a move he only showed me once and my limbs sprawled in the wrong direction. Hands grasped my leg and arm, that were precariously close to pitching me off the ledge.

"Calm down, little minx."

Aife's chuckle had me nearly begging for more of her touch. I cleared my throat and pulled away from her warm touch. I sat, albeit more tense than I had previously been. She sat next to me and crossed her impossibly long legs. Her sleek black hair spilled down her back, sleeves rolled up to show the beautifully inked labyrinths and runes that covered her tan skin.

She was unfairly gorgeous.

"Nocturnal?" Aife's voice was like a kiss on my heated skin, and I suppressed a shiver, or I think I did. If not, I imagine I looked like I had a miniature seizure. Her body was so close to mine that I could feel the heat radiating off of her. The smell of cedar wood and oranges tickled my senses as she settled beside me.

"Yes." I sounded wanton to my own ears and cleared my throat. "Unfortunately, I have about ten minutes before I don't get to enjoy it anymore."

"And what is it that pulls you from your reverie?"

"I have to go to the city." I glanced over to see her eyes on me. I met her eyes and noticed a small sliver of a purple so dark it was almost black around her pupils.

"The city at night. All that's out are sex workers, murderers, and those who are up to no good." A smile tugged at Aife's lips, a divot in her cheek peeking out.

Of course, she has fucking dimples. "Which one are you?"

"Wouldn't you like to know?"

Her head tilted in a predatory way. "There are quite a few things I would like to know about you."

"I could say the same..." I breathed.

Her brow raised and my attention went to the scar that crossed over it. Her scars were surprisingly less noticeable at this distance. Something about her drew me in and I found the marks that lined her face an afterthought. Not that they were imperceptible in the first place. When I did see them, the jaggedness of the lines concerned me for how deep they must have been dug into her skin. Along with the slight milkiness of her eye where the scar dragged down past it.

"I'm not a good one to know. You would be better staying far away from me."

"One could say that pulls intrigue more than fear." Where the fuck had that come from? I normally was not someone to be attracted to someone so obviously dark. I enjoyed an easy past, someone without the scars on the inside that made it easy to forget my own. Yet here I was, meeting the darkest eyes to see they had darkened into pools that settled within my core. Her scars ran deeper than any of mine. I licked my lips.

Her eyes flicked down to the movement. "Ignoring intrigue could make you far smarter than your prede-cessors."

"Good to know." I cannot explain why that upset me so much, but I lifted my feet out of the water and grabbed my shoes, shoved my feet into them and stood. Completely ungraceful to the point of almost tipping myself into the pond.

"Can I accompany you to the city?"

"I don't need protection."

Her lip curved up. "Believe me little minx, I do not doubt your ability to protect yourself. Just a little, company."

"If you insist." We walked in silence across the gravel pathway and to the concrete bridge, passing the sphinx statues on tall pedestals. "Why are you out so late?"

"I actually just came back from the city."

"Yet you are willing to walk back with me just to keep me safe. Who said chivalry is dead?"

"I'm not keeping you safe, as I said, I'm here for companionship." She slid her hands into her pockets.

"Why were you in the city?"

She shrugged, her black hair catching the light of the moon at the movement. "I do not typically stay in the Palace when we visit Austiria. This is the first time in almost twelve years I have set foot in there."

"That explains why I have never seen you before, neither has anyone else..." I tried off, almost kicking myself. I might have spent most of my morning asking around about her. To my dismay, it caused many of the females to blush, confirming what I thought when I first met her. No one that good-looking could be all innocent, not that being an assassin would make her innocent. Nor was I attracted to her. No, she was just an absolute dark Goddess, not my type at all. I need a white Knightess.

"Asking about me?" Aife asked teasingly.

My cheeks warmed.

"Curiosity is a dangerous thing," she continued.

"According to you, you are as well." I replied.

"Yes, well, I am an assassin." There was no shame and no regret. We started to cross through the archway where the city sat just beyond.

"You sound proud of that."

"Should I not be?" Aife asked coldly.

"Should you be?" I snapped back.

We were right below the archway when she turned towards me so quickly, I startled back into the wall. One of her hands drifted over the large swell of my hip and the other flattened against the wall beside my head, pinning me between her and the stone.

The warmth from her fingers spread through me like fire as I tried to breathe through the sensation, placing my hands flat on the stone behind me. I dug up courage and defiance and tipped my head up to meet her stare. She had to have been over six feet; she made me feel small. Which was no easy feat, since there was nothing small about me.

"Do not fool yourself into thinking I am one of the good ones, Elle. I am exactly who they make me out to be. I am the cold-blooded killer." Aife said, her hand left my hip and brushed back a loose strand of hair over my shoulder before returning to my side.

She continued, "I am good at what I do, not because I was ruthlessly trained and believe me, everything about my training was ruthless. I have the scars to prove it. But I am good at it because I enjoy it. I am the God that Kings and rulers fear." I almost whimpered at the feel of her lips that brushed the shell of my ear. "I am the monster in the dark, and I fucking love hunting." Aife pressed a kiss against my cheek and dropped her hands.

"Do that again, and I will kill you." I said, the breathlessness of my own voice made me blush again.

"Cute. Your first time is always the hardest. Watch yourself out there tonight, little minx. I am not the only creature who hunts in the full moon." Cold pressed in as she stepped away and walked back towards the Palace. *Sweet Goddess, I am in trouble.*

The Shadow District.

Such an apt name for what happens down here. Everything was dark and sexy, all black, red, gold, and hazy. A heavy scent of sex and musk trailed no matter where you went. Even in the open air it was a thick layer of it. Sconces hung from the buildings glowed a soft red. Beautiful people dressed in truly little walked in and out of the bars and clubs. It did not matter what time of day you walked into this corner of Austiria, this is how it always was. The sun seemed to intentionally miss spreading light across the cobblestones here.

Jesika's red heels clicked as she paced in front of me, where I leaned against a building a few hours after my interaction with Aife.

"Are you okay?" I had to ask because fuck, I was not all right. I knew who Aife was. I knew in my soul that she was dangerous. It rolled off her like clouds of thunder over the open sea. But I would be lying if I said it was not the most attractive thing I had ever experienced. She could dominate and possess me and the thought both terrified and intrigued me.

I was absolutely not all right.

Damn Katrina for not being here. She was not always the voice of reason, but if I could know how she felt about Aife, it would help put everything into perspective.

Maybe.

"Something isn't right." Jesika chewed on the corner of her bright red nail polish.

"Do you think so?"

Nika, another working girl I had come down to help tonight, had been gone for about fifteen minutes, which was not unusual. The male she had left with was a Teranomial. He had control over the earth's natural resources, and they usually were not aggressive. During past interactions with them, I chalked it up to the earth's calming aroma. The street was busy as patrons shuffled from bar to bar; the lights seemed even more dim than normal compared to the moon that blared down between the buildings.

It had not been long enough to normally raise alarm bells for me. I would never be one to doubt anything the girls said. They get enough of that from the males that frequented their attention.

"Yarmi Inn, right?" Jesika nodded, and I jerked my head to the door. "Head in and do not go anywhere until I get back."

She waved her hand as she walked into the bar. "Find her please, Elle."

I strode towards one of the four hotels within the district that specialized in hourly rates. It was one of the smaller buildings sitting on the corner just across from the center, shadowed by taller buildings, giving the illusion of privacy. That being the main reason, it was one of the most frequented by higher nobles and officials from all around Fursomerra. While they paid for the company, they would also pay for the privacy of not getting caught. The Teranomial must have had extra money to spend. Those beds were not cheap.

I reached but froze when a muffled scream from around the corner reached my ears.

"Fuck," I cursed, and grabbed the two swords that sat on either side of my waist, locked their hilts into the gripped gloves, and I crept around the side of the building. Two bodies towered over a smaller cowering one.

"This looks cozy." I held the swords out at my side as I walked into the dark alley. Nika's sob of relief tore briefly at the anger in my heart. The two large males paused and turned towards me as I approached. The blond one I did not recognize held Nika down by his boot. Their pants were unbuckled, and her dress was torn.

"Aren't you a pretty little thing, here to join the fun?" the male who had bought her time asked, his bald head reflecting the moonlight nearly blinding me.

"If you don't let her go, I'm going to cut off your favorite parts and you will never have fun again."

He scoffed. "Or what? You going to stab us with those little swords, pretty girl?"

I shifted my hand. The moon reflected off the newly sharpened blades. "Stab, maim, remove, kill, whatever it takes, really."

His brown eyes shifted as magic swirled in the air and shook the ground. I jumped forward, hooked my blade around his arm and, using my momentum, swung around his back, slicing his arm as he turned. I paused, the curve of both of my weapons at their throats. "Drop the magic, pretty boy."

My ears popped as the swell of magic dropped, and the earth calmed again. Magic over earth was scary. They have been known to bring down cities with their power. But it took a lot to build up, and it was only the particularly powerful ones that could do it. They were good in a battle, but never put them in the front because they were slow moving. It took a lot of coaxing to get the earth to respond to someone's desire but its own. "Remove your foot from my friend." The blond did, and Nika jumped up and ran behind me.

"Let us go. We didn't hurt her."

I pressed the tip deeper into his throat until a bead of blood touched my blade. "That is not up to me." I looked at Nika. "Are you alright?"

She nodded.

"What would you like me to do with these two? Kill them?"

Their mouths opened in protest, but stopped as I shifted the blades at their throat. The blond held up his hands and the bald one had his hand wrapped around the blade as if he might stop it from killing him with will alone.

"I... I don't want anyone killed."

"Pity."

"But..." We all paused at Nika's words; anticipation licked at my nerves. I am not normally bloodthirsty, I do not take pride in taking lives but situations like this where one person was being taken advantage of in the worst way, it was my undoing. "There was only supposed to be one of them, and they didn't..."

"Say no more." I twisted, and using as much force as I could, yanked the sword, taking the fingers off the bald guy's hand before I rotated and severing the rest of his hand off. Without giving the blond time to react, I brought down another swipe, taking his hand as well. Their screams disrupted the night before I took the hilt of both swords and hit them in the soft spot of their heads, knocking them unconscious. I snapped my wrists, cleaning most of the blood off the blades. Nika's freckled skin was paler than normal.

"Are they going to die?"

"They'll lose a good amount of blood, but unfortunately, no, they won't die." I sheathed my weapons and looked at her. Her previously elaborate updo fell in black ringlets down her face. "Are you alright?"

Nika nodded. "Just a little shaken."

"Did they..."

"No. We stopped at a..." Her mouth opened but her lips shook, and any further words refused to push past. I wrapped my arms around and pulled her into me.

"You're safe now, you're safe," I said, as she cried into my shoulder; her arms tight around my waist. "I'm sorry I didn't get here sooner."

Most of the sex workers here were Succubus. Nika was no exception. They had no natural inclination towards either violence or death. While Succubus were not hated in the Kingdom or the Empire they were not as welcome as others. Their natural sexuality led them to live like this. I had tried to teach them how to defend themselves, but it was typically against one assailant. Not two.

"Thank you, Elle." I tucked a piece of hair behind her ear.

"If anyone should be thanking someone, it's those men for your kind heart." She smiled, and I wrapped my arm around her shoulders, and we left the alleyway.

CHAPTER 17
AIFE

I had woken to a face full of hair and a pounding headache. The subtle light from somewhere behind my closed lids roused me. That and the slight suffocation from the blonde hair that seemed to have clawed down my throat.

The first thing I saw when I opened my eyes was a dusty chandelier that hung so low it almost touched the canopy of the bed. Though my vison was obscured by the hair that was probably wrapped around my lung by now.

I removed the arm from my stomach and stood, the floor an icy welcome to my aching feet. I went to the washroom and splashed my face with water before cleaning myself quickly.

My favorite part of Austiria was the whisky, and unfortunately, I tend to overindulge. The evidence of that throbbed behind my eye sockets.

Death would hurt less. At least it would have an end in sight.

Movement from the bed dragged me from the washroom and I watched as the female in my bed sat up. The blanket fell to expose her perfect breasts as she stretched. Her face pulled into the bewitching smile that caught my attention.

"Good morning," she purred.

"Sleep well?" I mused.

"You kept me up most of the night."

I gave her a wolfish smile. "You're welcome," I replied, and she laughed in response. At some point, I ended up at a bar and drank myself into bed with her. What was her name? Laura? Heather? Janice? I was not sure; it was just a haze of alcohol and sex. Mediocre sex if I am being honest.

I had no intention of going down to the city, but after my interaction with Elle, there was a need for a reprieve. I do not know what it was about her, but something pulled me to her in a way that unnerved me. I had to find something, and someone, to keep my mind off her seemed like the best way to keep my thoughts from driving to how it would feel to have her body pressed against mine. To feel those soft lips against mine, those odd hazel eyes, and that soft hair.

Feeling her desire leak through her pores like mine did, knowing I could taint that pretty, innocent soul with my own dark one, scared me more than it should have. I grabbed a pair of black pants and matching tunic as Marie...Rebecca finished lacing her dress.

While the room was nothing like mine back at Parnitus, they had been nicer to me with the furnishings than the last time I stayed here years ago. I know I could thank Zelu for that, as he had been unnaturally happy about the death of Angus. Guilt about the Allegiance Test might mingle in there as well.

After Naomi was adequately clothed in the little red dress, I distinctly remembered from the night before I walked her out.

Edith leaned in and pressed her lips lightly against mine, and simply said, "Goodbye."

With a smile I turned, only to be greeted with those hazel eyes. My gut churned as I saw an uncomfortable emotion pass through them. Jealousy. Elle turned and headed toward the kitchen, a large basket on her hip. My feet moved of their own volition, and I trailed behind her like a little puppy.

"Elle," I drawled.

"Aife," she sneered.

"Something bothering you, little minx?"

"Don't call me that."

I smiled. "Why not?" *Why would you ask that? Why are you interacting with this female at all?*

"You don't get to call me outside my name when you just shared a bed with another woman."

"Jealous?"

Elle stopped and met my eyes, her face wide with incredulity and round cheeks flushed. "What would I have to be jealous of?" She sent another glare before she stormed into the kitchen.

I stood there, enjoyment and guilt churned in my stomach. Why the hell was I feeling guilty?

Of course, I knew she was attracted to me. Everyone felt attraction to something dangerous. She was as attracted to me as I was to her for an inexplicable reason. I did not necessarily have a type, but she was not someone I normally pursued. Elle seems to be the type that craves passion, dating, love. I have no desire for that, nor do I have the ability to do it.

Being with someone else was supposed to cleave that attraction I had to her, give me back my right mind.

Yet here I was.

We shared two conversations and yet I felt guilty for sleeping with someone else. Someone I was perfectly justifiable in being with, even if it was a terrible lay.

I growled and shook my head. A little footman flinched and scurried down the hall. That made me feel a little better.

I squared my shoulders and walked to the kitchen. I did still have a job to do. I pushed open the door to the kitchen and was assaulted by the scent of herbs and meat.

"Ms. Aife!" The cook, Bernice said, and smiled at me. The dozens of people that bustled around moved with a distinct purpose that told me if I got in their way, I could and would get unceremoniously taken out. Steam, flour, and spices puffed into the air and people shouted. I was surprised I could hear her and that she could even see me.

"Hello, Bernice," I replied. She was an older female, gray hair piled in a tight bun and skin so pale her veins were visible. She was short and reached just below my chest.

"You look peakish." Bernice said as she ladled some porridge into a bowl for me.

"You sure know how to make a female feel special." I took the bowl and took a large bite. Perfectly balanced between cinnamon and apples.

My gaze found Elle embarrassingly quick as she moved amongst the kitchen workers, all who greeted her with smiles and thankful touches. Her long brown hair was braided out of her face, hanging over her shoulder. Her brown skin seemed to glow against her purple dress that hugged ample curves. My fingers tingled as I remembered how she felt beneath my touch.

Elle never broke eye contact with anyone she spoke to, not balking at the intimacy and was a magnet for the people's attention. After they spoke, the people seemed so much more relaxed. Her gaze would meet mine every so often, and the skittering of my pulse would have pissed me off if I were not so intrigued by her eyes. There was something unnatural about the color, like the held secrets and violence behind them.

"Ms. Elle, huh?" Bernice's voice cut through my thoughts.

"Hmm?" I asked as a child ran up to Elle, wrapped their small hand around her skirt pulled to reveal a long bronzed bare leg from the small slit of her dress.

She was breathtaking.

She nodded her head to the female in question. "Don't you even try, Aife."

I grinned at Bernice. "You telling me that only makes me want to do it more."

She thwacked my arm with her spatula. "She's worth a lot more than this place, and you will do well to know that."

My head dropped back as I laughed. Elle's lips parted in surprise. "Believe me, Bernice. I have no doubt about that."

Elle looked away, and I placed the empty bowl down. "I am looking for something, though."

Bernice froze, the ball of dough she had been kneading deflated.

"I just need you to point me in the right direction," she said with a swallow. "You know I would never lead you to danger."

I met Bernice when I first visited Austiria about fifteen years ago. She had been the only kind person to me here. After that, she had always found out when I was in Austiria and made it a point to visit me. Eventually, I started to let her know when I was in Austiria, so she did not have to track me down. She always seemed quite cranky when she found me.

"What is it, child?" She continued kneading, the tension in her shoulders brought them up to her ears.

"How would someone go about getting information out of the Palace?"

Bernice covered the dough with a towel in a dish and set it aside. She sprinkled another fistful of flour, slapped it down on the table, grabbed more dough and started the process again. Flour stained the front of her black apron. "Sounds like a question for the Igniris."

I withheld a groan. "Thank you. I will come by later for a snack."

She looked over at me, thinking of that scrawny child I was when we first met. Quite different from who I was today. While I worked to be lean for stealth, I worked hard for the muscle and weight I put on.

"See you later," she mumbled, shooing me away.

I walked out the door right as Elle did. "Hello again," I said, trying to keep my voice even, and not as if I were excited to be near her again. Which I was not.

"Are you stalking me now?"

"Not at this current moment. Although, I cannot deny that I followed you last night."

Her foot stilled, suspended over a step, eyes comically wide. I was about to ask why when she grabbed my arm and yanked me into a room on the right of the staircase. She slammed the door shut behind us and whirled at me. Where the hell did the room come from?

I looked around. A storage closet. What is it with females shoving me back into closets?

The top of her head came up to my nose before she looked up at me. She was so close that every breath caused her chest to brush against mine.

"Where did you follow me? What did you see? Are you going to tell?" Her voice was high and squeaky with anxiety.

"Take a breath, little minx. I am not telling anyone anything."

I do not think she took a breath; I do not think she even blinked. "I was curious as to what called you out so late last night, so I followed you." I chuckled. "I was surprised. I had not pegged you for the kind of girl who visited the Shadow District. But then I saw you head out of a brothel with some workers. I realized you were not looking for a worker or working yourself after watching you take on those two earth slingers. Which was probably the sexiest thing I have ever seen, by the way." I grabbed the tail of her braid and twisted the strands between my fingers. Just as soft as I imagined. She dropped her head against the wall behind her, her hair dropped from me.

"You don't get to talk to me like that when I watched you walk a female out of your rooms."

I pursed my lips; she was right about that.

"Do you do that every night?" I asked.

"Do *you* do that every night?" She parroted. I crossed my arms and waited. After a moment of silence, she relented. "Not every night. A few times a week if I can."

"Why?"

Her eyes swam with emotions; sadness, fear and, most prevalent of all, anger. This time, though, the anger was not directed at me.

"Because they cannot protect themselves and there is no one else who will. Because I feel the need to protect anyone I can within this miserable Kingdom.

Because this is the only fight I can handle right now. Because there are others out there living a miserable existence because a false...." Her jaw audibly snapped shut as the unsaid words tumbled like stones to the ground.

She pushed off of the wall. "I have the means to help them, so I will."

"That's very brave, Elle."

"Please don't tell anyone."

"Where did you learn to fight?"

She hesitated before responding, "A Caeruleus Knight."

"Explains the brutality."

"Excuse me?" she bristled.

"If you would have me. I would love to teach you some of what I know. Unless your Knight is possessive over you." *Aife. What the hell are you doing?* The desire to be near her was overwhelming. To learn as much as I could about her clouded my good senses. I wanted to take it back, to tell her to forget about it, but the words lodged in my throat.

Elle chewed her lip. "He was murdered, so I don't think he has possession over much of anything anymore." The desire to know more manifested in a physical itch.

Did he love her? She him? Why did he train her?

"Why do you want to help me?"

Great fucking question, Aife. Why do you want to help her?

"Because you're doing what I cannot do."

"You kill the people I save."

"I kill those who I must, but I would like to help keep you and your people safe." The assumption that I go around slaughtering people for fun gets rather tedious.

Her brow furrowed; three lines appeared between them as she eyed me distrustfully. "Why are you so concerned about my safety?"

"That is another great question, sweetheart." I opened the door and slid my hands into my pockets. "If you would like my help, I will be in the field behind the royal stables the day after next. If you show up, I will train you. If you do not...."

Now I had to find these fire bastards.

CHAPTER 18

AIFE

Sleep evaded me for the next two nights. It was up to chance if Elle would show up. Whether she would allow my promiscuity to deter her from training that she might not necessarily need but would prove invaluable, anyway. I had a rather insistent and annoying the urge to keep her safe.

Maybe it was how she risked herself, her position in court, and her life to help people. That she is doing what I could not, or rather, never had the courage to do. I have saved lives before, but only put myself at the risk she does for Joyce.

Then again, would anyone come to an assassin and ask for help? I did not have the most approachable job, or attitude, or empathy...or anything, really.

If Heptus ever found out what Elle was doing, how many nobles she potentially killed or ran out of town, nobles that gave him Knights and goods from their courts, who traded with him, she would be hung outside the gate as a warning. Heptus killed people for less and I doubt her Duchess would be much help.

Elle did make one mistake the other night though. She allowed those two pathetic Teranomial males to live. Something that could have proved detrimental. Luckily for her and unlucky for them, I was not as forgiving.

Hopefully, they were not too important. Regardless, no one would find them.

The field behind the stable was shielded from roaming eyes, blocked by the large barn and trees. There was one small pathway that led there from the Palace and another that went down to the water far below. Field was the best way to describe it. Mostly dirt with patches of yellow and green grass. It was not well cared for, but it would keep eyes away and give us privacy; if she showed up, that is.

With the incessant lack of sleep the last few days, I had more time to search for the Igniris that Bernice suggested might have more information. That turned into talking to the fairies, the nymphs, and some very handsy sirens.

I dropped swords, daggers, and a bow and arrows onto a leather canvas. I had seen her wield long and short daggers, like that one she kept tucked tight at her thigh. I remembered the parting of her skirt as she tucked it away, the smooth bronzed leg she revealed.

"I know how to use swords." I tried to contain the smile that threatened, but probably just looked like I ate a sour fruit.

"That is the second time you have snuck up on me since I've known you." As enduring as it was, it was irritating.

Elle shrugged. "Maybe you're not as good as you think you are."

I chuckled at her shiver and watched her hand move up and down her arms. Elle wore a simple tunic and pants that very well they might be the death of me. They hugged her plump thighs and sat beautifully on her...

"Do you know how many ways there are to train with swords and daggers?" I asked.

"Sigurd mentioned it at some point."

The name Sigurd ticked a memory. "Wasn't he killed by the Revolution?"

Elle's jaw clenched, and she looked down at the toe of her boot that was digging into the dirt. "That's what they say."

"Vanity has always been Josephine's downfall." Her eyes locked on mine. "The Knights in Parnitus honored him with a pyre and, after a few drinks, told me it was Josephine because he had refused her advances."

Elle blinked to rid tears from falling. "They didn't give him any funeral here. I don't even know where his body is."

"Were you and he... I mean... did you?" Since when did I have trouble forming coherent sentences?

Elle wiped her cheeks. "Jealous?"

Is that why my heart felt like it dropped to the bottom of my stomach? "Yes, actually. I do believe I am."

She barked out a laugh. "You sound surprised."

"I am not the jealous type, little minx."

Elle scowled to hide the smile I saw curve her full lips and grabbed a sword.

It took her a while to respond, like she wanted me to sit there in my jealousy. "There was nothing romantic between Sigurd and I, he was like a brother."

I closed my eyes and rolled my shoulders in a weak attempt to fight past the tightness. "Besides, you have no reason to be jealous. You made that pretty clear the other day." Elle continued.

"He may have been a brother to you, but that doesn't mean you were a sister to him." The air whistled and I dropped, the blade cutting across the air and embedded into a tree behind me. "That wasn't very nice."

"I thought you could prove you're actually the best."

I spun, catching her ankle with mine, sword in hand. I stood as she stumbled into a defensive position.

"Let's see what you Caeruleus Knights have taught you."

She lunged like a wild boar, power behind each strike.

I shifted away from a particularly wild swing and Elle lost balance, dropping to a knee. With a growl, she kicked back up and started again, her swings losing power, but her aim was still perfect. She was not an awful fighter, but it was obviously a male had taught her.

Males were all brute strength and ferocity, while females' strength lies in speed and balance. Fighting like this had made her stronger, but her real strength would show itself with proper training. I twisted away as her sword came down again. Her grunt and slow movements revealed how exhausted she really was.

Her footwork was dreadful, proven by her falling again. "Very good."

She rolled onto her back with a groan. "What is so good about falling on my ass?"

I squatted beside her. "You are good. Your footwork needs help, but otherwise Sigurd taught you well."

"Thank you."

"But it is obvious that a Knight trained you. Specifically, a male."

She peered up at me. "Are you saying I fight like a male?"

"I'm saying you fight like a female trained by a male." I stood holding my hand out to her. After a moment of hesitation, she placed her hand in mine. The hair at the name of my neck and my arms prickled as I pulled her up.

"Their strength comes from their arms and upper body; their center of gravity is higher. We carry ours lower, right at our naval." I moved towards her and placed my hand on my own stomach. "That is where we should pull the strength from."

"Put your feet shoulder width apart and don't lock your knees out. Think of each movement as a dance. The sword should be an extension of your arm, not a weapon to swing around like an armed ape. We can work on those weak arm muscles later." She glared as I pressed my hands to her middle back and stomach.

It was like I was a thirteen-year-old again, kissing my first crush. Every part of my body flared to life and every fiber of me went to the contact. Elle stilled at my touch as the waves of heat swept off her and nearly knocked me to my knees. Willingly to my knees.

It was unlike anything I had ever felt before, and I begged my voice to be steady. "Find the balance here." I kept my touch on her longer than was necessary, and it took an absurd amount of willpower to drop my hands and step back.

"Try again." The huskiness of my voice made her flush.

Elle glided onto the steps and when finished, she smiled. A smile that touched and relaxed a part of me that I had not felt in a long time.

"How did that feel?"

"Great," she breathed.

I indicated for her to lift the sword. I rolled her shoulders back and adjusted her grip on the sword. "This..." I told her, kicking her feet apart, "is perfect."

We continued the rest of the morning. I adjusted her stance and tried to break the male like habits she had been taught. She took what I said, used it, then twisted it into something that worked best for her.

"You're very aware of your body," I complimented, as we finished for the day.

She gave me a mocking smile. "I bet you tell all the females that."

"Is that what you think of me?" I rolled the weapons back into the tarp, securing them.

"I think you are very popular with the ladies and have all kinds of toe-curling compliments in your arsenal."

"Do you think there might be someone else on the receiving end of my compliments, Elle?" She paused, a bottle of water halfway to her parted lips; full, deep pink lips that glistened and begged to be kissed. I threw the tarp on my shoulder and walked towards her, my arm brushing against hers. I watched the goosebumps raise on her soft skin and revel in it. "You have no reason to be," I said, as I trailed a finger along the back of her arm and wrapped my hand around her elbow, leaning into her.

I brushed my lips over the shell of her ear. "You, by far, are the most deliciously distracting creature I have ever met. Same time tomorrow." I felt an irrational sense of triumph as Elle remained frozen.

I sat in the communal area within the servant's corridor hours later. Everyone was cautious of my presence and gave me a wide berth from where I stood next to a large hutch, a goblet of brown liquor clutched between my fingers. While the room was roughly the same size as the communal area of the Tributes wing in Parnitus, it appeared in better shape. The furniture was well cared for, the lighting brighter than I was used to, and the people seemed...well, happy. Which was odd, especially compared to the last time I was within these walls.

I remember the desperation as they worked as quickly as they could to get their jobs done and retreat. It had been during the War and there was no safe space. Now, this room was the safe haven, where they could be themselves. The Quinque being gone might be attributed to the overall lightness of the Palace.

The male I waited for set a public meeting place within the Palace so I would not be able to 'accidentally' kill him. He said something about being rather attached to his head. Not that I was one for beheading. I had not done that since I was a teenager.

Thus far, I had no luck in finding who the traitor was. They were either very smart, dead, or left the Kingdom already. Though Alhma and Zelu were convinced they were still within the walls of the Palace.

No one else seemed to know who they were. I initially thought no one wanted to give up someone that important. But as time went on, everyone seemed clueless as to who it might be.

A sweet scent hit my senses, like strawberries and chocolate. I glanced up to see a pair of giggling females looking at me. While everyone in this place had learned in the past few days who I was, it did not deter anyone from glancing my way with interest.

The thought that they could fix whatever inside of me made me this way. I raised my glass; the redhead smiled broadly and raised her hand, which was immediately knocked down by her giggling pink haired counterpart.

Fairies, such fascinating creatures. Their wings were as soft as silk and just as pliable. However, as they angled away from me, I noted the absence of the appendages. I guess Heptus really did cut the wings off of everyone; I had thought it a demented rumor. I was not innocent from the removing of wings, but mine were from rambunctious fairies who would have taken my ears if they could have.

"Assassin," a male said as he approached, and I reached out and grasped his forearm. I could feel him shaking beneath my hand, and it was both funny and exasperating.

"Ronaldo, thank you for meeting me."

He released me, wiped his hand on his pants seemingly subconsciously before waving to my goblet. "Let us refill your drink, then we can sit."

After he filled my glass and poured one of his own, we sat at a pair of twin wingback chairs next to the two giggling fairies.

He leaned back into the hard, cushioned chair. "What is it you need?" he asked.

"Don't worry Ronaldo. You have nothing to fear. There is no price on your head." I draped an ankle over my knee as I spoke.

His shoulder sagged, but tension still bracketed his mouth. "Then what do you want from me?"

"I heard that you might be able to help me find someone." My finger danced over the rim of the glass. The silver ring I recently purchased from the market within Austiria sung against the crystal. "Someone who has proved to be very elusive."

"Rumors led you right. I can find anyone."

"There is a traitor to the Quinque within these walls. I am simply looking for the wall cracks that will lead me to him."

"I know nothing of a traitor…"

"Lie to me again and I will rip your tongue from your mouth, shove it up your ass and make you tell me what it tastes like."

He flinched. "I did not mean...."

"I know there are traitors within these walls. I know there are some within this very room, possibly one I am sharing a drink with. What I do not know, is the one that clawed their way into knowing intimate secrets about the Quinque."

He was silent for a long while, probably considering whether to lie again and see if my promise held true, or what truth to tell me. I could smell the fear and tension that leaked from his pores like oil. He was either less brave than he acted, or he thought I knew his secrets.

Which would be correct. I know he is selling information to the Druids. Not for freedom or to help the Revolution, but solely for money. He liked to visit a few brothels down in the city and had found himself addicted to a few drugs as well.

"I am being sincere when I say I do not know who would be able to betray the Quinque in that way. It has to be someone with powerful magic on their side to have not been discovered." Ronaldo said, his pale blue eyes meeting mine.

"Unless they were very good at hiding."

His head shook vehemently, sloshing some of his drink out of his cup onto his lap. "The Priestess has some kind of magic that prevents anyone from spying. Like an anti-theft spell that should render the secret teller incapable of relaying anything about what they hear in confidence."

"What if the person isn't being told in confidence?"

"I don't see how they could overhear anything. The King and Queen have their chambers, studies, offices, and most meeting rooms are impenetrable to spies."

Interesting.

CHAPTER 19
AIFE

F or the next two weeks, Elle came to the field behind the stables for practice.

She remembered what I taught her with swords, as if she had spent her spare time practicing. Either being a perfectionist or she wanted to show me she could do it. Regardless, by the fourth day, I had decided to change it to bow and arrows. Which proved unnecessary after an hour.

She was a natural and regardless of how much distraction I gave her, she never missed. After we finished, she spent ten minutes apologizing to the tree that we used as a target. Joyce would have approved of her respect for nature.

I did tell her about Joyce, who she was to me. Elle laughed herself hoarse when I had told her Joyce referred to me as having "broody shit." I do not know what possessed me to tell her that, but she stopped laughing and gasped for air when I dropped her on her back in the hard dirt.

Elle told me about Sigurd, and how he saved her and became her combat tutor. Keeping her early in the mornings before her day started with Katrina, but how she was always late because she never wanted to stop. It gave her a form of control, the only control that she had in her life, since everything otherwise was dictated by someone else. She spoke like someone who had been trained in etiquette. When I mentioned this, she clammed up and said it was her lady-in-waiting training. I did not buy it, but changed the subject anyway. I studied her movements after that, noting the way she held herself and objects, a firm but steady grip on everything that she touched. How she walked with her shoulders back and chin raised.

My mind was distracted when we moved on to hand-to-hand combat, which, admittedly, she needed a lot of help on and luckily enough was one of my favorite fighting styles. Fists and daggers are so much more intimate, and I knew she would not have a problem with that because of her love of daggers. After the first week, I tried to convince myself that training her was to keep my skills sharp and help those who I could not.

It was a lie; I enjoyed spending time with her, and it helped keep me occupied with my lack of progress from the task both Joyce and Zelu had set for me. I could not find any information about Harenae since the Quinque left almost right after we arrived and they were not due back for another week, and finding the spy proved more difficult than I originally imagined. My mornings were spent with Elle, my days and nights consumed with those impossible tasks.

I pivoted off my right foot, twisted and swung my arm against Elle's chest and for the fourth time since we started about three hours ago, she fell on her ass.

Right when I was going to call it, she hopped up and shook her arms. "This is it. I got it now! Come on!"

I raised a brow; she was panting and drenched in sweat, but the excitement on her face melted my better judgment and with a small nod I attacked. She blocked my advances, defending herself with a refinement that left me near breathless. I kicked her foot to pull her attention down before I surged forward with a twist and threw an elbow at her head. She blocked it and I stumbled back. A radiant smile lit her face that left my head fuzzy.

"That was good," I said. She chugged her water, and I followed the little water pebbles that dribbled down her chin and dropped down the valley of her breasts before I cleared my throat. "Care to tell me how you were able to sneak up on me?"

She had not done it since that second time, but it made me nervous and was dangerous for my line of work. If I had a blind spot, I needed to remedy it immediately.

"I am quiet when I want to be." Her voice was soft, sending tingles down my spine.

I rubbed a finger along my jaw. "It's more than that. There are plenty of people who are quiet, quieter than you, that have never been able to do that."

She grinned. "Maybe I'm just better than everyone..." a loud grumble from her stomach cut off her words and her cheeks turned an adorable shade of pink.

"You need to eat."

"Would you like to join me?"

I stopped, "you want to have lunch with me?"

Her face flushed, and she nodded. "I mean, you're my friend, right?"

My feet moved of their own accord, closing the distance between us, the tarp of weapons over my shoul-

der. A traitorous hand reached out and tucked a strand
of hair behind her ear. "Of course we are."

If possible, her face turned even more red, and it was
annoyingly endearing. "Meet me at the city stables in
twenty minutes."

We parted ways, and I dropped the weapons off at
the armory before I walked back to the royal stables
and grabbed Rain, who had a lot of sassy commentary
for me. It had been a while since I had taken him
out and he was not happy about it. He was used to
being taken out multiple times a day by the grooms in
Parnitus. Apparently, they cared less for their horses
here.

The city was busy as always, but Threadbare was
closed and boarded up. I hoped that Molly had not
been the one to find her husband and got out once she
learned of his death. I turned down a less busy street
reached Aurora Row, where noble and otherwise houses were located along with the sole city stables. Trees
lined the street, hanging over like a ceiling of green-
ery and sunshine. Children ran around, played with
bouncing balls while parents lounged on balconies and
patios.

It was a beautiful vision of what life could be, the
comfort and security of being with your family and
loved ones. A life that would never I would never have,
even if Gregorovich let me go. There was no happiness
in the world for someone who killed as many people
as I have. There is no salvation for me. I wondered if
anyone in Elle's family had died by the end of my blade.

Rain's hooves ticked across the street. He nipped at
the low branches as we went. The stable was made of
oak wood, with grand white doors. I tied Rain to the
pole outside and pushed open the door, walking in. The
floors were an elaborate red and yellow mosaic tile; the

walls bare, allowing the natural wood to shine through. Dozens of stalls lined the walls, with a trough and a large faucet at the end.

Elle led a beautiful blonde mare with a long black mane out of a stall at the far end of the stable. She cooed and wrapped the reins around her hands, steering the horse out even at the grumble the creature emitted. The tight pants and tunic she had from our training were still slightly dirty from this morning; the white tunic untied and revealed a gold necklace hanging from her neck. Her brown hair hiked high on her head in a loose bun, her brown skin gleaming in the sunlight. Elle glanced towards me and smiled. A smile pulled at my chest; she was exquisite.

"You came." She was breathless.

I raised a brow. "Did you doubt that I would?" She did not respond but approached, pulling the horse forward again. "Who is this beauty?"

The horse whinnied.

"This is my stubborn girl, Koko." Her voice was honeyed as she looked at Koko.

"Stubborn like her owner," I said as Koko approached me, bucking her head towards my palm, insisting I pet her. I had no choice but to oblige. "You are a beauty, Koko. Let us hope you can hold your own against my stubborn boy."

We walked back out into the bright sun. The street in front of the stable started to fill as lunch arrived. Rain nickered as soon as Koko walked out. He batted at the ground and lifted his tail and head. If horses could roll their eyes, I am sure Koko would have been looking at the back of her head, but the smack of her tail told everyone she was not too upset with the attention.

"Just like his owner, I see, a shameless flirt," Elle murmured, and I chuckled.

"I get it. You disapprove of my extracurricular activities. I will make sure you are the next person I bed."

Her eyes widened. "That says a lot about you if you think I'd ever make my way to your bed."

Elle climbed on Koko's bareback as I unwrapped Rain from the pole, also bareback. Rain nipped at Koko, who snorted aggressively back at him.

Someone is feisty.

"It says a lot about your denial abilities that you think you won't, Elle." She snorted and turned towards the woods behind the stable. I had never done this way before and the thick tree line had no path and seemed overgrown and hazardous. "Are you planning on kidnapping me?" I asked. The trees were taller and angrier than in Parnitus and they grew in different enough angles to obscure the sunshine with a tent of branches and leaves. Brambles grew all over, sticks and overgrown weeds. It was like being in a wild forest. There was no clear path, no safe place to walk without the threat of breaking an ankle. The leaves that grew from the trees looked as if they would stab you from contact only grew thicker as we went.

"Tell me about her," Elle said casually as we carefully picked our way through. I kept Rain on the path that Elle carved for us.

"Who?"

"The girl from the other day." I was surprised she had waited this long to ask. After two weeks of being together for hours, she had not brought it up. Aside from the snarky comments.

"I honestly don't know anything about her. We met at the Longe."

"Do you do that often? Pick up random people in bars and sleep with them?"

"Yes." There was no reason to lie. I never found the point of it. I will either be accepted as I am, or I will not. Typically, it's the latter which is understandable. It is hard to accept someone like me and I have grown to prefer it that way. There is a perverse side of me that I cannot share, even before I was taken to Parnitus. My own kin feared the darkness that festered inside of me, told me that death clung to me like moths to a flame. I did hate everyone, so that might have had some influence on their feelings.

"When I fuck, how I feel, and what I know are the only things that I have control of in my life. So, I take advantage when I can. I fuck when I want to. I don't fight the feelings within me. I trust my instincts, and I try to know as much as I can about any situation."

That was the raw, honest truth.

Everything else in my life was dictated by what Gregorovich and Zelu instructed me to do. Occasionally, Heptus as well. Those had proved to be the ones that brought me closer to death. Unsurprisingly, he had been the one to send me into the situation that earned me the scars that covered my face and a majority of my body. They happened when I was younger, untested in certain aspects that left me vulnerable.

I learned pretty quickly that when Heptus gave me a job, to plan as much as possible and expect the most extreme unexpected. Especially traps.

"I can understand that," she finally said as the sun broke through. I wanted to lie back and bask in the warmth it provided.

"Please elaborate." I steered Rain up next to Koko and he strode closer than was necessary, but Koko maintained her lead over him. She was undeniably an alpha, and Rain was smitten enough to allow it.

Silly crushing horse.

Silly crushing elf.

Elle glanced at me before she guided Koko around some boulders and fallen branches, before she said, "There are not many things I have control of in my life, either. The last time I had any resemblance of freedom, I was twelve."

"Was that when you started working for Katrina?"

"Something like that," she responded, avoiding my gaze. Elusive, she had refrained from providing much information about her home life and family.

"What would you do with freedom, Elle?" I asked, as she led us across a small opening and onto a blooming path. It was surrounded by wildflowers and a full view of the sun overhead.

"I think I'll always trade one life of servitude for another."

"Why is that?"

The side of her lip lifted. "What would you do with freedom?"

Avoiding as usual. I wanted to push, to make her give me an answer. Nothing about her and Katrina's relationship seemed like it was poor or strained. If she had been working for Katrina since she was young, I could see why that would seem a reality; she had to be around twenty-seven. I knew if I pushed her, it would not get us anywhere; she held secrets she was not ready to or could not share. I could respect that she did not lie to me, so I answered her honestly.

"Freedom." I whispered, taking a deep breath as the reality of it hit me as I thought back to those families that relaxed on their patios. "That is something I can't even allow myself to consider, sweetheart. There is no option of it for me. It is either death or… something worse than death."

"Do I want to know what you consider worse than death?" My lips curved into a cruel smile at Elle's question. The memory of a rack and spiked whips crossed my mind.

"There are things in life that will make death seem like a mercy."

"Better enjoy the freedom while we can, then." Elle pushed into Koko's side and sped off into the space that had finally opened into a giant meadow with grass long enough to brush my ankles. I was on her heels.

Koko always a breath ahead and I wondered if Rain's allowed to allow her to win, though, the bites she aimed his way I reconsidered that he might actually be afraid of her. We ran for miles and miles before we finally slowed to a trot. Brown hair swung down to her saddle as Elle tossed her head back and laughed. The freeness echoed mine.

Elle's eyes sparkled as she looked at me and a strange red bled into the hazel irises, and said, "welcome to Price Point."

CHAPTER 20
TITAIA

The smile on Aife's face turned to wonder as trees to the left opened to reveal the marble statue. Aife dropped from Rain and walked towards the statue.

"What is this place?" she asked.

I had not really thought it through when I asked her to come to lunch, or when I made the decision to bring her to this place. I initially planned to take her to a cute little spring a few miles west of the city, but when we started talking about freedom and why she brought the girl to her room, I could not keep this place to myself. Not with the kinship we had formed over our assorted brands of prison. Our different forms of death, which we may hold for varied reasons but share the mutual understanding that death could be a mercy.

"Katrina and I found it a few years ago on accident." I said, as I dismounted and grabbed Rain's reins and led him and Koko to the field that she grazed when we were here. I grabbed the bag full of food and drinks and looked toward Aife, who stood feet from the statue.

The calm gentleness on her face was something I had not seen from her before. It reminded me of the first time I saw the Goddess. It was like I uncovered the reality of everything I had ever wanted to be, needed to be. Her power seemed to have been carved into the very stone she was made of. It hummed in an unearthly, very un-Visreala way that drew me in. Katrina had to pull me away from it the first time. I had stood there for nearly an hour just looking. It had felt like seconds.

Aife's breath was shallow as I approached. "Amazing, isn't she?" I whispered.

Eyes full of emotion met mine: envy, pride, hate, and a deep and ancient power. The power behind her gaze was intimidating, the subtle purple around her iris seemed to glow and spread through her pupil into the whites of her eyes like lightning bolts.

"I've never seen anything like it," she said as she blinked quickly and erased any trace of power in her eyes. "I've never felt anything like it."

"I know. The power is almost palpable." I inhaled deeply. The ancient magic seeped into my bones and settled around my soul.

"It's like she can see right through me, which is magic all on its own, since she doesn't even have pupils." Aife's eyes met mine again, so soft and kind that the stone wall I formed between us crumbled like dust in the wind. "Thank you for bringing me here."

I smiled. Katrina never felt the pull that I had towards the Goddess; it was not even something I fully understood. But I felt reassured to know that someone else felt it, that I was not alone. We dragged ourselves away and walked up to the castle ruins. Long fingers wrapped around the strap of the bag, removing it from my shoulders.

"I can carry..."

Aife held up a hand, silencing my protest. "I know you are perfectly capable of doing anything and everything on your own. You are a strong, independent female, and I would never dream of making you feel otherwise. Please lead the way."

We stepped carefully through the ruins and up the stairs, fifty flights with beautiful paintings lining the walls.

"Trodia," Aife whispered.

"What?" I turned to see her trailing her fingers over a painting.

"The Goddesses Trodia." I stepped down until I stood on the stair above Aife. The painting was of the Goddess whose black hair was blowing on an invisible wind, a red crown with moon phases adorned it. Her black dress was sheer, completely sheer, and she had her hands held out at a crossroads.

"How do you know?"

"My mother taught me about her when I was a child, about all the Old Goddesses and Gods. This must have been one of her temples." She looked over at me and my stomach dropped out of my body, completely lost to the stone stairs below at her proximity. If I leaned forward, I could press our mouths together, feel those soft looking pink lips against mine.

What the hell was wrong with me? Clearing my throat, I turned and walked the rest of the way up the stairs and up into the warm afternoon air. A gentle breeze floated up throughout, lifting my hair.

The snow was gone; the trees shook with life as they stretched on for miles, the mountains eating up the horizon. A small nest of birds had perched on the crumbling stone railing to the right. There were no walls for paintings here, just remains of what was once a great balcony. Now, gray derelict stone. Although this side of the world seemed to be left untouched aside from these remains, no other buildings populated the vast area before us.

"Be careful. Those stones are constantly falling. More fall off every time we come out here," I warned, grabbing the bag from Aife as she walked to the edge. I laid out the blanket and grabbed the bottle of wine, two glasses, bread, cheese, and meat, placing them out. I straightened to see Aife peering over the edge of the balcony pressing the toe of her boot into the stones, my heart rate accelerated as pebbles disintegrated at her touch.

"I would prefer not to be the one to kill the famed assassin. I am sure there would be some terribly upset people, specifically Joyce. I do not necessarily want to be on the bad side of a seer, so please do not fall." She looked over her shoulder at me, her hair swinging and a bright smile on her face. A dimple peeked out of both cheeks. Goddess damn *dimples*. Why?

That is the look I had when I first stood at the edge as well, the feeling of being untamed and free. Almost like I could fly. I do not think my smile looked anything like that. The flush that burned my cheeks proved that. Katrina did not blush.

I am pathetic.

Aife held her hand out to me and I walked over, stopping a step behind where she was. I looked at her hand, then over the edge. The stone was cracked and weak and waiting for a few hundred more pounds before it collapsed and sent us both to our death. I did not move.

I hate heights.

With a sigh, she grabbed my hand and tugged me over to her.

I squealed. Yes, I did. Full squeal as the stone crumbled but did not fall. I jerked my hand from hers with a scowl, ignoring the ache deep in my belly from her touch. "I could have died."

"I wouldn't have let you fall," she teased.

"That's not what you said."

She clicked her tongue. "Different type of falling, little minx."

I tried to ignore the quip and steady my heart rate, though my body reacted regardless. There was no stone beneath us, just a sheer drop to the edge of a cliff and a ravine far, far below. With the unsteady rock and standing at the edge of nothing, it was almost like floating.

My stomach ruined everything, letting out a loud, angry grumble, and her wide eyes turned to me. "Let's get you some food," she said.

Aife's hand hovered over my lower back, and she guided me to the blanket, as if assuring me that she would indeed not let me fall. I poured wine into our glasses as she tore the bread into pieces for each of us. The sun was warm as I dropped my head back, taking a piece of bread from Aife.

"Tell me about Trodia."

Aife leaned back, balancing on a hand. "Trodia, the Great Goddess of the crossroads, magic, the moon, empowerment. Some texts that say she is the original, that she created the stars, and the universe. They say she created her husband, Orbin, who proved to be her equal and in turn he created the planets. From there, everything else was created by their children. The mountains, oceans, Visreala, even humans. Her lover, Giua, Goddess of fertility, and fate was the creator of soul mates. Some say that Giua created soul mates specifically to immortalize her love for Trodia, which was completely unnecessary as Trodia loved Giua beyond anything we could fathom.

"Trodia was revered in the times of old; until new Gods were brought and claimed her to be the opposite of who she was. Said her power of the crossroads meant that she used that power to take souls before their time. She is the one who created the Realms, cleaved the world in three. There are a lot of rumors about why she would do this, but no one really knows why." Aife shook her head, the continued. "With the King and Emperor in charge, this might be the last temple of the original Goddesses."

I knew the Old Goddesses and Gods were being erased from history and life because of religion, or because a male named Heptus decided he was the one and only God. "What happened to them? The Goddesses and Gods?"

"Some text says they sleep, some say they died, some say they walk among us in hiding."

"When I was younger, I thought my dad built the moon and the stars for my mom. I thought my mom was a Goddess, and that my brother would protect me from everything." I said wistfully.

"What happened to them?"

She had asked me this before, but I managed to avoid answering. I did not want to lie to her.

Something deep inside me begged me to tell her the truth, "they were murdered, during The Great Übernehmen."

She sucked in a breath. "I'm so sorry."

I needed to change the subject before I started crying. "Do you have any siblings?"

"Almost, but my parents died at the start of the war."

"Your mother was with child when she died?" My heart felt like lead, heavy in my chest.

"It was a very long time ago."

"Did you mean what you said? When we first met, that you enjoyed killing?"

Aife laid back and placed one arm behind her head, her long legs stretched before her, crossed one ankle over her thigh, and perched the glass on it.

"I do." Again, there was no hesitation and no remorse.

"Why?" Nausea twisted in my gut as her depthless onyx eyes seemed to try to peel back my thoughts, my memories.

I have killed before, and I remember it in vivid detail. It was when Katrina and I had escaped to Austiria and was life or death. We were cornered, and he knew who I was. Gabriel, he had grown up with me and betrayed my family, planning to turn me over to the Quinque, to Heptus. The second time was protecting one of my girls. No matter what I did, he was going to kill her. It was different after that time, not easily different. I remember their faces ever last one.

"That is quite the intimate question." My brow furrowed.

"What makes it so intimate?" She smiled and lifted her hand, pushing a strand of hair behind my ear. I shivered at the tenderness and familiarity of it.

"I don't think my soul is one that you care to know, little minx."

I considered her, stopping the urge to nuzzle into her touch.

Right. Assassin.

And here I was alone with the deadliest assassin who worked for my enemy. I make great life choices.

Alone.

She chuckled. "You do not have to be afraid of me. I would never hurt you."

"You can't promise that." The words had more bite than I intended, but they were true. She could never promise me that and had no idea just how much I should fear her.

"Are you afraid of me?" she asked, as she looked at me with a patient curiosity.

"I should be."

I have heard of what she has done to people and while I had never witnessed it nor seen the aftermath, people talk, and I am enemy number one. Aife would be the one they send to kill me, the one that would hunt me down. But, for some reason.

"No." I finally answered.

We stared at each other in silence for a while. Her scars, sharp features, beautiful black eyes with a pupil rimmed in purple. The black coal that lined her face and accentuated her sharp features. Her pointed ears on display, body tense as if on constant alert as if waiting for the next attack. Physical or otherwise.

"Is Katrina as daft as she seems to be?"

I blinked. And then laughed. Loud enough that the birds scattered from the closest trees, their caws indignant. Her eyes glittered in amusement and the dimple that damn appeared on her right cheek. It was extremely unfair how attractive she was.

Katrina had spent our time here crafting her nativity to allow her into conversations that she would not have been if they had known how cunning she actually was.

"Which is it you prefer? The daft princess or the cunning warrior?" I asked.

Aife was quiet as she thought, before she finally spoke. "There are benefits of both. The daft princess never asks the questions that could put her in danger. Sometimes there's beauty in the naïve, beauty in never wanting to know or needing to know. Always by your side, regardless of what little they know is going on. The cunning warrior, well," she smirked, "they are able to stand by your side in dangerous paths you might find yourself in and fight with you. Fight for you, but there is always a threat. They always want to know more, need to know more."

"But?"

"But," she sighed. "I am a sucker for danger."

An inexplicable warmth spread throughout my body. A warmth that did not make sense because I could not distinguish which of those two I am. I never considered myself daft. I cannot run through life not knowing what is going on or who I am surrounding myself with. Although, I had not dug into answers, nor questioned what was going on or how to get through being here.

Cunning warrior? Could I be considered a warrior for refusing to fight when it mattered most? But I was cunning. I protected those who could not protect themselves. And I used what knowledge I had to my advantage. I was the hope for Fursomerra but what have I even done to prove that I deserved it? Am I worth the risk?

"What is going on in that pretty head?" She was sitting now, placing another piece of cheese against those perfect, full lips. I tried not to stare as her mouth opened and the cheese slid in, wondering what else could...nope.

No! Do not think about her mouth.

"Sometimes I wonder if fate made a mistake with me. If she gave me a task that I could never hope to accomplish. That I will never be good enough to achieve. That I am inevitably going to fail...."

I trailed off, both surprised and nervous, that admitted things I had never even admitted to Katrina. Glass still full in my hands, I stood and walked to the edge of the balcony, feeling her beside me a minute later. Aife stood so close that I could feel the heat from her body. My heart in my throat pounded incessantly against my ears. Her knuckles brushed mine, and that simple touch shook my knees and refocused me, calming the raging fire inside.

"I fear that fate placed me exactly where I am supposed to be, that she knew what I would be good at. I was born with a damaged soul, so living my life killing would not change my afterlife. Would not make it any worse than it was already going to be, would not change where my soul was destined to end up. Whether in this life or in the next, my soul will suffer and there is nothing I can do to change it." The hopeless acceptance of her words tugged at me.

"I don't think your soul is damaged."

Her laugh was void of any humor. "You do not know me, Elle. I told you that I am as dark as they say."

I knew that the darkness in her was tended by her own hand and that she thrived within it. I could feel it from the tendrils that seemed to curl around her, the darkness that followed her around like a leash. Both pulling her back and propelling her forward. But that darkness was not all bad, it was balanced, it was both light and dark. She was not good, but I could see that she was not all bad. Something in her drew me in like flies to the dead. I reached out and took her hand.

"I don't think you know what ladies-in-waiting are made of, Aife."

She threaded our fingers together as she spoke. "You're as much a lady-in-waiting as I am, Elle."

CHAPTER 21
TITAIA

Aife had a lot of suggestions for my fighting style. Part of me wanted to deny that she had been helpful, but the reality was she had been more helpful than Sigurd. She showed me how to fight in a way best fit for my body. She showed me how to disarm someone I was smaller and weaker than, how to fight hand to hand, which took longer than I would care to admit and how to handle weapons in a way that made everything feel more natural.

The week following our trip to Price Point carried much of the same. Training and occasionally eating lunch together but most of the time she had a task to complete for General Zelu and when we separated after training, I did not see her for the rest of the day. When I asked her what she was doing, she would ask me questions that I did not want to answer or say I was not working hard enough if I could talk.

I should take it as a hint to mind my own business, but as Katrina had said since we were kids, I am a busybody. Aife was as elusive as I was about her history and her family, and it irritated me. From what little she did say, she was from Matrador and had been taken by Gregorovich when she was nine. Making her two years older than me led her to believe that she was the wisest of us and continued to ignore my invasive questions while telling me to respect my elders. Who knew assassins could be so childish?

The one topic that she was never quiet about was Joyce. The love she had for Joyce was clear in the way Aife talked about her. How Joyce had saved her life and healed her from her from the many, many wounds she received. She alluded to the scars on her face coming from an assignment that Heptus had sent her on, one she realized was a trap as soon as she found herself in clutches of some bad males. She did not elaborate about what happened.

It was our last day before Katrina and the company returned, and I made my way to the field earlier than normal. The frequency of our training would become sparse with the return of the Quinque. If they continued at all. To my surprise, Aife was already there when I turned the corner, the rock pathway giving way to dirt and grass.

Instead of the usual array of weaponry, there was only a small pack.

"You're early," Aife mused as I approached, the pack slung over her shoulder.

"So are you."

Her hair was pulled back into a high ponytail, the ends curling over her shoulder. She was in her customary black tunic and unreasonably tight black pants showing off her toned legs body. Her shirt tucked in, and the top of her tunic untied at the top, the fabric folded out, showing her sternum and more tattoos that filled her skin right between her...

"No weapons today?"

Aife's smirk told me she knew exactly what I was looking at. "This is our last day of peace together."

"Since when has anything between you and me been peaceful?" She ignored me and walked towards a little path off the field that would take us down to the moat water's edge. "I didn't dress for a swim."

The wicked smile she gave me sent a pulse deep within my core and throbbed all the way down to my toes. I clenched my thighs.

"No swimming." Her eyes heated. "But I am perfectly fine going in with you naked."

I scowled to hide the blush that was spreading and heating my chest to nearly unbearable temperatures. "Then where?"

Silence was all that greeted me as she led us down the narrow path through the trees.

"Secrets, I get it. We all have them. Not like you are taking me to drown me, or throw me off a cliff, or stab me." Aife was silent. "I mean, you could hide my body in the trees, bury me somewhere although if you were going to kill me you should take me on the bridge and chuck me over, the water will wash away anything someone might find."

"I might do all of those things if you don't stop talking." Her voice was amused.

The path to the beach was a steep slope with trees that gave way about halfway down, it was already difficult to navigate through made more by the early morning darkness. It was roughly a mile and a half walk, full of slipping and sliding down dirt and rocks until finally we emerged onto the small beach. The ground was full of a thousand small white and brown pebbles mixed with the sand. The sun was just starting to peak over the horizon and sent soft sparkles off the rough water that splashed over rocks. Aife stopped and dropped the bag on a large boulder.

I stood rooted to the spot as she untied her boots and rolled her pants up to her knees, revealing toned, scarred calves and the tattoos that continued down both legs. I wonder if there is any part of her body that is not covered in some kind of mar.

"I thought you said no swimming."

"Standing in water is not swimming, sweetheart," Aife said.

"Sweetheart?" I squinted at her, and the corner of her lip tugged up while she beaconed to join her. She stepped into the water with a hiss and I, against my better judgment, took off my boots and rolled up my pants before following to where she stood about mid-calf deep. The water froze through my skin and gave my bones a chill I will never forget.

"Fuck that's cold!"

Aife held out a small purple stone with red and yellow veining.

"What is this?"

"It's a Volente's stone." Aife said, grabbing another one from her pocket and turned it over in her hand.

"Volente's stone?" I rubbed it between my fingers. "What do I do with it?"

"Some cultures believe that this stone helps heal. Purple takes the fear out of the heart and turns it into bravery and wisdom. Red is passion. It helps embed it into your heart and magnifies what you have, makes you remember it. Yellow is the pretty bow on the package; helping you see it all, feel it."

I turned the stone. "Sounds like witchcraft."

"Druids actually. To help seal the magic, push your desires, wishes, hopes, and yourself into it and throw it into the water."

I felt wary, borderline offended. "What makes you think I need this?"

"To help you find that freedom you seek." Her voice was soft and spread through me like water as I searched her eyes. They were open, honest, and a little hopeful, and the negative feelings disappeared like a fleeting wind. I closed my eyes and turned the smooth stone in my hand, spreading myself into it as much as I could. I cranked my arm back and tossed it against the rush of the water.

"You are Druid then?" She stilled; I think she might have stopped breathing.

"What makes you think that?" There was predatory violence in her voice that had my instincts flaring through me to run.

"I...I..." I hesitated. "You have a ring of purple in your eyes." A shudder raked through her body, and I realized that I might have put myself in the danger she said I would never face.

"You can keep a secret, sweetheart?"

It was a question, but I could feel the threat laced in the words and while the natural fear of being near a predator was there, I was not afraid of her. Not afraid of the realm's most lethal, relentless assassin.

Idiot.

"I'm possibly the best secret keeper in Fursomerra."

"I might be your competition in that." Aife grabbed my hands and brought them to her lips and gave me a soft kiss, so gentle my heart ached. "No one has ever looked at me close enough to notice, not even Zelu. The only person who knows is Joyce."

"Why is it a secret? I do not understand?" Aife's head dropped to our clasped hands, the sound of the water clashing against rocks and the feeling of it pressing against our legs faded as every nerve in my body focused on her touch. Focused on this one piece of herself that she is sharing with me, trusting me with. A piece that feels fundamental.

"Because it gives me magic, Druid magic." Her lead lifted, and she released one of my hands, intertwining our fingers with the other. I watched her long fingers wrap around mine, the feeling of our palms pressed firmly together. It was a sensation I had never felt before. It had a completeness and rightness that scared the shit out of me.

"The Quinque hunt for Druids every day and if they found out that I was one. There is every chance they will try to use me to get to them or kill me." I felt her thumb stroke mine.

"I won't tell anyone," I promised, meeting her gaze. "I will keep your secrets safe, Aife. Whichever ones you chose to share with me."

Aife was quiet for a moment, allowing my promise to melt into the air around us. My promise seeped into the wind and waves. "What about yours, little minx? Are you going to share any with me?"

I did not respond; my secret could end the war before it could truly begin. If the Quinque found out who I was, there would be no hesitation in killing me. No decision or potential leniency, it could start the and potentially end war while I am still on the wrong side of Fursomerra.

Aife's hands cupped my cheeks, and she bent down, her lips touching the tears I had not realized had fallen. Her mouth was warm and soothing, and the memory tucked into my heart. I let out a deep breath and turned my head to place a kiss on her palm.

"I'm sorry. I don't know why I'm crying."

"Secrets that you want to share but are not ready to because you do not trust me. I understand. You do not have to tell me anything," she whispered, curling a piece of hair behind my ear.

"I hardly think that's fair after you just told me your biggest secret."

"Well, you backed me into a corner with that one. It was either tell you or let you question everyone in the realm until you found out."

"You think mighty highly of yourself if you think I'd go through all of that." Her finger touched my cheek, drawing a line from the corner of my eye to my chin to tilt my head up. A pink tongue ran across her bottom lip, moistening the beautiful pout. My heart thundered; my blood pulsing so hard I could feel the wind in each pore.

"I thought your first option would have been to kill me, since you enjoy it so much," I gasped.

"You don't think highly enough of yourself if you think I could kill you." Her husky voice dripped with desire, and her eyes dropped to my lips.

"May I kiss you?" My already thundering heart stuttered, leaving me lightheaded. There was the logical part of me that said no, but every other part of me wanted this. I knew I should draw the line at friendship between us, but there was a reckless side of me that needed more. Needed to find out what this deep attraction to her was, why the fact of who she was did not quell my desire to be near her, to be with her.

Why did being with her feel so right? So complete. I nodded. There was a soft breath of relief before she closed the distance between us and pressed a kiss to the corner of my mouth. Electricity floated through me and as I leaned into the contact. Her lips were soft and gentle, and I wondered if she could feel the pulse that pounded through my entire body.

Leaning back a little, Aife's gaze was filled with an emotion that I could not decipher. "I will never do anything to hurt you, Elle. You never have anything to fear from me and I will do what I can to protect you."

My brain tried to process Aife's words, my thoughts focused solely on the warmth of her mouth. I brought my hand to the back of her neck, the silk strands of the hair at the nape tangled in my fingers. I lift my head and pull her lips to mine. My mind went blank but was also so loud. One hand cupped my jaw and angled my head up, the other wrapped around my waist, pulling me close the feeling possessive and delicious.

Her lips were not tentative, not questioning, or inexperienced. They pulled emotions and feeling out of me that sent my head into a spin.

This kind of kiss was written about in books.

A kiss of which I had only even dreamed. Aife kissed how she talked, how she is. The leisure, confidence and aura of sex and allure. Breaking any resistance and taking all of me hostage.

I am so fucked.

The hand around my waist tightened as she drew my body flushed to her, pushing a groan from her throat that fueled the desire in my body. Her tongue ran across my lips, and I opened to her. The touch of her tongue was like liquid fire melting into her. She pulled mine into an exotic dance that trembled deep within my bones. My arms were around her, pulling her closer. Wanting more. My body hummed from the way her tongue filled me, claimed me thoroughly.

She pulled back, resting her forehead on mine as we worked to catch our breath. "You made a mistake by letting me kiss you, my little minx."

My mind was a hazy fog of ecstasy. "Why is that?"

"Because now that I kissed you, I'm not going to stop." Her lips brushed against mine again. My body tingled in response.

"I have made many mistakes in my life, but I wouldn't put this on the top ten." Aife laughed, her breath smelled of cinnamon across my cheeks.

"Maybe I do think too highly of myself if I can't make it into the top ten of your lists."

"You've made it to the top of other lists."

"What lists are those?" she whispered, nibbling my jaw.

I gasped as her lips trailed down to my throat, pressing against the beating pulse, and I felt her smile. "Just...a few."

"You are sinking your claws into me." The purple in her eyes was vivid and swirled as she leaned down and kissed me again.

So soft and so sweet that my heart melted in a puddle that only she had hopes of cleaning up. Aife had sunk her claws so deep in me that I had no hope of pulling them free.

CHAPTER 22
AIFE

I leaned back against the wall next to General Zelu outside the War Room as it filled.

It had been two days since I saw Elle. Since I kissed her. The Quinque arrived and, as expected, they bombarded our time from the moment their carriage appeared. It had done nothing to keep Elle off my mind, though. The memory of her soft lips and body pressed against mine haunted me every minute.

The entire ordeal had been annoyingly distracting especially while I continued to interrogate the Palace residents. Zelu had not been surprised by my lack of progress. He and I were disappointed. There was a point where I started second guessing my extraction skills. I knew how hard it would be. No one embedded their way into the Quinque by shouting from the rooftops. Nevertheless, it nagged at me. No one knew anything. The names I was given dragged me around the Palace so much I felt like I was chasing my own ass.

I picked at a particularly stubborn piece of blood from beneath my nail with a dagger. Of course, Zelu came back from Aurdina with another task. One that I had to take care of this morning, one of the guards had been selling information to the Revolucija. He had not been working with anyone. There had only been an exchange of money and information on where weapons were stored and where they were traveling.

Because of that, I had dried blood beneath my fingernails. I used one of my favorite methods that Gregorovich and Zelu had trained me to withstand. Of course, training to withstand torture included using the methods on me. Pulling fingernails was the most effective. They eventually grew back, but there was nothing that could ease the pain of that feeling.

I was twelve when they pulled mine off; it took a year for the nails to return to normal. My screams had been lower than the pitch the grown male hit earlier today. It became a goal of mine to see what octave I could reach. Currently in the lead was a male from Marinoara. So high I was surprised the windows did not shatter. He could have been a great soprano singer.

King Heptus and Emperor Gregorovich were feral with excitement and power when they returned and immediately sent word to the noble houses of Austiria and Parnitus to make their way to the Palace the day after their return. They did not want stand ins; they wanted the fifteen highest noble houses. It put me on edge to consider what they might have been so keen to get the nobles together for. Especially after Zelu told me we would be here for another month. More time to find the spy, gather the information Joyce needed, and spend more time with Elle.

Elle had told me about her time here in the Palace, that there were servants specifically working as spies for the Quinque and she did everything she could to avoid them. She mentioned a Javier that served as Queen Alhma's bedmate; he was on my list. My awfully long list.

I finally got a particularly nasty spot from beneath my nail when Zelu elbowed me.

"Ow." Blood pooled from where the dagger stabbed my nail bed. I stuck my finger in my mouth and pushed off the wall as Brock approached with Katrina on his arm. My eyes honed into her hand that was wrapped in gauze. Behind her was Elle in a tight blue cotton dress that flared at her waist and flowed down to the floor. I did not try to hold back the heat in my gaze as I stared at her before meeting her eyes. The pink in her cheeks spreading down to her neck and I recalled the delicious taste of her skin when I kissed her neck, like sunshine.

"Prince Brock," Zelu said as we bowed.

"General!" Brock's voice echoed in his enthusiasm. *Why is this family so loud?* "Can't wait to hear the news my father and Gregorovich have for us."

"I still cannot believe they refused to tell us anything! They were all in a tizzy in Aurdina." Katrina pouted and Brock kissed her non-injured hand.

"They disappeared for days and were so excited we thought they stumbled into Hespath during their absence!" Brock walked to me, and I bit back a groan when he grabbed my hand.

"One day soon, assassin. I will come to Parnitus and train with you. I look forward to your tutelage." He grinned with all of his teeth.

"No need to wait Prince, let's start now." Zelu let out a bark of laughter and tried to cover it with a cough. Brock furrowed his brow.

Idiot.

"After you, your Highness," Zelu said, guiding Brock into the room.

I winked at Elle as she passed, and her smile had me aching to pull her down the hall into another closet. However, after her vanilla and jasmine scent hit me, I considered ripping her dress up and sinking my fingers into her right here on the wood floor.

Zelu pinched the skin on my arm, and I hissed, pulling away before following him into the room. The nobles were gathered around a large circular table in the center of the room, on which sat a map of the Realm. Guards surrounded the room against the walls and Brock took his place at the table, with Katrina by his side and Elle behind them.

Zelu was at the table opposite Brock, and I stood behind him, which granted me a perfect view of Elle's face. I met the eye of one of the biggest Guards to ever guard. Seriously, he must have been half ogre. His brown eyes bore into mine. A muscle twitched in his bicep, which was as large as my head. He would be fun to tussle with. I winked, and his pale face flushed with anger or a dare. Gods do I hope it is the latter. I have not had a good fight in weeks.

His gaze cut over to Elle. Eyes roving over her full figure, stopping at her ass before climbing back up slowly. A brow raised, and he leaned over to whisper to the Guard beside him who chuckled, and eye fucked Elle as well.

"Excuse me a moment," I said to Zelu. He gave me a curt nod before returning to his conversation with a male noble, Roy. I walked to the two Guards who kept talking with their eyes on Elle.

She was *mine*.

They had not even noticed I was behind them. Some guards. I leaned in and was able to speak into their ears thanks to my height advantage.

"Look at her like that again, and I will rip your fucking eyes out and wear them as a necklace."

They jerked back and by the time they took their next breath, I was back on the other side of the room, dagger in hand, sliding the blade between two fingers. They looked over and blanched, diverting their attention immediately. A heartbeat later, Heptus and Gregorovich sauntered in with Alhma and Josephine trailing.

"Your Majesty!" one of the elder nobles roared. "I hope the news you brought is worth us dropping everything to get here for!"

Gregorovich laughed. "Still have to pay to get your cock sucked at brothels, Urmin?"

His gray eyes sparkled like shining steel. That is never good. He tortured me my entire life but always made it seem like it was my fault and made me apologize for it. When I was younger, I did everything I could to make him happy with me. I did the best I could to dreg some compliments out of him, which, of course, was a fruitless task. It took a long time and Joyce beating some sense into me to realize that nothing I did would ever be good enough.

He was the perfect manipulator. Having people continuously search for your unobtainable approval kept them working hard. Even if they could never achieve it.

When he tortured me, the glint in his eyes was identical to this one.

"In due time, Urmin!" Heptus said.

Heptus and Gregorovich made their way to the table. I toned out the idle chatter and looked at Elle to see her watching me. I pulled my lower lip between my teeth. Her eyes zeroed in on the movement.

She tilted her head towards the guards, and I threatened them with a raised brow. I gave her a feral grin, lifting my brows quickly. Elle rolled her eyes in exasperation, but the humor sat on the corner of her lips. It was worth it when I looked back at the guards to see their eyes pinned directly in front of them.

A Caeruleus Knight walked in, holding a small wooden box cradled in his arms like a newborn baby. He approached the table and placed it in front of Heptus, bowed, and exited the room.

"Lords and Ladies!" Gregorovich started his delicately on the box. "Try to guess what this contains."

"Deeds!"

"Money!"

"Spells!"

"Power!"

"Sex!" The guesses became more obnoxious as they all yelled over one another.

"Close, but no. Go ahead friend, I will allow you the pleasure." Gregorovich said as he bowed to Heptus.

I had never seen two people with so much power so faithful to each other. Heptus could destroy Gregorovich without a second thought, and Gregorovich is charismatic and liked enough to turn all the Realm against Heptus. Yet, they are entirely loyal to each other.

From what I learned, they had been friends since they were children and had schemed and worked their way into power together. Rumors were rampart that Heptus killed his father to take the crown of his then Kingdom, Engrich. As soon as he did, Gregorovich was named his second. They had wanted to replace the Old

Goddess and Gods and align themselves as the most powerful in the Realm.

When I was younger, I struggled to understand how anyone could do what they had to people. Joyce told me there were three reasons someone would want dominion over others: power, money, and religion.

Power. Heptus and Gregorovich ran the two most powerful territories within Fursomerra. The Kingdom of Austiria held the most functional farmlands outside of Hespath, leaving the rest of the Realm to suffer with tainted ground or limited usable lands. Parnitus Empire was rich with fabric and textiles. The strength in their abilities and the majority of the Realm bowing down to them kept them in power. Heptus was effectively named King of Fursomerra after the Great Übernehmen. There is no greater power than that.

Money. Holding the best lands, they are the richest. Taxing everything in Fursomerra and forcing everyone to pay. Even those outside of their dominion, although there is nowhere outside of their dominion. They control all of the trade, both land and water, and love to tax it. Using the money to keep the rich rich, and giving the poor enough to survive.

Barely.

Religion. Heptus and Gregorovich had successfully eradicated religion that focused on anyone but themselves and the Gods they chose. Books were burned, monuments and statues were destroyed, only to be replaced with ones of their own likeness. Heptus was convinced he was a descendant of Linx and worked to turn himself into a religion.

The question is, since they hold the entire Realm, what else do they want? Heptus flipped the lid of the box open, and a bright light emitted from a scroll of paper popping up from the box. The room was silent, eyes on the parchment and the King.

"Tell us what you know of Galvidore." Heptus' voice was bright, and a bolt of warning shot down my spine.

"Galvidore is a big trading post with crop and livestock," a noble in the back said.

"Yes, we know what it is now, Lyle. What about ten years ago?" Heptus said, exasperated.

I looked at Elle, who had gone utterly still, her eyes on the box.

"It was one of the five main Kingdoms," Zelu supplied.

"Good, General!" Heptus' excitement was palpable. "What else?"

Katrina's smile was as fake as Josephine's nails.

"Zane and that bitch Peele dictated that place with their pathetic children," Lyle spat.

Gregorovich chuckled. "Yes, what else?"

"Was the lead ruler of Fursomerra."

"What was that?" Heptus barked. "Speak up Marlie."

One of the few female nobles cleared her throat. "Within Galvidore the Normaran family was believed to be the true rulers of Fursomerra."

"And what Visreala were they?" Heptus asked with a bright smile.

"Phoenix."

Heptus slapped his hand on the table, causing everyone to jump. "Yes! Exactly. The Normaran's were the last Phoenix line in Fursomerra."

"Some great line," Gregorovich muttered, and the room erupted in laughter. "What happened to them?" The laughing teetered into silence and some nobles shifted uncomfortably. They all knew what happened to the family. Half of the nobles in this room betrayed the Normaran's and caused their death.

"Don't be shy!"

"They were burned alive!" Urmin jeered. "Every last one of them!"

"Ah." Heptus tapped the lid of the still opened box, the light still shining faintly, his green eyes almost inhaling the light. "Were they all?"

Once again, he was met with silence. "One was never found. Do you remember who that was, Gregorovich?"

"The daughter, Titaia Nomaran."

"Exactly, four Nomaran's, three bodies. You all know this, do not pretend now. We have all been looking for the last decade to find the child."

"Well, she wouldn't be a child now, Heptus," Gregorovich countered. "What do you think, Katrina? You grew up there."

Katrina's lips were pale, but the rest of her face was pure curiosity and interest. "She was around my age. I would say probably twenty-six or twenty-seven." Elle had the slightest tremor in her finger, her chest rising and falling in deep, calming breaths.

Curious.

"There were rumors," Heptus said. "About a Prophecy that foretold the war."

"We don't believe in Proph..." Urmin started.

"I do!" Heptus yelled, and Urmin's entire body quaked as Heptus pinned him with his stare.

A curl of magic filled the room as Heptus' power pushed against Urmin. Alhma placed a hand on his forearm and his rage filled eyes cut to her. He took a deep breath. With a blink, the rage dissipated and Urmin gasped, holding a hand to his chest. A servant handed him a glass of water that he swallowed in one go.

"We knew the girl was alive. We knew she had been hiding like a coward. While we were searching for her, there was no real fear that she would take the crown, as she had no real claim. The throne falls to the eldest male Phoenix, who, of course, was killed with the rest.

"This," he tapped the scroll, "is the Prophecy." Gasps echoed around the room and rolled my eyes. All this talk about Galvidore and a Prophecy and they had not figured out what was in the box yet? These are the great leaders that are in charge of the Realm.

A fucking glowing scroll.

Yet they are shocked it is the Prophecy?

Give me a break.

"Will you read it?" Marlie asked.

"There are words here that we have agreed to keep between us." He nodded towards Gregorovich, who inclined his head respectfully. "We do have a traitor amongst us, and one can never be too careful." He and Gregorovich chuckled at some joke that sat amongst themselves.

I watched Gregorovich's eyes roamed the room and settle on Elle. The look had nothing to do with a traitor and everything to do with the promise of conquest. The beast within my chest unfurled in anger and wanted nothing more than to rip him open from ass to forehead. Why do all the males in this room insist on looking at what is mine?

"However, this does confirm that Titaia is still alive. This female is the only one who holds a threat to us, while she should not have a claim to the throne, she can birth a male heir who would be one to unjustifiably end our reign. Although," Heptus looked around the room meeting each nobles eye, "this Prophecy eludes to her holding the power of three Phoenix which makes her more than just a birthing canal for an heir."

"Is there any idea of where she might be?" Marlie asked, her eyes on the scroll.

Gregorovich pursed his lips, finally looking away from Elle. "We can guess that she is not with the Rebellion. We think she might be within Hespath, which is one of the reasons they have kept themselves as locked up as they have," he said.

"We need to double our efforts to get into Hespath and see if she is actually there or not. Search every single corner of the Realm, no stone unturned, no village left free. Do not kill her if you find her. Bring her to us. It has to be us. Search your own homes, interrogate anyone you deem appropriate." The thought that the Phoenix would come back could be cause for concern, but there was something they were holding back. Something key to the start of this hunt. They continued talking, but I was focused on Elle, who trembled.

Katrina had noticed and walked back towards her while the focus was on Heptus and Gregorovich. She whispered in her ear and rubbed her arm. Anyone else might think it had been to comfort her from Gregorovich's attention. It was such an animalistic desire that I was not the only one who noticed. There was something else, though. Her reaction started before his attention. I wonder if she has some connection to the Normaran family.

\#

CHAPTER 23
TITAIA

I had to have worn a path in the plush tan carpet that filled Katrina's room, having paced it for what felt like hours. All the while, Katrina sat on the bed chewing her nail.

We returned to her chambers as soon as we could after the meeting and revelation of the finding of the Prophecy.

After the meeting, the Quinque decided to host a large formal dinner, and I had to stand there for two hours while they ate and laughed and I had a panic attack. I felt Aife's eyes on me the entire time. I may have been hiding my feelings for the last decade, but she is observant.

I have been searched for ever since my family was murdered, but it was always a secondary hunt. Yet this was completely different; this was hunting.

"Shit. Shit. Shit," I repeated, running my fingers through my hair which was oily and sticking up in all directions. "Fuck Katrina!" I dropped to a chair, pressing my palms to my eyes until starbursts appeared.

"We have to get out of here soon," she said, the nail on her thumb a mere numb from her chewing.

"Do we? They are looking everywhere but here." They are going to every village, every city, every farm and find out how to break into Hespath. Right now, this Palace is the only place that they are not looking.

"Titaia." Katrina's voice was soft, and I looked to see her standing in front of me. She dropped to her knees and grabbed my hands tightly in hers. I did not realize until that moment how cold I was. Her hands felt scalding in mine. I knew what she was going to say.

I looked into my best friend's mossy green eyes and chewed my lip. It was only a matter of time until all the searches came back negative, no sign of me anywhere. Only a matter of time before they start to look within their own walls. "I have nowhere to go."

"We, have the seers," she said, squeezing my hand, "and it might be time to tell them who you are."

That was what Katrina did, what she had done since we were children playing mermaids in the castle.

Protected me from anything and everything. If there was a boy picking on me, she would start shooting rocks from her slingshot. If I were getting in trouble with one of the maids, she would cause a distraction large enough for them to have to run off. As soon as my life was in danger in Galvidore, she got me out. I owed everything to her, my life. There was nothing I would ever be able to do to adequately thank her.

"I trust you," I whispered.

Katrina's smile could rival the sun. She sat next to me and pulled me into her chest, her arm around my shoulders. I snuggled into her warmth, breathing in the ocean scent that always was a part of her.

"My next meeting with the Seers is in eight days. We just have to wait until then. For now, we will rest your glamour every night. Just to be sure."

The roaring in my ears was deafening. I had been afraid most of my life, especially living within the home of the beast who wanted to kill me. But that fear had reached a tipping point. They had not known that I was alive for sure, but it seems like whatever was written in this Prophecy confirmed their fears and betrayed me.

Katrina pulled back, looking into my eyes. "What is going on with you and the assassin?"

"What?" I spluttered.

"Don't you get shy on me!" she squealed, slapping my arm.

"Stop hitting me!"

"I saw the way she was looking at you! Made my panties wet," she said, and I barked in disgust, trying to stop the heat from coating my cheeks.

"Katrina," I whispered, fear dousing the pleasure. "She was watching me; I know I reacted...do you think sh..."

Katrina shook her head. "I think most of us were barely breathing during that exchange, Titaia. Do you think Aife would turn you in?"

My initial gut reaction was to scream no. But can I really say that? I barely knew her. Spending every day for two weeks together means hardly anything.

"No. I don't think she would." I felt it deep in my soul, the truth in it.

"Titaia. She is a literal killer," Katrina said slowly, as if talking to a child.

"I know!" And I did. Aife never gave me any notion that she was anything other than what was said. She told me repeatedly that she has no remorse for what she does. I should rightfully be terrified of her, feel disgust about who she is, what she was.

But I was not.

"I cannot explain it. I just..." I shrugged. There was no logical way to explain how I felt or why.

"You're falling for her."

I scoffed. "I've known her all of ten minutes, Katrina."

She hummed at me with a wink. "They will be here for six more weeks. Plenty of time."

"Goodnight, Kat." She laughed as I slammed the door behind me. The halls were still crowded. Most nobles were staying here for the night, which means their servants were running around taking care of their needs.

I know Aife saw my reaction as soon as they brought up my family and when they mentioned the prophecy. Whether she thought it had to do with me being a Normaran or I might know something about the missing Princess, she knew there was something going on with me.

The logical side of me said that I needed to avoid her. That even though I knew deep down she would not hurt me, I needed to be smart. Even the thought of that physically and emotionally hurt. While logical, it was not realistic. There was no way I could avoid her.

I could pretend that I had no idea what was going on. Me? A Normaran? A Princess? What is that? Who? That is laughable.

Aife extracts information for her job, so I do not know how well that would work.

Looks like I will just have to say absolutely nothing and hope that she does not ask anything. Solid plan.

\#

CHAPTER 24
AIFE

"We have ten thousand within Lorngastein, ten thousand within Galvidore, and twenty-five thousand between the King and Emperor in the Caeruleus Legion," Zelu said as he leaned against the table in the war room, pushing little statues across the map. He had a strong and powerful voice, one that commands attention and reaches into the tiny crooks within the room. I clenched my jaw to keep from yawning. "We know that the Druids are in the hidden city of Harenae, unfortunately that's all we know." Balled up paper hit the side of my head and I opened my eyes to see Zelu glaring at me. "I am not sure what part of this you thought was optional for you to understand, but let me clarify. None of this is optional."

I rolled my eyes and strolled to where he stood. I braced my forearms on the table and looked at the map. "I do not know why you find this necessary for me, General. I do not command legions; I do not fall into pretty lines on the battlefield. I work in the shadows," I said.

He raised a brow. "Does that make you feel powerful? Hiding in the shadows instead of standing on the front line?"

"I do not hide."

He tipped a broad shoulder, and I glanced back at the map. Lines depicted territory borders, blue showed batches of water, horizontal triangles and half circles annotated mountain ranges and rolling hills throughout the realm. Major cities and their known names and large places within each territory that remained without any depiction. Fursomerra was surrounded by islands, most unknown but a few identified. The largest part of the map was on the edges and was completely black. Elegant gold letters foiled over the ink, Holuranda and Pomulola Realms.

"Why are you showing me this, General?" I met his guarded blue eyes, noting a lingering unspoken word beneath the depths. A shadow floated beneath the ice, like a goddess damned shark.

"Are you forgetting the most important lesson I ever taught you, Aife? Did you become so bloodthirsty that you neglect that one skill I said would save your life?" His eyes bore into mine so deeply I wondered if he could see the black that covered my heart.

"Information."

"Information!" Zelu yelled, his hands hit the table in a sharp thud. "Yes, information is what will save your life one day. Not how good you are at fighting, creeping into the shadows, or how skilled you are as an assassin. Information. Facts. Knowledge. That is what wins wars, battles, and saves lives."

I felt like a child being scolded by a parent. It had been years since he talked to me like this. I remember the last time he did. It was my one and only time being captured, what put those scars on my stomach and back.

4,379 days ago.

Even though he was able to pull me out before they got the chance to kill me, Zelu did not hold back from reprimanding me while the healers patched up my wounds. I do not even remember what he yelled about exactly; I only remember him being angry. He burned down the building I had been kept in and tracked down everyone single Visreala involved in my torture and killed them.

When he dragged me out, I was barely hanging onto life. They used a spelled dagger that caused my blood to not clot. At least that is what they told me; I was not necessarily chatty during the torture session.

"There is going to come a time when what you know is going to save your life." Gregorovich said, his voice hard as if he was trying to tell me something he was unable to say aloud. "You want me to sell information to survive?" I asked. He gave me an incredulous look. "I am just asking; you keep talking about what I know and staying alive. Obviously, you want me to abandon the Empire and save myself." I shrugged.

"You're a child."

I grinned.

My smile dropped as the feeling of burning hot metal on my skin flashed into my mind. A memory of the training Gregorovich had given me to make sure that I would never sell information, willingly or otherwise. It felt as if Zelu knew where my mind went; he walked over and placed heavy hands on my shoulders, making my knees buckle. I craned my neck to look up at him.

Fucking Minotaurs.

"Knowledge and information help us deter enemies. It gives you the advantage of knowing where safety is, where to avoid, and where your enemies might be." He patted my shoulder and left.

What the fuck?

I stood there for a heartbeat, trying to figure out what the hell he was trying to tell me. Some round-about way of a secret that made absolutely no sense. If I was in trouble, the last place I would run would be to the legions and Knights of the Empire and Kingdom. I had killed plenty of their friends and most of them were terrified enough of me that they would try to kill me at my most vulnerable.

I went to step out the door and ran into Elle. Quite literally.

I grabbed her arm and steadied both of us, pulling her body into mine. She gasped, grabbing my biceps.

I chuckled. "Told you that you'd fall for me."

Elle repressed a laugh and pulled back. "You do keep saying that. Although I did not actually fall." Her voice was soft, guarded even as she smiled. "What were you even doing in there?"

"Planning my world domination, obviously." I bent to grab the books she had dropped.

"Library?"

Elle nodded, reaching for the books. I lifted them just out of her grasp and slid my hand into my pocket, offering her the crook of my elbow. She looked up and down the hall. I smirked as her scowl increased when she saw the lingering looks of the females and interested and terrified looks of the males.

"Don't want to be seen with me, sweetheart?"

She scoffed before placing her arm around mine. A pleasant current shot through my skin at the bare contact. "Can't you get in trouble for fraternizing or something?" she asked.

I laughed. "I'm sorry, are you the Queen?"

She mumbled.

"What was that?" I responded.

"It wasn't a stupid question, just wondering what would happen if someone saw us."

"Besides them being jealous of my incredible luck?"

She rolled her eyes.

"Nothing at all. I may be indentured, but I do have some freedom, remember?" I asked with a shrug.

"Fuck, feel, and know. So, everyone is going to think you are feeling something for me or fucking me?" My hand flexed at her words; I do love the way she says the word fuck.

"Something wrong with either of those?" I asked as we turned out of a main corridor, and she led us down a deserted passage. The halls were warm, heat seeping from the stone walls, deep red carpet lined the floors, and paintings scattered over the walls with torches every few feet.

"I just don't need people thinking I'm going around sleeping with everyone."

Everyone?

Jealousy. Green and sticky made me clench the books in my hands tighter. I looked over at her, but her eyes were straight ahead, her face an unreadable mask. We turned another corner, and a door appeared. A tall and wide wooden door with a silver serpentine handle, the top of which held a mosaic glass arch with some picture I couldn't make out. I opened the door, allowing her to step inside first. Closing it with a soft thud behind us.

Elle took the books and placed them on a silver cart just inside the room to the right. This must be the smallest library in the Palace, it did not have as much grandeur as the main one. No statues or large paintings of the royal family lining the walls. A lack of dust in the air and the dull glow of lanterns was surprisingly inviting. It was well-loved.

There were no windows. Hundreds of shelves created a path down the center of the room and along the walls. The smell of books and old parchment filled the air, transporting me back to my mother's study in Matrador. The image of her body hunched over notebooks flashed into my mind, her brown hair curled over her shoulder and hand moving across the pages.

Elle walked in front of me, every step creating a delicious sway in her hips. She walked to the back of the room where the books got older and thicker. When she turned between two shelves with books that appeared to be older than Fursomerra itself I realized that she was either ignoring me or forgot that I was here. Neither of which I enjoyed.

I grabbed her wrist and twirled her around, pressing her back against the shelves. I pinned a leg between hers, lifted her arms over her head and leaned into her neck and inhaled, enjoying the delicious smell of her. The heat from her body was intoxicating. The flutter of her pulse made my palm itch to wrap around her throat.

"Let go," she grunted weakly, trying to wiggle out of my grasp. The darkness of my laugh sent goosebumps on her flesh.

"Not until you answer my question," I whispered, licking the arch of her neck.

"You didn't ask anything." She said, trying to sound impatient, but she was breathless. The arch of her back and the skipping of her pulse told me she did not want me to let go.

"I am getting there, sweetheart. Let me just enjoy the moment." I said, pushing my nose in the dip where her neck met her shoulder, breathing in jasmine and vanilla. She knew how to get out of this. She could easily maneuver out of my grasp. But she did not want to, enjoying this as much as I did.

"Tell me, little minx." I murmured, kissing up the column of her neck. "Are you sleeping with someone else?"

"I'm not even sleeping with you." The mirth she threw in her voice turned into a gasp when I bit her ear, pulling her earring into my mouth.

"That doesn't answer my question," I whispered.

"Are you jealous?" I kissed right below her ear, trailing my lips down her jawline, saying nothing. She laughed incredulously. "You are!"

"I don't like to share," I murmured, enjoying the sounds that came from her. My own arousal all but soaking through my pants, especially when she pressed her chest into mine and I felt her hard nipples.

"Little assassin jealous of who's tumbling in my sheets." Elle giggled.

I nipped at her jaw, and she squeaked.

"Not just your sheets, little minx. Of whose touching this jaw." I pressed my lips against her. "Who's whispering in this ear?" I took her ear between my teeth. "Whose fingers are running through this soft hair," I let go of her hands and ran my fingers through the loose strands of her braid. She grabbed my waist. "Who's kissing these lips?" I ran my lips over hers and her fingers tightened on me.

"All *mine*," I growled. The certainty and possessiveness that filled me was both terrifying and intriguing. Something about this female drew me in and if I were not careful, I could fall into an obsession with her.

I tilted her mouth further into mine. "I belong to no one," she said, her voice hardly above a whisper.

I chuckled into her lips, "we will see."

"Mighty highly." Her words turned into a moan when I pushed my hips into her, pressing my leg firmly into her center.

I brushed my lips over hers again before pulling back and straightening my shirt. She gaped at me.

I tapped her chin with a finger. "This is a library, Elle. Not a brothel." I walked away scanning the shelves, not comprehending a single title, as I tried to pull myself together. I love females. There is no question there. I knew when I was a child that I did, but never has one caused me to be so unhinged.

"You are insufferable." Elle straightened her skirts and hair, her cheeks pink with a flush. I wonder how she would look freshly fucked.

Calm down.

"Looking for something specific?" I asked, watching as she ran her fingers across her lips in thought.

Why was that so erotic?

Elle's eyes shifted so quickly over the books I wondered if she could actually read what the titles said or if she was pretending.

"Katrina asked me to retrieve a book for her," she said. "Something about the history of Fursomerra or the Realm. I do not know exactly, only that I would know it when I saw it."

"Not cryptic at all. Is the Duchess planning to save the world?" I asked in a little chess match that I constantly played, a game of hide and seek. Ask the right question to get the right answer.

"This is Katrina we are talking about," Elle said with a snort. Her eyes cut over to me quickly before going back to the titles. She was hiding something; I knew that. She had a secret and a big part of me wondered if she would ever trust me enough to tell me. A bigger part wondered if it was because of a desire to know all about her for myself, for Zelu, or Joyce.

"Have you ever heard of the Normarans?" Her fingers jerked as she ran them down the spine of a large leather book that looked as if it might crumble beneath her touch.

"Who hasn't?" Elle responded.

"You're from Galvidore right?" I asked.

She nodded.

"Did you know them?" I pressed. Her reaction from the prophecy and now tickled my curiosity too much to leave it alone.

"A lot of questions without asking what you really want to know," she turned towards me and leaned against a shelf. "Out with it."

"You know what I'm asking, Elle." Her bottom lip disappeared between her teeth at my question. Her eyes swept from my feet to my head before she closed them, as if trying to erase this conversation from existence.

"I have a lot of secrets, Aife." Her voice was barely above a whisper.

"*I* have a lot of secrets, Elle."

The corner of her lip tipped up. "I don't think I can trust you with mine."

I studied her, and for the first time in my nearly twenty years of being with Gregorovich I was considered betraying him for someone other than Joyce.

"Who do you trust? Katrina?"

I did not wait for her answer as I weighed my options, options that I had no idea why I was weighing. This should not be a discussion; this should not be a topic between us. I should not even be around her as much as I have been. I could lie and say it is my mission for Zelu, to find who the spy is although everything within me said she was not the spy. For some reason I trusted her, and I wanted her to trust me. It had nothing to do with Zelu, Joyce, or anyone else.

It had everything to do with us.

"Meet me tonight at the beach." I paused, then added, "Bring Katrina."

Those strange hazel eyes were wary as she asked, "Why?"

"A secret for a secret," I said. My heart was pounding so hard I thought she might be able to hear it.

"Why don't you tell me your secret now?"

I snagged a loose piece of her hair. My knuckles brushed her cheeks as I twirled it around my finger. "Because I have a feeling our secrets require more privacy. And I think earning your trust requires someone you trust learning my secret." I tilted my head down, brushing my lips against hers, not fighting the groan that clawed up my throat.

Her taste was just as I remember, the sunrise and everything I do not deserve. Elle leaned into my kiss, her lips molding around mine in a rhythm that was insistent and not enough. I pulled back and leaned my forehead against hers.

"We will be there at two," she promised.

CHAPTER 25
TITAIA

Nervous, upset, mad, irate, frustrated. All of the words to describe Katrina's feelings.

A secret for a secret. Was I a fool? Anyone could lie about a secret, especially someone like her.

When I reached Katrina's room without the book but with the ultimatum from Aife, she yelled at me for an hour before dinner and glared at me throughout the meal. I could see Aife's eyes twinkling in amusement from across the room.

Katrina noticed and glared at her so darkly it knocked the amusement right off that elf's face. Served her right.

Katrina continued to yell at me after dinner.

It was not that I had agreed to share a secret; it was that Aife had clearly discerned there we had a secret to tell, big enough that she was potentially willing to share one of her own. If we trusted that what she shared was factual. Katrina also freaked out about having to potentially kill her, which was laughable that she had any notion she might be able to get close enough to even attempt it. I tried to talk her down about that, but she started planning how I could seduce Aife and while she was occupied with my 'lady bits,' Katrina would sneak up and stab her.

Not only had she wanted me to play decoy by having sex with Aife, but she also wanted to kill her while we were having sex. After much discussion and a few more hours of her freaking out, she finally agreed to accompany me.

It helped that I said I was going whether she went or not.

I already had a secret about Aife, a life ending secret, according to her. I have known it for a few weeks now and she had not assassinated me, so there's that. Was that a reason to trust her? After Katrina agreed to accompany me, she strapped half a dozen blades to my body and hers and strapped a sword across my back.

I did not have the energy to fight her.

"I hate nature," Katrina growled, swatting at the bugs with her hand as we trekked through the woods.

I snorted. "Funny how you think we are going to be able to escape Austiria without being knee deep in the forest and nature."

She ignored me. "Bugs, slimy creatures, nasty creepy things that want to suck your blood and eat your bones."

"You have been reading too many horror novels, dear." We slid down the last bit of the decline the metal on us clanged like bells. Aife sat on the lone boulder staring out at the water and glanced up as we approached. She undoubtably heard the moment we started our descent with Katrina's incessant complaints. Aife smiled, and I considered telling her to never do it in the presence of anyone else ever again. It was devastating.

"Look here, assassin!" Katrina shouted, stomping at Aife with her finger raised.

"Oh Goddess, Katrina." Aife's brows rose in surprise, her smile morphed into a smirk.

"If you are here to trick us or try to kill us, we will kill you first! Elle knows how to wield a blade!"

"She helped me train, Katrina," I said, exasperated. "She thinks I can kill you with two shakes of my wrist."

"Or a shake of your ass," Katrina murmured.

Aife chuckled, looking back at Katrina. "I promise, Duchess. Neither of you have anything to fear from me, especially not Elle."

I gestured to them to join me on the blanket I just laid on the ground. They sat on either side of me, forming an odd triangle and in silence we looked at the rushing water.

"Secret for a secret," Aife said.

Katrina glared. "You first. Assassin."

"Katrina," I groaned. I looked back at Aife, and her tanned face was pale, her bottom lip pulled into her mouth. I wanted to take that lip between my teeth.

"I indirectly work for the Rebellion."

Silence.

"What?" Katrina whispered.

"Fifty-seven Rebellion leaders and sympathizers that I was assigned to kill are quite alive and well. They are in hiding with the Seers and even some with the Druids."

My heart thundered so hard I was surprised I could not see it pounding through my shirt. Then Katrina howled with laughter. The sound of a cackle obnoxious enough that the water shifted it is current in response. I tried to shush her, but tears streamed down her face in her hysteria.

The Quinque knew there was a traitor amongst them, knew someone within their circle was passing information to the Seers. Katrina was so skilled in deception that they had never suspected her and would never suspect her. But their very own trained weapon was also betraying them. That was something they had not seen coming.

"By all means, keep laughing," Aife grumbled.

"I'm sorry…" Katrina gasped. "I am sorry. That is just bizarre; you expect us to believe that *you*. You! The assassin trained by the greatest General to ever walk the Realm is a traitor. If this is a trap, I promise I will throw you into that water and no matter how skilled you are, assassin, not even you can survive the rapids."

"Yes, because while Zelu trained me, someone else saved me. I would have surrendered to the darkness without her, and while I have succumbed to the horrors of what I do, I am not lost to it." Aife spoke as if Katrina's threatening words had only been a comment on how warm a summer night it was.

"You kill people for a living. You are the horrors in the darkness." Katrina spat. "How could you claim that you haven't fallen into it?"

"Katrina," I warned.

"No, Elle. She is right, I am a monster. I had a choice in the beginning. It was kill or be killed. I chose survival. At nine years old, I had to find a way to live with everything being asked of me and adapt to the circumstances I had been given. If I did not, I would not be here with you. I would have been killed. Regardless of what you might think of me, Duchess. My soul may be bound to burn, but I do have a heart that has not been lost to the darkness."

"Who?" Katrina asked.

Aife's long fingers rubbed her lips. "Her name is Joyce."

Silence pressed into the darkness. Aife stared at her fingertips as if they could tell her what we were thinking. I did not question what she told us; I could feel the honesty in my bones.

The raw truth. The thought that the Quinque had taken a child of war and threatened her with death or servitude, because that is what she was. A murderous servant for the Quinque and their whims.

"When I arrived at Parnitus Joyce sought me out. I was the youngest recruit they ever brought in and the only elf. I am still the only elf. Their kind is not very welcome amongst the Quinque, and Joyce knew that. She also knew what they planned to do with me. Somehow, she thought my life was worth fighting for, even when I killed people she knew and continued to kill. Joyce is why I betray them."

Katrina watched Aife, who looked out at the water glowing in the moonlight. This side of Katrina was every bit the best friend that I remembered, the smart and fast thinking Duchess who had saved my ass from getting in trouble since we were kids. Who thought fast enough to get me out of Galvidore, saving my life and keeping me alive? My best friend looked over at me. She had come to the same conclusion that I had. Aife was telling the truth.

Guilt and envy clawed at my gut, puncturing vital organs as I looked between them. These two brave women were putting their well-being, their lives on the line for the Revolucija. Ultimately protecting me, waiting for me to take my place within the fight. And I was a fucking coward.

"Are you going to fight with the Rebellion?" I asked.

I had seen the hatred for Gregorovich she tried to keep hidden. That was when I saw true evil in her. Whenever he was near, the threat rolled off her like a thunderstorm over water and I wondered he did to deserve it. If he was as responsible as Heptus for some of those scars that littered her body.

Aife looked up at the sky with a heavy sigh. "I have been trying to figure that out since I spared the first Rebellion leader. Joyce had told me once I did that, regardless of what happened after I was a rebel. That is not necessarily true. Since then I have killed many more than I have saved, but..." she took a deep breath.

"I think she knew that I would never be faithful to Gregorovich. Not after he slaughtered my mother and father in front of me." My heart shattered for the little girl with black eyes and an untainted soul.

"Heptus killed my family after they betrayed their friends. Said they could not be trusted, which was ironic." Katrina said. "Cannot say that I blame him. I wanted to kill them myself. His promises aligned with my father's idea of freedom and led to the betrayal. Being able to rule as he saw fit and not having to live under the righteous rule of the Normaran's. I did what I could to right their injustices, but nothing will ever be enough."

"That's not true, Katrina," I said as I grasped her hand.

"Do not try to comfort me on this. I will live the rest of my life trying to fight against their betrayal. What they cost Fursomerra, what they did to yo..." She took a deep breath. "I understand what it is like to live with those who killed your family. To want revenge."

Katrina, who pulled me out of Galvidore and thought to shield me within the Palace beneath the eyes of those who hunted and killed my family. Who has protected me all these years, not just out of friendship but retribution.

"If we had to make up for all of the decisions our families made, we would all be apologizing for the rest of our lives and no good would ever come from the world," Aife said.

"I figured working with the Seers might be the best way to make up for it, and to put some good back into it," Katrina admitted.

My heart tumbled to my stomach, making it flutter with nausea. Katrina was not supposed to divulge that she was working with the Seers. She wasn't supposed to say anything at all. We agreed to hear Aife out, but not what to say. Aife's confession had hit too close to her heart for Katrina to keep hers hidden.

Aife laughed loud and deep, her eyes twinkled with delight, and I captured the sound and sight in a glass case within my heart. "When I first met you, Duchess, I thought you were the densest woman in all the Realms. But I think the rest of us are foolish to have ever underestimated you."

Katrina flipped her hair and gave her a mock bow. "We do what we must."

"I admit I had suspicions, but you were not at the top of my list. I thought it might have been you," she said, jutting her chin at me.

"No, I'm not brave enough for that." I tried at jest, but it fell as flat as my voice was. Aife opened her mouth, but I interrupted. "I'm the one they are all looking for."

Concentrating, I lifted my glamour. The glamour that hid my identity, and that I had worn faithfully for ten years. The one Katrina had so carefully placed and detailed. It was like lifting a blanket off your body after hours of being stifled by the itchy heat. My brown hair faded to white, and the burn of my eyes let me feel the hazel eyes turn to the darkest red wine. A ripple across my face and my features changed, sharpening at some points, and filling out in others. Unfortunately, no matter what form I was in, it was impossible to hide these chubby cheeks.

"I am Titaia Ellaine Normaran, Princess of Galvidore." My name felt weird, foreign on my tongue. I had not spoken it aloud in years.

Aife's reached out and touched my hair, making it visible from the corner of my eye. I had forgotten how bright it was.

A whisper from Katrina and the sensation of being covered in a blanket fell over me again.

"Whose idea was it to place you in the heart of the enemy?" Aife watched the hair on her fingers fade from white to brown.

"Mine," Katrina said, pride evident in her words. "It was our only option."

"I was promised to Brock before the war, and they kept the engagement in good faith even after the war started. Heptus convinced my family that doing so would ensure their safety in the war. Aligning our two families would be beneficial, which was a lie, of course. Even before the war, the Queen and King had never trusted Heptus the way my father had." Katrina looked out to the water again, her eyes filling with tears. "I did not find out about the attack on Galvidore until right before it happened. I wanted to save everyone, but I could only reach Ti."

"You both serve the Revolucija in your own rights, in your own ways, how you can." My eyes burned as tears streamed down my cheeks. "I have been a coward all of these years."

"That's not true..." Katrina started, but I held up a hand.

"It is. I do what I can in the city, but I have been spineless. Hiding while everyone looks for me."

"It was the smart move. If you revealed yourself, it would have been a death sentence," Aife said.

"Depending on what you do with what we told you, you might sign it for her," Katrina said carefully.

Aife looked positively offended at that comment. Offended and angry. Her obsidian eyes were like shards of glass, her back stiff, even the air took a deep breath. Katrina was right. I did not know what Aife would do. She could end this war by identifying me. I mentally smacked myself for being so stupid. I watched Aife, who, in turn, watched me. I saw the ice shards melt and resolve settle in her gaze.

"Do you remember what I told you the first time I brought you here?" I tilted my head in a nod at Aife's question "You will never have anything to fear from me..." Aife grabbed the dagger strapped to her side, flipping it to hold the hilt out to me. "Take it."

It was the same dagger that was always at her side. The hilt was wrapped in black leather bindings shaped like an inverted hourglass. The cross guard was shaped like two wings and silver runes I could not read were carved down the center of the black blade.

I grabbed the hilt, holding it between us as she released it before moving closer to me. Her knees pressed into mine and Katrina watched anxiously. Aife lifted my empty hand and placed her left hand in mine, palm up. She grabbed my hand that held the dagger and placed the tip of the blade to the skin below her pinky. I jerked and tried to pull away when she dragged it diagonally through her palm to right below her thumb.

She looked at me and I noticed her eyes were so dark and bottomless it felt like they could save me and end me at the same time. Like she was the beginning and the end of life.

"I, Aife Cirdorn Awing Amamion, pledge myself to you, Titaia Ellaine Normaran. I will protect you until my last breath. I will set this world on fire and watch it burn until that crown sits on your head."

A glow pulled my eyes from hers. Symbols appeared from the blood on her hand and swirled, wrapping around her hand and mine. She moved her hand, and I watched the gold symbols fade into my skin, leaving a soft, nearly invisible tattoo on my own palm.

Aife's eyes bore into mine as Katrina asked, "Why is your name so long?"

CHAPTER 26
AIFE

It had been a long, exhausting night. Katrina and I agreed we needed a sacrificial lamb to keep the eyes off her and Titaia. And since I virtually tied my life to Titaia, it was important to me in many ways. Though Titaia disagreed vehemently, we were out of options.

It was odd to consider. The female who had caught my attention so thoroughly was the one that I had searched for. She was always a secondary target for me. If, at any point, I had found out who she was, I was to take her to Gregorovich. Instead, I had a scar across my palm, binding me to her. I had no intention of performing a pledge, but I did not regret my decision. I knew that Elle had a secret. One that she hid for a long time, but I would have never guessed she was the Princess.

The last living Phoenix.

And when Elle... Titaia gave me that secret, it showed the trust that she had in me. After that, the desire to protect her and tie myself to her was just too strong. I had known Titaia for a little over a month but the connection and draw I felt to her did nothing to ease her anger when I explained that I had tied me to her as her personal warrior. It started an argument about how she was trained to not need protection.

Until Katrina told her how sweet and romantic it was, and Titaia blushed so red I was sure the color was permanently ingrained in her skin.

She was grumpy, but accepting when I told her it would be a way for me to find her and a way for us to know if the other was in danger. The binding meant that I could not betray her in any way; I had pledged loyalty to her and the consequence for betrayal was severe. I neglected to say it would kill me, but I do not think it was necessary.

I underestimated the Duchess. I had known her in passing for years and what I knew of her was bubbly, doe eyed, and ignorant.

The Seers chose the perfect recruit; she played her part well. Someone within the castle that was trivialized and had a deep hatred of the new regime. Although Katrina's trust with the Seers was not enough for her to confess that Titaia was her lady-in-waiting. Katrina had been the mastermind of the Phoenix's survival and I knew that tore Titaia apart.

When Katrina spoke, I could see the appreciation and humiliation that Titaia had in what she had done, that she felt less than worthy of her title. Of saving and freeing Fursomerra.

But tonight, that was going to change.

Or it would if this party would ever end.

I wanted to gouge my fucking eyes out.

The nobles were leaving after four days of driving me out of my mind. I had been propositioned with various kinds of jewels, land and property, money, even females. Humans and Visreala. Lord Kiom offered his wife and eldest daughter. Both of whom were beautiful and looked more than willing to...be with me. It took an icy glare to get his daughter to stop staring at me. If she had touched me, I would have broken her hand without a second thought.

His wife, Harah, said, "I don't normally go elves, but I do have a thing for elves." All this to kill their enemies, most of whom sat with them at the war and dinner tables. Quite ridiculous.

"The Emperor is getting restless," Zelu said whilst standing next to me. He somehow was able to fold his large form into a black jacket and matching pants. This was the fanciest he had been in a long time. Courtesy of the farewell black-tie affair Heptus and Gregorovich decided to host.

During the four days of their stay, there had been many more meetings where they discussed the search for the Phoenix. Heptus made it apparent that her being barely alive was perfectly acceptable as long as there was still breath in her lungs and blood pumping into her heart. Gregorovich had offered tips on a few torturing practices and smiled at me when he talked about blade tipped whips.

Zelu also shared that the Revolucija had executed a dozen well timed attacks at the same time all around the Realm that stretched from Liladon to Tropera. That was a surprise to me. I thought they executed smaller strikes. With the revelation that the nobles promised more numbers, an additional 60,000 were added to Quinque's force. After the promise they were assured the tripling of their lands, stretching their allotment into the Land of Hespath and Harenae after they won.

"This Palace is full of idiots; they wouldn't know a lion if it bit them on the ass," I said, staring at

Elle... Titaia who shadowed Katrina across the hall. She dressed for the occasion, wearing a delicious black dress with a scooped neckline, and long fitted sleeves. The bodice was fitted and flared right at her full hips, her long brown hair down in curls. She was beautiful now, but knowing how she looked behind that glamour, in her true form? It left me breathless; she was the most striking creature I had ever seen. Her beautiful wine-colored eyes, the moon white hair that contrasted her dark skin beautifully. I would never look at another female again.

"The Emperor has given us seven days, so I will be assisting in the search. We do not want to reach that deadline, Aife." He passed me a meaningful look. "You don't want to meet that deadline."

Zelu dropped his brows before turning on his heel and stocking away.

After much drinking and more bribing from the nobles, the crowd was sparse and distracted enough that I could slip out unseen. Titaia and Katrina had left a few hours earlier, Katrina feigning illness, which was not that hard to believe, given her state. She showed up for breakfast this morning with a hand sized bruise around her throat that she attempted to cover with makeup. Titaia physically restrained herself from Brock by grabbing fistfuls of her skirts, breathing so deeply I thought she might pass out for exertion. I was able to corner her and held her in my arms while she told me Brock had gotten into his argument with his father and decided to take it out on Katrina. He choked her to the point of unconsciousness, sending one of his Guards to wake Titaia to retrieve Katrina.

I spent the rest of the day imagining the several types of fun I could have with him. I could drag it out for days. We have all kinds of devices in Parnitus;

suspension tables, racks, I could sever his Achilles heel and one I had yet to use, a large metal coffin that conducted heat very well and was full of sharp nails. I never asked Zelu where he found it, and while I am lucky to have never had to endure it, I would love to test its efficiency.

The hallways were clear as I made my way down to Katrina's room, only passing a few servants and they were not as interested in where I was going as they were in giving me as wide a berth as possible. When turned the corner towards Katrina's room, whispered voices reached my ears and I slid back around the corner and leaned against the wall.

I watched the tall form of Gregorovich drop a strand of Titaia's hair. "Maybe next time, pet." He turned and sauntered down the hall.

"Are you alright?" I asked, approaching Titaia who had dropped back against the wall holding her chest. She jumped, looking alarmed, before relief colored her face when she saw it was me.

"Aife." Goosebumps pebbled my arms at my name from her mouth. It always sounded so good coming from her. "Gregorovich...."

Titaia walked into me and wrapped her arms around my waist. "Let's go inside."

We closed the door to Katrina's room, and I grabbed Titaia's hand, leading her to an ugly flower chair that sat before the roaring fireplace. The bathroom door was closed and the sound of water was just audible. I knelt before her, bracing my hands on her thighs.

"Are you alright?" I asked.

"He has been so relentless these last few months." She tried to smile, but it faltered. "He has never shown any interest or even acknowledged my existence until recently and honestly, it's terrifying." Titaia leaned back and a glass of brown liquid appeared on the arm of the chair.

"I have learned how to woo a female," I murmured, kissing her knee. It trembled beneath my lips, and she inhaled softly.

"Is that what you are doing? Wooing me?" Titaia smiled and took a long sip before offering it to me.

I sat up on my knees, leaning over her legs, staring into her eyes. The real color burned through the hazel and sparked with desire as she placed the glass to my lips and tilted. The liquor slid down my throat in a delicious burn. Her lips parted as she pulled it away, her eyes tracking my tongue as it traced my lower lip.

"Is it working?" I whispered.

"Depends on who you stole it from."

I placed a hand on my chest in mock offense. "I would never steal, my dear Princess."

"Ugh, don't call me that." Titaia rolled her eyes, her smile fading. "I am scared. After ten years, I am putting all of my trust into a head in a fireplace."

Before I could answer, the bathroom door banged open and Katrina stepped into the room, pointing to Titaia.

"I want…" another glass and a large decanter full of whisky appeared on the small table that sat between the two horrific cushioned chairs. Honestly, who picked out this décor?

Katrina smiled before collapsing into the empty seat pouring herself a drink.

"Sometimes I forget how wonderful magic is." Katrina threw back her drink and poured another. Titaia nodded slowly in agreement. Her eyes focused on my fingers as they found their way to the slit in her skirt that tortured me all night. Her skin was smooth, and the softness just begged for my touch. The softness of her is such a contrast to the rough scar lined skin of mine.

"Excuse me, but I would rather not watch my future Queen get finger fucked before we meet with the Seers." My head snapped to Katrina at her words and her eyes flicked between my hands and my face, an eyebrow raised in warning.

"Are you saying, Duchess, that you would be willing to watch in other circumstances?" The leg under my hand tensed and I chuckled. "I am not saying we oblige her, little minx. Just a question."

"You are intolerable," Katrina said with a wave. "The Seers might be unsettled once they see you, especially before I can tell them what's going on."

"Shouldn't they be able to, I don't know, see us?" I knew that was not necessarily how it worked. Joyce had explained it to me hundreds of times. But these are supposed to be the greatest Seers, the ones presumed to save Fursomerra.

"When it comes to Elle, they cannot see anything. For some reason she is blocked from their sight."

The more I listened to and watched Katrina, the more I felt like a fool for not suspecting her as the spy in the first place. I chewed on my lips; I do not think Zelu would make the same mistake.

"Are you going to make us hide?" Titaia asked. I perched on the arm of her chair and grabbed the glass from her.

"I think maybe if you stand out of sight when they arrive until I can explain. Which should be anytime now. They are pretty punctual for old biddies."

I snorted.

"Just stand over by the fireplace." Katrina set the glass down and waved us away, her jaw tight. I know her tension matched mine.

I stood, holding my hand out to Titaia, who took it. I placed her against the wooden mantle, angling myself so we could both see the fire without being seen. The only sound for the next few seconds was of wood crackling and our breathing.

Titaia stared at the wall on the other side of the room, her eyes glazed with thought, her thumb moving absentmindedly across mine. It was a calming effect that drew my mind to my goals after this conversation. I would make my way back to Parnitus with the Emperor to keep suspicions at bay but once there I would get Joyce there somewhere safe and then I was coming back to Titaia.

As surprising as it had been to find out about Katrina's dalliance with the Seers, I was even more surprised about Titaia. There was something regal about her, but she never struck me as Royalty. There was no comparison to the other Royals I met. I had assumed she adapted to her life as a lady-in-waiting and molded into the role, taking on a casual grace and refinement for her position.

The more I thought about our interactions, though, the more it made sense. Not her position with Katrina, or her years of training in combat, but the desire she had to protect people, people that were not within her reign. That could have stemmed from the royalty within her, but the difference was clear. Most royals would fight with words and money, Titaia fought with blades and bravery.

Her face was pale when her hazel eyes met mine. I reached out and brushed my knuckles against the soft skin of her cheek. A small whistle from the fire and a scoff and shuffle let me know that she did not enjoy my attempt at heroics as I pinned her behind me.

We watched as the flames licked higher in the hearth and the fire took turned a shocking blue. Katrina's back was stiff as her gaze flicked to Titaia, then away again. The flames parted, and a face appeared, surrounded by blue wisping smoke.

"Good evening, Katrin." The voice sounded like the very flames it appeared out of, raspy and commanding. The female was weathered with age, but her eyes were alive and bright blue. Making her seem years younger.

"Gunnuti," Katrina's voice was casual as she crossed her legs.

"We know you're there," Gunnuti said and Titaia tensed. I looked over to Katrina, who had a small smile on her face. "Come out assassin."

Seer indeed.

I cut a look to Titaia, telling her to stay put, and she glared back but made no attempt to move as I walked towards the fire, setting myself in the chair next to Katrina.

"Good evening, Gunnuti." I placed an ankle over a knee and sat back, glass in my hand. I poured some more whisky into it and used every ounce of my self-control to not look over at Titaia, whose eyes were like a brand on the side of my face.

"Care to explain Katrina?" Gunnuti looked between us, her face unreadable, but that haughty Seerness that Joyce possessed was mimicked. It must be a Seer thing. Tegan had the same look on her face, one of knowing too much.

"Aife is one of us..."

"This I know. Our sister Joyce has told us all about the assassin. Yes, dear. Our sister has spoken highly of you, and we know what you have done for us. Angus was all in a tizzy when he arrived." I rolled my eyes.

The idiot. "He wears his scar like a badge of honor, and still has not shut up about almost besting you."

"I should have just killed him," I grunted, and Gunnuti chuckled.

"Yes, well. Even if he did not come close, it seems that neither of you have done good at hiding your loyalty." I clenched my tongue hard to fight the urge to argue. I had no loyalty to anyone but Joyce. And now Titaia.

"We actually have a mutual friend who introduced us," Katrina said.

Gunnuti tilted her head, which was an odd movement for something with no neck.

Or body.

You know, floating head and all.

My mind drifted back to a Wraith I had been assigned to a few months ago. Her head looked similar to the Seer's when I sliced it off her body, but covered in black smoke and bright red flames. She also was not speaking much...sometimes I miss the quiet.

"Who? Why do I not..." she trailed off. "Did you find the Princess?"

"I prefer Titaia, thank you." Titaia stepped over to my chair and took my previous position perched on the arm of the chair. I could feel the small trembles that wreaked her body. I wanted to touch her, to pull her into me, but she had the strength to stand alone.

Gunnuti stared, and Titaia shifted uncomfortably under the harsh gaze of those bright blue eyes.

That or the headlessness.

"I apologize, I just. I never expected." Gunnuti glared at Katrina. "How long?"

To her credit, Katrina did not balk or apologize. "We escaped Galvidore together. I have known who she was the entire time."

"Why didn't you say anything? We could..."

"Could what?" Titaia challenged. "Katrina was quiet at my request, and we had been here long before you recruited her."

"We can discuss this when she is safely out of the Palace and far from Austiria and Parnitus lands. For now, we need to get her out of there," I said, before this turned into an unnecessary argument.

CHAPTER 27
TITAIA

"Goddess, Ti," Katrina gasped, falling to the ground again. I dropped my stance and offered my hand to her. It had been two days since we had talked to Gunnuti, and I found myself surprisingly calm about the entire situation.

Whether it was because I would finally get out of this hellish place or because I was going to be with Katrina and Aife. Aife had left for an 'assignment', as she called it.

"I will be gone for a few days, but when I get back, we will discuss how to keep you and Katrina safe until we can get you two out of here." Aife said as she tucked a strand of hair behind my ear.

Only certain words broke through the fuzz she created in my mind. Her mouth was so close to mine that comprehension seemed a farfetched idea. I think I nodded, or I might have said something, I am not sure. The leisurely confidence and allure that surrounded her had completely fogged the world around me.

Her answering chuckle sent goosebumps across my arms. "I'll be back soon." Soft lips pressed against mine. Her kiss was insistent and deliciously seductive. I might have tossed her to the floor and ripped off her clothes, had Katrina not been a few feet away.

Kissing her was like waking up from a long sleep to find all of your dreams and wishes had been answered. Her long fingers wrapped around my neck, tangling in the braid that hung down my back.

I pressed my body against hers, and her groan echoed down to my toes.

"If you start having sex right now, I'm going to be very upset." Katrina's voice cut across the fog in my brain, but instead of pulling back, Aife's arm curled around my waist and lifted me off the ground.

I giggled into her mouth and felt the smile. Out of everything I expected from Aife, affection was the last on my mind. However, every day she showed a little more.

Aife kissed me before lowering me to my toes, her hands still holding me tightly against her. I could feel the hard lines of her body, and the sensation sent tingles straight to my core.

"Please be safe," I said when we finally parted.

After she left Katrina made fun of me for a solid ten minutes before I attacked her, using everything Aife had taught me to my advantage, effectively keeping my mind away from what she was on her way to do. I know it is not her that picks the assignments she receives; it is not her who actively seeks missions and people to kill. But it is still extremely difficult to come to terms with the female who kisses me as if I am her reason for breathing, being the same one who has killed dozens of people.

I had just used one of her ass dropping moves and now Katrina was sprawled on the floor, ignoring my proffered hand.

"I think I might be dead," Katrina grunted. I laughed, dropping down next to her, the uneven stone floor surprisingly comfortable and cool on my tight muscles. We were quiet as we tried to calm our breathing and erratic heartbeats. The sun finally peaked over the horizon in the early hour, and I knew we needed to head back to get ready for this summons with the Quinque. With any luck, I would be able to attend as well.

Now that we are going to be leaving, I wanted more information; I needed more information. Everything I learned would only help when we escaped, help the Revolucija and the Seers. And I guess...me.

"Did Brock tell you what this meeting is about?" I asked, breaking the silence.

"I don't think he even knows," she sighed, slapping her palms on the floor and slowly climbing to her feet. I followed her lead and stood, wiping my back. The sun was over the horizon when we descended the stairs and made our way back to the Palace. "There is no part of me that's sad to leave this place, but I am going to miss how beautiful it is." Orange rays drifted over the limestone walls, giving an ethereal glow. The black roof and statues reflecting the light, sending it back into the sky. It was a stunning view.

"I don't think I'll miss anything about this place," I responded, running my fingers through my sweaty, damp, and tangled hair. "I am relieved you will never have to marry that pretentious male, though."

Katrina sighed, threading her arm through mine. "Definitely. I will just have to find a new rich male to convince to take my hand," she added.

"Duchess Katrina, Maiden Elle." The Guard said as we walked into the Palace.

I rolled my eyes. "I'm sure it's going to be so difficult for you."

"If only we could all be as lucky as you, just walk into a room and the most dangerous creature possible picks you for their own."

"I belong to no one but myself," I retorted, my cheeks flushing at her words.

Katrina snorted. "Yes, your Majesty." Being inside these walls made it impossible to swat her, and she knew it. "I just hope I'm lucky enough to find someone who looks at me the way she looks at you."

The blush was a permanent color of my skin, I am sure of it. There is no denying that Aife looks at me in a way that makes me feel like I was the sole focus of her attention. I knew one person who looked at Katrina that way. My brother, Titus.

Getting Katrina ready for any affair was a chore, which tripled when Gregorovich was present. I have reached the point that I am convinced it has nothing to do with him taking notice and everything to do with pissing Brock off. Which is why I shoved her into a tight emerald dress, which complimented her red hair beautifully. Then tightened the corset until her breasts touched her chin. Her hair coiled down her back, half of it in a bun with an emerald bow tying it up. Of course, with as much work as it took to get her ready, we were obviously going to be late, but Katrina walked as if she had no care in the world. I wondered if she leaned that apathetic strut from Aife.

I followed her across the wood floor, my heels clanking. Ever since Gregorovich had taken an interest in me, trepidation flooded my system and I wanted to flee. Taking deep breaths, I moved in front of her and grabbed the golden handle opening it, the murmur within the room died and Katrina threw her shoulders back picked her head up and walked in. It was one of the smaller Council chambers in Heptus wing, used when he wanted more privacy than normal. Anxiety gave way to curiosity as I sidled into the room standing along the wall, noticing that it was just the six and their direct servants. Phoebe stood flush with the wall behind Alhma, I gave her a small smile and her fingers shook when she raised them in a wave.

"Fiancée," Brock growled, standing to pull Katrina's chair out.

"Apologies for my lateness," Katrina said, ignoring the threat in his words, and glided across the room to the chair. It was a small circular table Gregorovich and Heptus at opposite ends, Heptus between Brock and Alhma, Zelu between Alhma and Josephine and Gregorovich was between Josephine and Katrina. The room was dark but comfortable, with black walls with wooden accents.

"No need." Heptus waved a hand before turning back to Gregorovich, who looked positively thrilled to have a bust filled Katrina next to him. "You sent the assassin to Baron?"

Josephine nodded, the corner of her lip turning up. "Left this morning, your Majesty. She seemed extremely excited to question him," she said.

Heptus chuckled. "Hopefully she gets creative. Did you tell her to drag it out?"

"Oh yes, I told her to make it as painful as possible. Deter any of the other Nobles from thinking their lives will be better if they join the Revolucija. I told her we want Revolucija associated with pain and death." Josephine said.

I remember Aife and Baron's interaction from the welcoming party. It seems the threat that she had interjected was not a lie. I thought back to what she had said to him; she made it seem like she heard something that he might not have wanted her to know. I wonder if that is why they sent her, if she shared whatever she heard with Zelu. As much as I do not like Baron, I never considered his death.

"Our little elf is quite versed in the art of pain, causing and taking." Gregorovich's amused voice made the hair on the back of my neck stand on end. There was an amused chuckle echoed around the table.

"I would not like to be the one on the end of that blade," Katrina murmured. My stomach roiled at the casual conversation about murder.

"If she decides to use a blade," Gregorovich said with a laugh. A large crash jerked me back from the conversation and I looked over to see Phoebe scooping up shards of the wine glass she dropped. I was glad for the distraction and walked over to help Phoebe clean up the mess.

"Can... can you fill up their cups, please?" She held up a decanter full of wine.

"Whatever you need," I said with a smile, and grasped her hand that was holding the glasses, squeezing it. I rose and walked around, topping off the drinks as the discussion continued.

"We have a rough estimate of where Hespath is." Josephine took a large enough drink of her wine that I had to fill it up again. "We are looking south of Pearl City."

I moved towards Zelu. "No thank you," he said, waving me away, and I moved to Alhma.

"Why do you think that?" Brock asked.

Josephine smirked, "Let us just say the Revolucija is not as impenetrable as they thought. They are unable to pinpoint exactly where it is location is, but they have significantly narrowed down our search."

"Don't move yet," Katrina muttered as I filled her glass. I stood amused as she guzzled the wine, handing me the cup to fill it up again.

Lush.

"Should we send reconnaissance to Asherana?" Brock asked.

"Already taken care of, dear Prince." Gregorovich plopped a grape into his mouth, his eyebrow raised seductively at me. "We sent Clayton to see what he could find."

Clayton came here during one of his travels last year. He was running an errand for Gregorovich and came into the Palace covered in so much blood and dirt it took the maids three days to get the floors clean again. I swear he is part giant, tall and bulky, large tree bark eyes, and a strangely attractive greenish hue to his skin.

Brock whistled appreciatively. "As impressed as I am by Aife, Clayton is a whole legion on his own."

"We keep only the best in our arsenal. We sent Daniella with him." Gregorovich said.

Heptus chuckled. "That little nymph. You will be lucky for him to return loyal to you still. She is a tricky one."

I assume Daniella is one of the dozens of Tributes that Gregorovich keeps prisoner in his household. They fill a large reason of why Alhma hates when Heptus visits Parnitus alone, his sexual appetite is just as insatiable as Gregorovich's. The glare she gave Heptus' let me know she was annotating Daniella's name for potential death in the future. She was not a forgiving female, especially when it came to her husband.

Heptus chuckled at Alhma and kissed her knuckles. "No need to fret, dear wife. You are my one and always."

"We also discovered a temple." Josephine said, causing Heptus' head to span back to her, her colorless eyes glowing with information. "To Malakai."

"Of all the false Gods to choose. Malakai? Why not Linx?" Brock grunted. Malakai, the God of Righteousness, the irony of Brock not understanding why Linx would not be chosen to be worshiped was almost enough to make me laugh. "Who was protecting it?"

"The Sirens," Josephine said.

"I want that temple destroyed, and every last Siren brought to Austiria, I want to remind them of who the one and only God is."

"I will join you in the teachings, father," Brock said, practically vibrating with excitement.

"Now." Gregorovich met the King's gaze, and deep understanding crossed their faces. The latter nodded and Gregorovich continued, "Two nights ago, Landreasken was burned to the ground by the Revolucija; Visreala, humans and children murdered in cold blood."

"How did I not know about this?" Zelu's minotaur form rippled beneath his fair skin, drawing taunt against his face. His already intimidating aura seemed to reach out and squeeze my throat. Zelu took a deep breath, pulling back his rage after noticing the servants lining the room lurch.

"Apologies, General," Gregorovich said placidly. "Heptus and I decided to keep it close hold until we found out what exactly happened, aside from us you are the first to know."

"What happened?" Katrina asked, her voice barely above a whisper.

"They slipped in like cowards in the middle of the night, took out the Knights guarding the upper city, and started killing everyone they crossed paths with."

"This is it," Alhma said. "The official declaration of war."

"Yes, my Queen it is," Gregorovich said.

"Are we ready?" Brock asked.

"Yes. We are," Heptus said with a dark chuckle that raised every alarm in me.

CHAPTER 28
AIFE

A few days after I returned from disposing of the pathetic fire stick Baron, I found myself heading towards the Knight's armory that sat deep within the Palace. Nerves made me chew my lips raw as I stomped down the stone steps.

Zelu made little progress with finding who the spy was. He narrowed it down to a Noble but not much else. His mind was on much larger matters currently. The Quinque was officially at war with the Revolucija. Titaia had told me what happened after I left.

The summer made the Palace unbearably hot and somehow even being deep beneath the ground did not help with the rising temperatures. It was almost Lughnasadh, which meant the heat was going to peak soon. I did not do well in the heat. I was made for the fall; I blame it on the elvish blood.

I was pleased to find the arms room empty save for one female who stood at the back of the room sharpening a blade. On the extensive list of things Austiria does better than Parnitus at the top are the weapons they forge, right before the whisky.

The room held rows and rows of bow and arrows, swords, daggers, axes with three sharpening centers and practice targets. This place was a dream, my dream. I cleared my throat, and the female jumped, tightening her grip on the hilt of the sword, and turned to face me with it aloft.

"Going to stab me?" Humor floated through my voice as she took me in with wide eyes. I walked into the room, touching the intricately carved handles of axes that lined one side of the walkway. The walls were white, and the floor was a beautiful mahogany that amplified my steps, and the metal heels of my boots echoed throughout the room.

"You scared me," she said, lowering the sword, but her fingers were tight enough on the hilt to turn her fingers white. She watched me, her brown eyes bright with suspicion. Not that I could blame her.

"I apologize," I said, picking up an ax. The handle was leather, the blade was double bitten, but even the side intended to be dull was sharp as could be. "I didn't mean to scare you. I thought everyone would be at breakfast."

She eyed the weapon I wielded. Her own hand was still tight on her sword. I inhaled deeply and the scent of ocean water tickled my nose. Armoras.

Water singer.

"I have seen you around, assassin. You have been asking a lot of questions." Her eyes betrayed her fear even as she fought to keep her voice was hard.

"What can I say? I am a curious Visreala." I kept my steps slow, not wanting to scare her, but knowing my aura said otherwise. I had seen her with Titaia before and they seemed like good friends. Although, good friends of Titaia does not mean good friends to me. Her hold on that sword told me she knew how to wield it, and I had rather not put myself in the precarious situation of underestimating someone, especially after Titaia showed me my ass when we first met. The female watched as I approached, her eyes wide and stance defensive.

A mouse watching a cat.

"I've seen the injuries caused by your curiosity."

I shrugged. "I hate being lied to." Before I found out Katrina was working with the Seers, it was my own life on the line. Even worse, knowing who it is now, I have to continue as normal, which includes the aggressive means of interrogation for which I am known.

"No one likes being lied to," she countered.

I smiled coldly. "Everyone doesn't have a violent streak." I leaned against the wall next to the grinding wheel, ax still in my hand, twirling it. I had no desire to hurt or intimidate her, but I had a reputation to keep, and anyone who walked in would think that is exactly what I was doing. "You have me at a disadvantage. You know who I am, but I do not know who you are."

She sneered. "Why? Do you like to know the names of the people you kill? Want to carve my name onto your chest with all your other scars?"

I clicked my tongue. "Well, that is not nice. I have seen you around with Elle. I thought you would be as welcoming as she has been to me."

"You know Elle?"

I lifted my shoulder and ran my finger along the top of the ax.

Her black hair was pulled back in a tight ponytail, her brown eyes pinned me. Her right eye twitched. Uncertainty turned to resolve, and she rolled her shoulders back, before saying, "I am in search of a merchant who is selling goods worthy of the King."

My blood froze, the words I heard months before being parroted back to me. "I have no goods worthy of a King, unless he would like fresh spirits." I whispered back.

She placed the sword on the table and moved over to a small bench in the corner of the room near the spear lined wall. I moved to stand before her and the feeling of being underwater dropped over me, hollowing out my ears and giving a small squeeze to my lungs. She had dropped a sound bubble of water. I glanced around to see a small ripple of water clinging in a tight circle around us. "That was quite the risk," I said.

"The Seers told me that someone completely unexpected would find me. I figured there was no one more unexpected than the assassin who kills at the whim of sociopaths," she said with a shrug.

"Yes. Nothing more unexpected." I tried to find the guilt or horror in meeting someone who had been directly affected by it. Armoras were Gregorovich's favorite to dispatch, especially when they got out of line in Galvidore. Indira stretched her legs in front of her, crossed her ankles, and placed her folded hands on her dress.

Waiting for me to speak.

"I apologize if I killed anyone you may have known…" I started, and she held a hand up.

"Fate decides punishment however she sees fit. We all have a role to play in righting our world. When it is time, you will get what you deserve."

Yes. Fate had a nasty plan for me.

The first time I spilled innocent blood, I knew I was going to suffer in the afterlife and every life I have taken since then has only tainted my soul further.

Moreti, the God of Death and the Underworld, was going to have the best time with me. Regardless of Joyce's opposing beliefs, I would make up for the pain I caused. Indira is an example of why I know there is no retribution for me, there is no purifying my soul.

"How did you get involved with all of this?" I asked.

"The Quinque is responsible for the destruction of my village, killing most of my family. It did not take long for the Seers to find me and invest in my ability." I angled my head. Water singers are a great asset, but not uncommon. "Words that are shared in secret don't remain that way. There's always a trace of conversations left."

"I don't understand." I said, my brow furrowed. She was talking in riddles like Joyce loved to do. I was never good at riddles.

"There's more truth to the walls have ears than you could possibly imagine." The water singer said.

"You talk to walls?"

She laughed; it was a loud echoing sound, like waves crashing on rocks. Surprisingly pleasant. "In a sense yes."

"Do they talk back?"

"More often than you'd believe."

I huffed out a laugh, definitely an asset to any leader or rebellion.

"Unfortunately, Queen Alhma become paranoid enough that she started casting protective circles that inhibited my abilities. I do not know if she realized someone was spying or was just that paranoid in someone finding out what they were planning. Which is when they..."

"Recruited someone else who wouldn't need those abilities to hear the conversations."

Ronaldo had mentioned that Alhma found a spell to keep conversations confidential. This must be the effect of that.

She nodded. "They asked me to keep an eye on her and protect her since she was able to get information that even the walls aren't privy to hearing anymore."

"Does the Duchess know that you are spying on her?" I closed my eyes. The sinking sensation in my gut battled with the constant names I called myself in my head. She had not even said the name of the spy and here I was babbling. Where the hell were the twenty years of training?

"I hope she doesn't trust you to keep all of her secrets."

I did not say anything, amateur.

"I am Indira."

I flipped the ax, clearing my throat, thankful for the reprieve. "Indira, you must have a plan, then?"

"Plan for what?"

I lifted a brow. Indira worked for the Seers, but it seemed she had no inkling of what was going on. "Alhma believes someone is passing secrets to the Seers. She shared that theory with Zelu, who then tasked me to find them."

Her mouth opened and closed, trepidation spreading on her face.

"I thought you were looking for someone else to..."

"I, I didn't, I didn't know." Tiny beads of sweat trickled from her hairline, and she dropped her head into her hands. "I did not know. Shit. Shit."

"Katrina can't die," I said. Titaia would not survive the loss of her best friend.

Head shaking, Indira pressed the heels of her palms into her eyes.

"The seers told me she knows the Princess." Her eyes were painful when they met mine. A shimmer of blue crested behind the brown. "Is that true?" she asked.

I had already put my foot in my mouth, and this could put Titaia in danger. At this point, though, I was desperate regardless of where this conversation went. Now no one else would hear.

I gave a sharp nod and her head dropped into her hands again with a groan. "I don't know how I missed this."

The urge to comfort her was overwhelming, and I felt disgusted with myself. I am not the comforting type; I cause the pain, I do not ease it. Titaia was making me soft. "Take a deep breath. We can figure this out."

"How the hell can we figure this out, assassin?" she snapped whilst glaring at me. The water bubble around us pulsed, causing the air to thin. This female was going to drown me. "We have to find someone willing to take the fall for her."

"Yes, we do." Was it the worst possible suggestion? Probably. Did I feel any remorse? Absolutely none. The truth of what I was looking for settled into her as she met my eyes. We needed someone to take the fall for Katrina, someone to sacrifice in her stead. If something happened to Katrina, Titaia would break. I would do anything to keep her alive.

"I will do it," she said, her voice breathless.

"Are you sure?"

"Do not pretend to care for my life, assassin. There is no one else. It is only a matter of time before they find out about me. I would rather die quickly than risk telling them anything, and I would rather to it at the hand of someone who is fighting for the future of Fursomerra."

I stared at her, her brown eyes resigned and solid. She was going to die for Titaia and Katrina. "You are right. We do not have time to find another way. I am sorry, regardless of what you think of me. I am not completely heartless."

Indira sighed, looking up to the ceiling, blinking back tears. I looked away, allowing her the vulnerability with some form of privacy.

"We all know the risk we take. I can die knowing my family would be proud of me." Taking a deep breath, Indira met my eyes, the golden flecks within hers bright. "Will you tell the Seers?"

"Of course."

She chewed her lip before saying, "I have a sister, Penelope. Six years ago, she was in Parnitus, but I know that at some point she left. Will you find her?"

Guilt clawed at me so deep I thought I might bleed. "I give you my word. Your sister will know what you died for." Setting the ax down, I grasped her forearm, before adding, "I will find her."

She met my eyes. "Tell me," she said. "Have I met her, the Phoenix?"

"Yes."

"Make sure they survive, Aife. Keep the Princess alive." At the use of my name, I thought guilt might buckle me.

"I swear."

CHAPTER 29
TITAIA

A month.

That is how long we had.

One month for Aife to get back to Parnitus, get Joyce to safety, and come back. Then, we go to Doumland, to the Revolucija. Katrina has been buzzing with excitement since Gunnuti laid out the plan. She was sending word to Doumland for them to prepare for our arrival. We would be meeting with Valkyrie from Hespath on the way, and they would take us to Doumland.

I tried to convince everyone that Katrina and I would be fine to navigate to the meeting place. Gunnuti and Aife insisted that we wait for Aife to escort us. Gunnuti argued that once we left, we would be two of the most hunted Visreala in the Realm, and it did not hurt to have a trained killer on our side.

Aside from finally getting the hell out of Austiria, meeting a Valkyrie is what has me the most excited. The Valkyrie had been almost eradicated from our history long before the war even started. My mother used to tell me stories about them, and I would pretend I was one of the warriors. Mother had one of the tailors in the city make me an outfit similar to what the Valkyries used to wear, and while my brother made fun of me, he would always play with Katrina and me.

Currently, we were in the lavishly decorated throne room as another party commenced. A celebration on behalf of Gregorovich, Zelu, and Josephine leaving in three days. Thank the Goddess. The room had been bedecked in gold silks with dancers on elevated marble slabs and seductive music. It felt like being in the Shadow District as Josephine danced with an overly excited local noble. I know that the departure had stressed Aife, and I had hardly seen her since the Lughnasadh celebration yesterday morning. She had been acting very odd when I saw her, refusing to meet my eye and giving me the briefest kiss when we parted. Katrina had been preoccupied with worrying about Zelu finding out about her.

I was watching Katrina giggle at something Gregorovich had said when the double doors at the back of the room flew open, hitting the walls hard enough to shake the room. The Guards jumped up and unsheathed their swords. Gasps and screams sounded as the pathway from the door to the dais cleared. Apparently, if someone were attacking, they would have clear access to the Quinque.

The top of a hood came into sight. Aife stalked down the room, her hands wrapped around a set of bindings at the end of which was Indira. My heart seized and fell to my stomach as her bleeding face came into view.

Heptus and Gregorovich watched Aife with rapt interest. Her face was cold and distant, the trained assassin making a disruptive appearance. Aife reached the first stair of the dais and yanked her arm around, tossing Indira to the ground. She hit it with a sickening thud. Priestess Josephine grimaced at Indira's bloody and bruised body and moved beside Gregorovich.

"I have found your traitor, Majesties." Aife's voice was cold, a deep sinister excitement spinning into her words.

She sounded nothing like the female I had come to know. Her shoulders thrown back and face feral with pleasure. She stared at the King, not bothering to bow or show the formal respect expected. General Zelu appeared next to her, his face blank as he looked down at Indira and back at Aife.

"This maid, Indira," she said and kicked into Indira's back, who had tried to push herself up on her arms, "has been passing information to the Seers since she arrived at the Palace."

"Is this true?" Heptus asked.

Indira spat and bared her blood red teeth. The blood landed at the feet of Heptus. "You pretenders will die. The heir of Fursomerra will rise in the...."

"Pretenders!" Heptus yelled. "You are a traitor to the crown. The one who will die is you!"

Indira's laugh was full of malice and hysteria and sent an icy chill down my back.

"Shut her up," Josephine hissed.

Aife glared at Josephine before stepping to the side and hit Indira so hard her face whipped around sending blood flying towards Katrina and I. Katrina stepped back with a squeal and Brock smirked at her before wrapping an arm around her waist and pulling her into him.

"So delicate," Brock growled in her ear. "You do know what the sight of blood does to me." His hand trailed down to her ass, and he pinched it.

"What do you think?" Gregorovich asked Josephine, whose eyes were glued on Indira. The air in the room

THROUGH THE EMBERS - VOLUME ONE   271

shifted, magic spearing through it. Josephine was attempting to look through Indira's memories. Katrina's hand grasped mine. Regardless, if Indira had been involved with the Revolucija or the Seers, it was obvious she was not the one they were looking for.

"She was taken from her family during the siege of Liladon," Josephine said. "What the assassin says is true. She is working for the Seers." Aife's head twitched, and Indira's face was twisted in agony as Josephine pushed further. "It also looks like she has a sister," Josephine looked over at Gregorovich, and continued, "within Parnitus."

Indira turned her swollen eyes to Aife to give her a nod so imperceptible that if I had not been watching intently, I would have missed it. "Penelope," Aife answered. "I will find her once we return."

Gregorovich chuckled, relaxing back on his throne. "Well, Zelu. Your assassin was the right thing for the job."

"She has proven very useful, Emperor," Zelu responded with a bow, his voice full of pride.

"Yes, well done assassin," Heptus growled. "Not bad for an elf. Now kill her."

"You want to kill her now, Heptus? What about information? What about what she knows?" Alhma argued.

"She knows nothing of importance," Josephine stated. "We know what she has passed to the Seers, and she has not had contact in a few weeks. Seems they abandoned her."

Indira scowled. Her eyes glazed over Katrina and me before reaching Brock, where she spat again.

Indira did this for us.

I looked at Aife who was staring at the blood. Her eyes flicked to mine before looking back at the thrones.

She had no emotion in them. She was a blank page of coldness and savagery.

"And why would we trust a whore like you?" Alhma sneered.

Katrina covered her snort of laughter with a cough and Brock's fingers tightened on her waist so tightly she gasped, grabbing his hand. Josephine's face turned bright red, but oddly, it looked to be in embarrassment.

"Come now, wife," Heptus chuckled, walking around to kiss the side of her head. "No need for name-calling."

"I mean no disrespect, your Majesties," Josephine said with a bow and returned to her seat. The entire room stared at her. Never has Josephine acquiesced to an insult from the Alhma.

The Queen looked just as taken aback, but the King nodded.

"Kill her," he ordered again.

Aife pulled the dagger from the scabbard on her hip, flipping it between her fingers. Moving to stand directly behind Indira, Aife grabbed her chin and forced her head up, meeting Indira's eyes.

"Death to the pretenders!" Indira shouted, before, in one swift movement, Aife shoved the blade into the base of her throat severing her spinal cord and she fell over.

Dead.

Aife forced Indira to watch her, not for the thrill of the kill, which is undoubtedly what the Quinque thought. But to have one set of eyes that knew who she was, and what she was dying for.

She killed my friend.

My friend who was looking to save her sister, to help bring down the Quinque in any way she could. My friend kept me from trouble.

Aife wiped her blade off Indira's dress and put it back in the scabbard before bowing.

My friend's body was dragged out by guards. Then the party started again, the spot of blood the only indication that Indira had been killed. I looked up to see Aife talking to Zelu across the room.

My lips tingled and bile sat in my throat as she deliberately avoided looking at me. She was an assassin, a killer, and somehow a savior. My savior. Katrina's savior.

I know why Aife did this. Deep in my bones, I knew that this was the only choice she thought she had. But that was my friend. And she had killed her without hesitation, without remorse.

We had reached Katrina's room before I realized we were moving, and when we got there, I ran to the toilet and got sick. Over, over, and over. Hands rubbed soothing circles on my back as I emptied the contents of my stomach repeatedly.

Katrina did not know Indira, not in the way I had.

"She saved me," Katrina said, more to herself. I realized then that I was sobbing. Katrina pulled me towards the basin, holding my hair back as I splashed icy water on my face and rinsed my mouth out. When I was done, she sat me on the couch in her room and took the spot next to me. "Aife and Indira, they did it for us. They saved us. You must understand why she did it, why they both did."

"It was so easy. So easy to take the life of my friend," I croaked. My throat was dry and hurt.

Katrina pulled me onto her shoulder as I started crying again. Aife has killed before, I knew that she was an assassin, it was her job.

There was no peace that I could make with it, it was not something I could accept. But I was able to see around it. It is not what defined her, not who I saw her as. There is always a price in taking a life, whether it be sanity, morality, or bits of your own soul. There is always a cost. Aife adjusted herself to live with what she does, continuously told me that there was no saving her.

"You know her, Elle. You know who she is, how she feels about you. She had to make it believable, for all our sakes, Indira knew as well. Anything else would have been suspicious."

Aife gave Indira as honorable a death as possible. She did not draw it out as it would have been if it had been given by anyone else. But Indira had been beaten up. The proof was of her appearance in the room. Was that necessary? To beat her senseless.

There was a tentative knock at the door, and I started to shake.

Katrina opened the door enough for Aife to slide in. She threw her arms around Aife. "Thank you so much," she cried.

"You should thank Indira. She was willing to die to keep you safe." Aife's voice was docile.

I stared at the table, unable to look over at Aife, afraid I would see the monster.

"I will never forget her. We will honor her." Soft footsteps and the cushion beside me compressed as Katrina sat and Aife on her other side as if seeing the turmoil that burned within me.

Katrina was leaning back, and I met Aife's black eyes. Full of sorrow, of guilt, and a bit of fear.

"I am sorry, Titaia," Aife said, the whites of her eyes pink with unshed tears.

I swallowed, and it felt like sand lining my mouth and throat. "I do not know how to feel. I do not know how to deal with any of this," I said.

"There is nothing that I can say to make up for what I did, for what you had to witness. An apology is not enough, but it is all I have." I could hear the remorse and sincerity in Aife's voice. I chewed my lips.

"How did you know Indira?" Katrina asked.

"I met her in the armory a few days ago. She told me that she was protecting you, Katrina. The Seers told her you know where the Phoenix was and to keep you safe."

Me, to keep me safe.

The Phoenix. The supposed Princess. The coward who allowed everyone to die in her pathetic name.

"I did not know. She had never spoken to me. I did not really know her at all. I wonder if that is why she befriended Elle." Katrina said.

"She was my friend long before you started with them." The bitterness of my words tasted sour on my tongue.

"I never wanted anything like this to happen," Aife said. "After we met and talked, I promised her it would be me who did it. If it were someone else, they would have dragged it out to make her suffer. I gave her a quick death. She did not feel any pain."

I scoffed. "How could you possibly know that?"

"I have been doing this for a long time. I know how to make it quick and painless."

"Yes, because you're so good at your fucking job," I spat and regretted the words as soon as they came out. Aife's eyes hardened.

"Yes, I am. I never tried to convince you otherwise. I never wanted you to believe any different because it is who I am. I was ruthless because hesitation for me means failure, and failure means death. Indira would not have been alone in her grave."

Katrina was barely breathing beside me.

"I know who you are. You never apologize for taking mothers and fathers from children, never regret taking siblings or friends." My anger was poison, and the only antidote was spewing it on her. "You take the lives of others to save your own skin. You can pretend that you do not fear death and that you care, but I know the truth. You are just as much of a monster as you claimed."

Utter silence filled my head. My words settling between us like a mile thick wall.

Aife's voice was cold, her eyes like jagged pieces of obsidian as she said, "I told you that I would protect you. I am sorry if the way I do that does not fit into the picture you made of me. But I meant what I said. I will do anything to protect you, Titaia."

"Why?" I seethed. My blood was fire, my ears were ringing, and all I wanted to do was cause pain. Aife stood and walked towards the door. Pulling her cloak close around her, she grabbed the handle.

"Gregorovich decided to leave tomorrow. Heptus and Alhma are going to join us." Her eyes met mine, inviting me to see the soul she offered, and white-hot shame trickled down my spineless back. "I will be back in a month. Be ready."

With one last glance at Katrina, she walked out the door, closing it softly behind her.

CHAPTER 30
AIFE

The last time I truly cried was the day I was the one and only time I was captured and given a majority of the scars that mar my body.

I did not see Titaia when I left Austiria, but Katrina had hugged me so tight she nearly crushed my ribs. She told me to be safe, she would see me soon, and would protect the stubborn ass female.

After the long ride back to Parnitus, where the Queen told me, 'I have always wondered what it would be like to be with an elf.' It took me three days to face Joyce. I had the feeling she never sought me out, knowing I needed the time. On the third day when I saw her friendly brown eyes, I broke down and cried for hours, recounting what happened in the three months I was away.

I told her about Titaia and Katrina, the oath I swore to Titaia then how I ended up killing her friend. Joyce listened, offering words of encouragement, but otherwise she was the silent ear and comforting heart of my closest friend. I did not regret the decision to take

Indira's life, but Titaia's reaction had affected me so deeply that I found it hard to look at myself in the mirror anymore.

The two weeks following our return were filled with meetings that not even Zelu had been invited to. Heptus and Gregorovich locked themselves in studies and war rooms occasionally inviting Alhma and Josephine, whom had been spending an odd amount of time together. Heptus appeared jumpy and aggravated, but whenever in public, he was stoic and confident in their ability to win.

I stood in a corner of the meeting room, Heptus sorted through notes while we waited for Gregorovich. The way he was scribbling over papers made me think he blocked out everything else and forgot I was even there. He was seated at the head of a long table; maps lined the walls between bookshelves holding history books on war and drafts of books he had been writing to account his life as a God. He sent copies to Gregorovich who decided to keep them for sentimental value.

"She killed my general, Heptus!" Gregorovich screamed, as he stalked into the room and slammed his hands on the back of the chair next to Heptus, who had looked up in surprise.

Alhma and Josephine trailed after him, the former covered in blood, a sadistic grin spread on her face. The females were standing close together, the backs of their hands nearly brushing. They had always been at opposite ends of everything, especially when in the same room.

"He needed to die; he was a traitor." Alhma's voice was calm, even with her purple eyes wild.

"She speaks the truth, your Majesties," Josephine agreed, stepping between Alhma and Gregorovich.

Gregorovich's face turned purple with anger. "What is this? Are you siding with that crazy bit..."

"Take care of your next words, brother," Heptus growled. "I sympathize with your loss of Zelu as I found him a friend, but that is the Queen and my wife you speak of." Heptus' face flickered between the ethereal glow of the Sphinx and who he showed to the world.

"He was my friend Heptus," Gregorovich slumped in his chair, his voice breaking. "Our greatest asset. Our General."

"What do you have to say for yourself, Alhma?" I realized though Heptus calmed Gregorovich down, he was just as angry, if not more.

Alhma shrugged. "There is nothing else to explain, dear husband. Zelu was providing secrets to the Revolucija. We caught him mid-transit."

I gaped.

"It is true. He was just about to send our plans for the Pomulola Realm to his conspirators." Josephine said.

"Zelu would never betray us," Gregorovich said, and blanched.

"It's the ones who are closest to us that can hurt us the most, Emperor," Josephine said with a slight bow.

Something in this interaction had my body tense and on high alert. This was not the truth. I tried to steady my breathing as the compulsion to run pierced me like an arrow. I might have gained partiality with Heptus and Gregorovich by killing the would be spy, but the rumor about Zelu did me no favors. Heptus allowed me to live by the grace to Zelu, I doubt even if Gregorovich wanted me to stay I would be safe. The Kings hated elves and had always wanted me dead.

Pushing the brick wall behind me, I slid into the passage, closed it, and sprinted through the shadowed hall to Joyce's room.

Joyce did not jump or so much as shift when I burst in.

"Zelu is dead," she said before I opened my mouth.

"Alhma said he is a traitor, caught him passing information."

"He passed no transmission, Aife." Joyce's voice was strained. "He overheard a conversation he should not have."

The thundering in my ears worsened. "What did he hear?"

Joyce grabbed her chest and rubbed a soothing circle before giving a small laugh.

"Josephine told Alhma the truth." I raised a brow. "Come now, child. You do not see the family resemblance?"

"What? Family?" There were similarities between them, both were expert brooders, insanely bloodthirsty, and of course physical resemblances. With all that, though, I never expected them to actually be related. With the mutual hatred that was so well known, how could they be?

"They are sisters, Aife. Josephine is the eldest," Joyce was wheezing as she spoke. "Their mother left Josephine with Druids where she eventually found her way to Gregorovich's servitude specifically be by Alhma's side."

"Why kill Zelu?"

"Soror Augurium," Joyce said, as if it was the most obvious thing in the world.

"Soror Augurium, obviously, how could I possibly forget?" I rolled my eyes.

"It is a powerful type of sorcery that can only be found within sisters. So powerful that it can destroy any type of being. It is specific within twins and only female twins."

"Twins are real?" I had thought they were a myth told to spread the rumor that there is another, more powerful source of ancient magic.

Joyce nodded. "Their mother knew the danger of having twins. Not just the decimation they could cause, but because their powers together would make them hunted, so she decided to only keep one."

If it is true, together they could very well destroy Heptus or...

"Alhma was a great child. Her mother sent her to work with her family's clan of Druids, separate from where Josephine went. Seems that even with the distance and not having been with each other since birth, Josephine's natural darkness had spread to her sister. Alhma was drawn to dark influence and somehow found the way to avoid the cost of using dark magic. She was sent back to her mother when the Druids found her trying to sell her soul to Odvis, God of Death."

I shivered. "Does that mean they can kill Titaia?"

Joyce pursed her lips and nodded once, her face paling with the movement.

I reached over and grabbed her hand. "What is it?"

"I am going to die in three days, and I must be in Hespath before the last breath leaves my body or I will not have a rebirth."

I jerked back, feeling like I had been kicked in the stomach. My ears started to ring as I stared at her. She had said it with such certainty that it had brokered no room for argument.

"I... no."

"It is time, Aife. I am at peace with it. You will come to be as well."

"I'm not ready to lose you."

Joyce's shaky hand covered my own, and I cherished the feel of her smooth skin beneath my fingertips.

"I will never leave you, foolish elf."

"You're all I have." I hated the weakness in my voice, the way it cracked. Joyce was what kept me balanced. She was my constant.

"I cannot imagine why. You are such a joy to be around."

"We will get you there." I stood. "Get ready. We leave in an hour."

The path back to my room from Joyce's was long. Even though the halls were clear, it felt like a risk to be wandering around. I turned a corner and ran directly into Heptus and with one quick motion his arm was pressed into my throat, my back against the wall, my boots grazing the floor.

I relaxed my throat and body, releasing the pressure. He leaned into me, shoving his hairy arm deeper. Sometimes I forget how tall he is. Standing at well over seven feet, he kept lifting until I no longer touched the floor, and he was still tilted down to me.

"Zelu is dead," he growled, whisky and anger seeping through his pores. "Your death is going to be a great pleasure of mine, elf."

He spat in my face and dropped me back to the ground. Before I could react, his large fist sunk into my stomach and knocked the air from my lungs. Pain radiated up to my chest and down to my feet. My legs slipped, and I dropped to my hands and knees. Definitely leaving tonight. I coughed, blood sprouting from my mouth as he stomped away. His alcohol fueled stench lingering in the air.

Nausea clogged my throat as I pushed off the ground and stumbled the rest of the way to my room.

Fuck, that hurt. If he had been anyone else, I would have killed him immediately, but that male could have snapped my neck if I blinked wrong.

I closed the door and leaned against it, staring into the small space. The hole in the top corner of the ceiling that always dripped, the loose floorboard that held weapons and letters from Joyce, the cracked brick that allowed a sliver of sunlight to peak through. I grabbed my bag and started shoving twenty years' worth of pain, torture, and learning into it. I would never see this room again, this room that housed me since I was a child. Where I first met Joyce and she pulled me out of my self-pity and hatred and nursed me to be a somewhat functional member of society.

Strapping the bag to my back, I turned for one last look. It was a disgusting space that led to more sickness than one person should ever go through. But it had been my home, where I lost every piece of my innocence, where I had been patched up by healers more times than I could count. I had many firsts and lasts in this room, and I hope to never see it again. I slammed the door behind me and took the painting passage at the end of the hall to Joyce's room. When I got there, all she had done was move from the chair to the bed.

"Alright, Joyce. We have to go, help me with your cloak." Shuffling through her dressers I grabbed clothes, shoes, and bathing supplies before helping her don her cloak ignoring her apologies for not being ready.

"Do you…" she started, her voice croaky with exhaustion.

"Save your energy," I said, putting on her bag.

I wrapped my arm around Joyce's waist; she leaned heavily against me as we toed out into the hall. It was late enough that only those that desired silence and anonymity were out. Still, I decided that one of the passages would be the best route. I did not want to run into Heptus again.

"Aife," a harsh whisper reached my ears. I adjusted my grip on Joyce's waist as she stumbled, trying to keep up with my quick pace. "Aife," she said again.

"I can't talk, Emily." I said as we turned down the small stairway that led to the servant's entrance.

"Aife, just wait."

"We don't have time."

"I know, you stubborn elf. We're here to help." Emily snapped.

I paused, looking over my shoulder to see Emily carrying a basket and half a dozen people behind her.

"What's going on?" I asked, startled, as one of the males walked up and placed one arm behind Joyce's back and the other behind her knees, picking her up in a fluid motion. I pulled a dagger out and pressed it to his throat with a snarl.

"We are here to help you get out." Emily lowered my arm and dumped the contacts of another bag into my bag. They ushered us outside and when we emerged, I saw that Rain and another mare had been saddled, the mare holding a special saddle for Joyce. It looked like a short basket with blankets and pillows to keep her comfortable.

Taking the bags off my shoulders, two of the males loaded them onto Rain. A sense of gratitude overcame me, and I hugged Emily. Even though I spent my life in Parnitus I had not socialized aside from Joyce. It was a way to protect myself because I did not want to put myself into a situation where I had to kill a friend. I could not count how many times I had to assassinate someone from within these very walls.

I pulled back, and uttered, "Thank you."

Emily pushed on her tiptoes, pressing a chaste kiss to my lips. "It never would have worked out between us anyways. You would have broken my heart. Now hurry."

I jumped on Rain's back, grabbing the reins of the horse Joyce was on.

"Good luck." Voices followed us as we took off into the tree line.

"Told you she liked you," Joyce snorted.

CHAPTER 31
TITAIA

I let the scalding hot coffee burn my throat, soothing the relentless ache. After Aife left, I spent the days keeping myself busy, without the overbearing presence of the Quinque we all thought the palace would be rather peaceful again. With Prince Brock in charge, though, everyone seemed to be on edge. Waiting for the rage that swam beneath the surface to strike.

There was a charge that set my teeth on edge in the Palace. Katrina spent her time with Brock trying to glean information from him about anything he might know, which is proving to be not much. Gunnuti ensured continuously that Aife would be back. She had been in touch with Joyce and mentioned the old Seer confirmed as much. Which was surprisingly of little comfort.

My head was torn between anger at Aife for what she did, and anger at myself for letting her leave without saying goodbye. Because of whom she is, because of who I am, there is every chance I might never see her again. Either one of us could die.

I relaxed within the brothel. Madam Nebia walked around, greeting the room. It was Jesika's birthday and instead of the usual night out, she decided to throw a party. The normally bright house was covered with scarlet red and gold drapes, cutting out all light from the large bay windows. Gold chandeliers were turned crystal, tables were laden with food and drinks and platforms set up with dancers and a dance floor in the center of the room.

Dozens of Nobles were expected to frequent along with patrons and close friends of the females. I would not normally attend events like this since it is within the confines of Madam Nebia's walls. She had a rigid attitude that brokered for little fuckery and was able to keep the rabble out. Tonight, however, was a full moon and Nebia had expressed concern, especially with what was happening with the Revolucija. Word spread about Landreasken and Austiria had been abnormally quiet since. Discipline by the Knights increased, resulting in many Visreala being injured and human slaves killed.

I was dressed comfortably in a pair of emerald pants and a matching long tunic that was loose over the belt of blades at my waist. In my boots were another two sets of daggers, and hidden within my shirt was one more, just in case.

The party had been tame for the last two hours. Bodies gyrated against each other. On walls, couches and I swear I saw an ass cheek on the dance floor. The smell of sweat and sex filled the air, overpowering the aroma of my coffee.

I noted the movements of all twelve girls within the room, Jesika atop a platform in a ridiculously small bikini, her face bright. Succubus magic filled the air to the point of suffocation, and I shoved my nose closer to my cup. Madam Nebia had given me a tonic to help dull the lull of the draw. It worked for the most part. I still throbbed and my thoughts drifted to Aife, and her mouth and fingers more than I would ever admit aloud.

The way she kisses, full of a leisurely confidence and danger, was like a magnet in my mind. The feel of her body against mine was full of hard lines and a feminine softness that was at complete odds with her demeanor. I spent countless nights imagining what her body would feel like against me. If she would be gentle and caring or rough and fuck me into oblivion, I could not decide which would be better.

Her long fingers trailing down my bare skin digging into me, marking me, while her tongue caressed my mouth letting me know exactly how she would own every part of my body. How her hands would grasp my ass before moving to the front of me. I was perpetually soaked for her and I knew how satisfied she would be, that she would fuck me like she did everything in life. In no rush and enjoying every lick, every touch, every feel.

A shriek jolted me back, my body warm. I rubbed my thighs together, trying to contain the fever pulsing through me. Damn that elf. A giggle followed as Madam Nebia ran into the embrace of a tall, dark male.

I sighed and placed my cup down. I shook my arms, trying to rid the delicious memory of Aife and focus on the room around me. One, Jesika. Two, Amanda. Three, Yuma. Four, Kisinda. Five, Iorina. Six, Jila. Seven, Nika. Eight, Olivia. Nine, Rebeka...I stood on my tiptoes. Ten, Ornita. Eleven, Rugara. Twelve, Tristia. No, wait. Where is Rebeka? I walked through the hot room trying to spot bright pink hair.

"Rebeka?" I asked Kisinda, Yuma and Tristia who were dancing together in the middle of the floor.

Their glazed eyes met mine. Alcohol was not the only drug in rotation tonight, "dunno." Yuma said, her thick accent dragging with whatever was in her system.

"Tha' wa'." Tristia pointed towards the stairs, "Roda'po to'k ha'." Her words slurred so hard I could only make out sounds.

I turned toward the staircase, my body on high alert, warning bells ringing in my head. The situation was not out of the ordinary, but instinct was telling me to check. The feeling was going to nag me until I put eyes on her and got verbal confirmation that she was all right. That itchy feeling that something was wrong tickled down my spine as I took the steep stairs to the second floor. It was unusually quiet. As if I walked through a sound barrier that separated the sleeping quarters from the loud party downstairs.

Rebecka's room was the third door on the left of the hall. I placed my ear on the cool wood and listened. I heard nothing.

I grabbed one of my blades and I touched the door-knob, jerking back quickly with a curse.

The metal was scalding hot, my skin an angry red. I growled. Rebecka was a Succubus like all of the girls in this brothel. The only way the door would be hot is if someone else made it that way. An Igniris.

Aife and I shared our special hatred for them. They loved causing chaos. Where Teranomial's take a while to gather power from the earth, Igniris were able to gather fire from anything and they used that as a reason to state that their power, and lives, were greater than anyone else's. Not that great because they did not have the ability to create fire.

Taking a step back, I braced and kicked as hard as I could into the weakest part of the wood. Right by the knob. It crashed into the wall behind it; I froze at the threshold in horror.

The room was covered in blood. Bedsheets ripped haphazardly off the bed and were spotted in red. The nightstand in the corner was overturned, and the lamp shattered beside it. Pools of blood scattered around the floor and on the walls.

I stepped in attempting to avoid the blood, but it was everywhere. "Rebecka," I called, my grip tightening on the knife. "Rebecka?" I called into the silence again.

I had one job, one responsibility.

Keep the girls safe.

Guilt was led in my stomach as I moved to the washroom. The door was covered in bloody handprints. Taking a deep breath and moving as quietly as I could, I opened it. If he killed her, I would bleed him dry....

Soft, feminine crying reached me. Rebecka was standing leaning over the basin, her shoulders shaking. She was coated in scratches and blood, a body slumped in the tub.

"Rebecka," I whispered, placing a hand on her shoulder. "What happened?"

Her light brown eyes met mine in the mirror and I realized she was not crying, she was laughing.

"Asshole tried to kill me," she said, looking over to the tub. "I won." Her head fell back, and she laughed loud and maniacal. Tears streamed down her face and when I turned her to me, she buried her head in my shoulder and cried in earnest.

"I'm so sorry I wasn't here," I murmured, running my fingers through her pink hair, trying to comfort her even though I failed to keep her safe in the first place.

She just wrapped her arms around my waist and clung to me. This is exactly what Madam Nebia was afraid of, exactly what she knew would happen. It made my anger tick further and my resolve tighten. As terrified as I was to fight, it was the only way to protect the people.

My people.

To keep them safe and give the hope of a better future for them, fuck. I was going to have to put that damned crown on my head.

Goddess help me.

The next day word came of the King and Queen returning, and the Palace could not have survived a moment longer. The party ended quickly last night after Madam Nebia came upstairs and saw what happened. She took care of the body and tried to convince me that it was not my fault, that the only reason Rebecka was able to protect herself was because of the training I had given them. I tried to find comfort in that, but I could not rid the guilt.

When I returned to the Palace, I found Katrina in her room pacing.

The Queen killed General Zelu.

Something in Brock broke when he heard the news. His blood thirst took a turn for the worst. Within the eighteen hours since finding out, he had become volatile. Murdering four servants, including one of Heptus's favorite cooks, whom he killed over a stew that he tried to make everyone eat, anyway.

The younger children, Erin and the twins, Mathilda, and William, had been confined to their wing of the Palace. Locked off from the terror their eldest brother wrought.

Katrina had an ice pack in her eye and a limp in her gait. Her green dress was covered in rips and mud.

"Brock has lost his fucking mind," she said simply. "He threw another five servants into the stockade, demanding allegiance and loyalty, which they obviously gave right away. But he convinced himself that it was a lie, and they were going to betray him."

I gestured with wide eyes at her obvious injuries. Servants be damned. What happened to her?

"I made the mistake of stepping in to ask if I could do anything for him, which he immediately took as me initiating an uprising against him. He slapped and started kicking me. The Captain finally pulled him off me long enough so that I could get away." She shook her head exasperated, and continued, "He finally snapped. I always knew he would. I do not know how much longer I can do this. He has never been so..."

Katrina trailed off when I pulled her to a chair. I poured cleaning salve onto a cloth and started wiping the cuts on her arms. Katrina dropped her head back on the chair, feeling relieved as the cooling salve reduced the swelling and redness. Brock's love for Katrina had always bordered on obsession. He had violent outbursts that seemed to have gotten worse with time, but nothing like this. He had never outright beat her in front of others.

"Why did the death of Zelu affect him so much?"

"Well," I said, putting the salve down and wiping her arm with hot water. The cuts healed immediately, leaving puckered pink skin. Unfortunately, there was nothing I could do about the bruises. "Zelu helped train Brock. He was pretty close to him. Well, as close as anyone could be to Brock." I paused. "I think he might be afraid. Zelu betraying them means that there is no one he feels he can truly trust."

Katrina was watching me when I finally met her gaze.

The moss green illuminated in the firelight. "Everything is about to change," she said.

There was something in her words, in her eyes that made my pulse studder. "What happened?" I asked.

"Aife ran." Sadness and fear swam in her eyes.

My hand froze, blood pooled in my ears. "Ran?"

Aife ran. She ran. Did she run here? Was she planning to come back? Was she running away from us?

"Zelu was the only one keeping her alive there, even after she…" Katrina cleared her throat, then continued, "earned their favor. If she stayed, Heptus would have killed her before he came back or Gregorovich would have, even if he found her useful."

I walked to the basin and washed the salve off my hands.

"She took an old Seer with her."

"Joyce," I interrupted, turning to face her.

Katrina nodded. "They left two days ago. Gregorovich sent scouts to bring them back dead or alive. They have not returned, whether it is from failing and not having the guts to come back, or Aife killing them first."

I waited for the feeling of disgust at her taking another life after Indira, but all I could think was that she was still alive. I did not blame Aife for what she did. She protected Katrina. I would have done the same. I would have taken as many lives as I had to, to save my best friend and would have had no regrets or remorse.

"Do you think she will come back for us?" I asked, hearing the unease in my own voice. I had no doubt that we would be able to escape on our own, but there was that extra comfort that I had in knowing that Aife would be there with us. If I were honest with myself, I was terrified that she would never forgive me, and I do not think I deserve her forgiveness.

CHAPTER 32
AIFE

A pained groan roused me from sleep, it was still dark when I opened my eyes. Our fire still had small flames burning in it. I looked to where Joyce laid to see her holding her chest, her breathing dull and rasping.

I jumped up and packed, my nerves flayed. I had to get her to Hespath as quickly as I could. Joyce sat up and handed me the blankets she had been wrapped in. "Only a few more hours," I said, helping her up, her entire weight against me.

"That's good," she panted, as I hoisted her onto her horse. "I can hold on to a few more hours."

I grabbed the reins and jumped onto Rain, who reared before taking off. He could feel the urgency, my desperation, and Joyce's pain. She stirred every so often, giving me directions.

The sun peaked between the tree canopies burning through my black shirt and sweating body as we ran through the forest. I did not give myself the opportunity to think about why we were heading to Hespath, about what would happen once we got there. I just knew I had to get Joyce home today. I also tried not to think about Titaia and how we left things. How I left things, how I broke her heart. In nine days, I would be traveling back to Austiria to retrieve Titaia and Katrina. Although the recent circumstances would make it more difficult. Especially since I have killed three different groups Gregorovich had sent for me.

They were pathetic, really.

Like Zelu had not trained them at all.

They did not check their surroundings when they trampled through the forest like a herd of elephants. I did not even descend the tree for the first group or the second group that followed shortly after. The last group, I decided to get my hands a little dirty, a welcome distraction from my dying friend. Part of me was insulted that Gregorovich thought so poorly of my training that he imagined the dismal Knights he sent after me would be effective.

We reached an encapsulated batch of trees with a pond and double waterfall; flowers and plush grass lined the edge of the pond. The paths forked in a ridiculously disorienting way, and I had no idea where to go. Joyce having been quiet for the last hour of our ride, pushing my urgency higher.

I dismounted, walking over to my companion. "Joyce. You have to tell me where to go."

She sat up groggily and tried to pinpoint where we were, her eyes fogged and slightly crossed. "The water," she rasped.

"I see it. There's nothing here."

"Foolish elf."

"Dying, and you're still an old hag."

"Take me to the pond," she snapped.

I eased her off the horse, sliding an arm around her back and knees. I hoisted her up and took her to the water's edge. She pointed to a small gray rock, and I led her to it.

"Cut my thumb," she said. I hesitated, but she glared at me with impatience.

I grabbed a knife from my boot and after a breath, I pressed it into the pad of her thumb and a small bead of blood formed. Dropping it beneath the surface of the water, she groped before jerking her arm and lifting it out of the water.

The surface started to shimmer before it lifted in a swirling tornado. A bright light burst before turning into a set of translucent stairs that trailed up to the trees.

Joyce rolled onto her back and started gasping. "Through, go through."

Her face was pale, and she was covered in sweat. My heart tightened when I picked her up. She somehow felt lighter than moments before.

I clenched my teeth and looked at the stairs. Of course Seers would produce water stairs. Taking a deep breath, I picked up my booted foot and sprinted up the stairs. There was no room for hesitation anymore. The stairs would either hold me or I would be going for an extremely uncomfortable swim.

The sensation was odd, as if the water were pulling onto me but repealing me at the same time. I stayed dry and steady as I sprinted up the water stairs.

At the top was another waterfall, like a curtain. Joyce's breath became sparse. I took my lip between my teeth and stepped through it. We were met with a bright sun, chirping birds, and dozens of females and children standing in a half circle around the entrance. The children holding flowers stepped forward and gestured for me to put Joyce down. I watched in fascination as it curled towards her in an almost protective embrace.

I dropped to my knees and rubbed my hands along the grass beside her.

"Please, Joyce," I whispered; her breathing was imperceptible.

The group surrounding us moved in closer, sinking to their knees and putting their hands through the blades of grass and started singing. I did not know the language, but the timbre rose in pain, sorrow, joy, and happiness. Pain that I had never experienced before gripped me to suffocation as I watched the grass wrap around her body.

Then I heard it.

One last shutter of her heartbeat before it stilled. Flowers were placed around her, and I felt touches as if they were fingers on a breeze. I had lived my entire life in the darkness. Grew in it, thrived in it, loved it. The many different forms of darkness had made its way into my life over the years. But this one. This is the one that burns the heart of even the strongest of creatures.

The grass and flowers enveloped her body. I had the urge to rip it all away; but my body was not my own to move. I was held to the will of those touching me as the song peaked before crashing down. At least, what I could hear over the buzzing in my ears was the never-ending crescendo of high-pitched ringing.

"You saved her, Aife. She will be reborn." My eyes were heavy as I dragged them from the flower covered mound that was once Joyce to the female before me. I stared back at the earth, at my friend, the last of my family.

The woman who raised me. Kept me from breaking, from fully surrendering to the monster that clawed at me from within.

"This will not be the last of Joyce. That female is too stubborn." Blue eyes leveled with mine. "Let's get you cleaned up."

Gentle hands reached down, grabbing mine, and I loosened my hold on the grass, allowing myself to be lifted. Almost against my will, I dragged behind her, my steps moving from soft grass to a solid surface as we walked. Two lines formed on either side of our path, females and children standing with males and warriors.

I knew those leathers.

Valkyries.

The female led me further along the path to a cabin with a large red door. There was a small porch with a lounge chair in the front. A child ran by and yanked the door open as we approached. My throat burned and I could not form words of gratitude, the blur in my eyes distorting everything around me.

"Rain." The name was painful to say, like a blister erupted within my throat. I was pushed to the bed by invisible hands, and I dropped heavily, as if my heart really had been turned to stone.

"Rain will be retrieved. Now you rest. When you are ready, Chloe will bring you to the Council."

I did not argue. I did not speak. I could hardly breathe past the ball that settled in my throat and my heart. A squeeze on my shoulder, a shuffle, and I was enveloped in darkness. A darkness that seemed too bright for the darkness that settled within me. I placed my head onto the pillow, rolled on my side and cried until my eyes burned and sleep finally took me.

I do not know how long I slept; how much time passed. I vaguely recall the feeling of hands brushing my forehead. A soft breeze caressing my face is what made me open my eyes. I blinked away at the haze that threatened to lull me back into my slumber. The bed beneath me was warm and plush. A silk pillowcase rubbed at my face and a furry blanket covered my body.

My head throbbed, and my face hurt. With a groan, I sat up and threw my legs over the side; the warmth of the floor was a welcomed feeling.

I took in the room and noticed that aside from the main area I was in, there was a kitchen, a small living area, and a bathing room. The center of the floor held an ornate rug with a giant phoenix holding an eagle and a crow in each taloned foot. The furniture was beautifully crafted, not the mediocrity I thought there would be from a place cut off from society.

All the furniture bore the same symbol. The Phoenix with an eagle and crow in each claw. Symbol of the Revolucija. The walls were white, the ceiling high with exposed beams and lights strung across it. The small kitchen held limited counter space and a double burner oven.

A flood of emotion and pain brought back the reality of why I was there. A short knock broke my thoughts and as the door flew open, I was on my feet, dagger in hand, watching a Valkyrie stroll in.

I had been so out of it; I thought I had imagined it. But here one was, beautiful mixed gray and white leathers embroidered with winged horse stitched on the left breast. The top was sleeveless, solid white with braided gray leather wrapping around from front to back. The pants were white with a gray stripe down the side of each leg. The female had russet brown skin; her hair was a black afro that was adorned with a white headband with another winged horse matching her leathers. White tattoos covered most of her exposed skin, from forehead to. But what caught my eye was the feathered wings peaking over her shoulders. Wings that emitted their own light, shifting with every movement she made.

Her light brown eyes sparkled as she smiled, crossed a fist across her chest and leaning at the waist. "Assassin, I am Chloe."

She closed the distance between us in a few steps and extended her hand. I stared at it.

Joyce is dead.

"How long have I been asleep for?" It hurt to speak, and my voice was cracked and warned.

Her lips pursed. "Three days."

I stared at her, and she dropped her hand.

"If you did not wake today, Gunnuti was going to...well. I will let her tell you what she was going to do." She stepped back and pointed to the door beside the kitchen, and continued, "Freshen up, take all the time you need. I will let the counsel know you are ready."

She closed the door softly as she left. I went to the bathing room to find the tub already filled with steaming water. Goddess, sometimes I love magic.

My pants and tunic were dirty enough that I would never wear them again. I would potentially burn them, so I tossed them away as I undressed. I had sunk into the tub slowly in delight when hot water sizzled against my skin.

Joyce was gone. Had been gone for three days. I wonder if I missed her burial, or if what had happened when we got here was considered her burial. She had rarely spoken of her home, never mind the dangers of talking about Hespath. I think talking about it made her sad.

I do not think Gregorovich knew she had ever lived in Hespath. I lowered my head, allowing the heat and water to cover me. The ceiling rippled through the water. It was painted with a meadow, animals grazing and running about.

I stayed submerged until my mind was light with a lack of oxygen and the corners of my vision started to blacken. I sat up and ran my fingers through my hair. I grabbed the roots and tugged, reveling in the physical pain that distracted from the emotional.

Joyce was gone.

Gone. I thought she was indestructible. She had to be four hundred.

I got out of the tub and dried off with a fluffy tan towel. The softness felt like a brand of a false life, a life that I would be forced to continue without her.

When I emerged into the main room, I found clothing similar to my usual attire on the bed, along with the rest of my weapons. I changed and strode to the door, swinging it open to reveal Chloe, who was sitting on the lone chair. She smiled at me from the doorway.

"Much better! Let's go." I stepped down the three stairs and took pace next to her through the village. Again, I found myself awed by how normal this place seemed. Wood and brick houses lined the street. Children laughed and sang.

The sun had long since set by the time we started walking, but the sky was clear, and the stars were as bright as I had ever seen them. Joyce would never be able to see the stars again. I had been through so much physical pain; scars decorated my skin like a nagging memory. But the pain of losing Joyce, that felt like it seeped into my bones, into my being, pulsing deeper into me with every beat of my heart.

"Joyce was a wonderful person, and a fantastic seer," Chloe said. The houses parted into a large courtyard that forked in four directions, including the one we had come from. We headed right.

"Did you know her?" I asked, surprised.

Joyce left Hespath long before the war started. She had not stepped foot in Hespath in almost thirty years. It had been about twenty-five since she found herself captured by Gregorovich, the same age the Valkyrie looked.

"I have lived sixty-seven years," she laughed.

I forgot. Once a Valkyrie completed their training and Liturgy, earning their wings, their aging is slowed. I resisted the urge to stare at her wings as she led me along a pathway where flames were high in the sky, dancing. "She trained me before volunteering to go to Gregorovich."

"I didn't realize she was a willing participant in her capture." I did not stop the bitterness from my words. I had known Joyce most of my life, but really did not know the old hag at all.

"There are a lot of things you do not know, assassin." Chloe's voice was sympathetic, causing an oily path of shame to slide down my spine. "The Elders will help you fill in some of those gaps."

I stopped listening when I realized how large this place truly was. Hespath had always been described as a little village with barely enough to sustain itself. Running on female leadership and evil magic.

From what I could see, it was thriving. The houses were made of more than mud, like some slums within Parnitus and Austiria, the roads smooth and level and endless crops. I had never seen anything like it.

We made it through a thick tree line and approached about a dozen females sitting on tree stumps surrounding a bonfire. The fire was odd, translucent from the base up to the flames that reached for the stars.

"Blood fire," Chloe explained as we approached, pulling an apple out and rubbing it against her leg. "It's burned here for the last two centuries." Her bite was loud, and juice ran down her chin. "As long as the fire burns, a Phoenix lives."

The females rose as we approached one, I vaguely recognized, approached. It felt like ten years since our last interaction. Next to her was one I met when I arrived.

"Aife Amamion," the latter said, holding her arms out to me. I glanced at her hand before looking back at her face. Before I could react, she grabbed my elbow and yanked me towards her, her arms a steel cage around me.

I have no idea what it is with these old seers being strong as oxen. Her hug was solid, but warm and grandmotherly, like Joyce's had been. I did not want to be touched, but I felt myself leaning into her embrace before I pulled myself away sharply.

"I am High Priestess Eira. I believe you know Gunnuti." Gunnuti inclined her head. "Thank you for bringing our sister, because of you, Joyce took her last breath on this land and because of that, she will be reborn and live another long, albeit bossy, life."

Everyone chuckled, and I cocked my head.

"I am sure you have many questions," Eira said.

"You could say that," I huffed.

I followed her over to the fire, where names were exchanged, and more hands were proffered. I avoided all of their touch. Hugging Eira put me on edge. I am a Goddess damned assassin. I do not cry.

I focused on the fire. The flames danced around each other, pockets of it appeared to jump and spin to the music of the embers as it burned steady and strong.

Titaia would love this fire. The movement was so strong and solid, utterly beautiful. A crunch tore my eyes away from the fire and I saw everyone staring at me.

How. Uncomfortable. Chloe's lips twitched under another aggressive bite of her apple.

"Chloe said Joyce volunteered to join the war," I said. I would have screamed there were flying carriages and Heptus was in a kilt to get the attention off me. I was not used to it and decided immediately I did not like it.

"She was the bravest of us all, that Joyce. The true High Priestess and named me in her stead while she was gone." I sat at the stump she led me to. Everyone eased back onto their respective ones.

"She never talks about her home." I tried to swallow the guilt. I never really brought it up after the first time we briefly discussed it.

Joyce told me about the sunrise in the spring over a stream deep in the forest. How she would wake up ridiculously early every morning, hike the four miles to a large overhang of rocks and watch the sun rise. The sadness in her voice made me never ask again, but it was enough to pull me out of whatever hole I had dug myself in. The guilt I felt now though, from not asking her more questions, not begging for her to tell me more, was burrowing me deeper.

"Our sister spoke very fondly of you, Aife. She trusted you and knew you would bring her here when it was time. She never saw your future, but knew you would be invaluable in the fight." Eira said.

"I don't think I helped the right side of the war at all."

A few Seers chuckled and my eye twitched.

"That is not the one I speak of. You know the real fight is brewing between the false King and the rightful heir," Gunnuti responded.

"War has already been declared with the Revolucija."

"While those who are deep within do not know their fate to endure it, the time is coming where they will all be active participants," Gunnuti said, and I stared at her.

What the fuck?

"Soon Heptus, Gregorovich and their sightless followers will learn fear at the hands of the Phoenix and her assassin."

CHAPTER 33
TITAIA

I had not heard Aife in the days following her escape. Concern and anxiety crushed my spirit. I
thought that she might not come back for us, that she
might have been hurt or captured. Katrina reminded me that if she had been, Heptus and Gregorovich
would have shouted it across the lands.

Shouted that they had killed the famed assassin, and
what would happen if anyone else betrayed them? Instead, they were working to keep her escape a secret
and naturally, the Palace was buzzing with rumors.
Rumors that she escaped to join the Revolucija, that
she became a mercenary. The most ridiculous of which
is that she found a husband and settled down into the
sedentary life of a homemaker.

I rolled my eyes so hard I gave myself a headache.
I am not sure what about Aife ever screamed house-
wife type to them, but it was borderline amusing how
ridiculous they were being. There was also envy from
those inside and outside the Palace walls from those
that wished to shed the fear and control of Heptus.

But there was an evil festering in their anger and hatred that made my skin crawl. As if their own feelings
were being stoked with an unseen flame. Something
that threatened the reality that they might forget who
their actual enemies are and fight with Heptus and
Gregorovich instead of against them.

Heptus and Alhma were due back at any moment,
and not a day too soon. Brock's reign of terror had not
eased since Aife's escape. He seemed to fear that she
would show up here and kill him. He was paranoid
enough that he started killing in meetings and during
his outings in the city. Katrina worked to keep me in
his good graces and keep me out of the rooms he was
in. I wished I could do the same for her, but the one
time I tried stating she had another engagement, he
slapped me so hard my vision went blurry. My cheeks
are tender.

I was in Katrina's room, hanging up her dresses and
straightening up while she tried to keep Brock calm
for the arrival of his parents when the horn sounded
announcing their approach. Dread sunk down to my
toes. Ever since the night with Rebecka, trepidation
seemed to float just beneath my skin, as if my body
were preparing me for devastation.

I stroked the fire and threw in more wood, allowing
the room to warm up the chill that the first of October
brought before I straightened the skirt of my dress.
The deep purple lace reminded me of Aife's eyes, and
longing lodged in my throat like a boulder. I knew she
was not dead, but I also knew that she left with Joyce,
which means that while she might not be dead, she
might not be okay.

I stood next to the road with the rest of the Palace.
Katrina stood next to Brock feigning boredom, but I
could see the wrinkle in her chin. She was worried.

Katrina did what she could to keep Brock from turning more people into wall mounts and I could see how it exhausted her. The crowd stirred restlessly as carriages crossed to the front of the Palace and, as if the world took a breath, everything stilled. Even the birds and insects had gone silent.

Katrina leaned into Brock and kissed him on the cheek and the tension that had drawn his shoulders to his ears released. The carriages pulled around and the Captain dismounted his horse, opening the door. Heptus' laugh leaked out as he stepped down from the carriage, his hand firmly in Alhma's.

Her cheeks were pink with happiness, her dress askew. He had not even bothered to buckle his belt, wanting to send the message that they stood together even with the death of one of their own at their hands. Their eyes grazed over us, my heart faltering when the Queen's lingered on mine a little bit longer than was comfortable.

"Welcome back, father, mother," Brock greeted his siblings, mumbling a soft greeting beside him. They were quieter than I had ever seen them and all three had lost some color during the weeks their parents had been away. We bowed as they walked over to Katrina and the children with broad smiles on their faces.

"How has it been, my handsome son?" Alhma asked, her voice lifting with a happiness I had never heard. It burned my nerves.

"All is well, your Majesty," he said with a smirk. "We had a few issues, but I handled them."

Bodies shifted, the anger and frustration potent. Issues of his own making, and he handled them in the most unsatisfactory way imaginable. Heptus always had a temper and was not one to quell from murder, but he normally had an illusion of a reason. Brock killed the cook because he did not want lentils in the stew.

"Fantastic! Let us go in. Your mother and I have some business to attend." Heptus grabbed Alhma's ass, and she giggled, smacking his hand playfully.

I might be sick. The group wandered inside with the rest of the servants trailed but I detoured to the pond, lights sparkling off the water like fireflies.

Katrina and I had agreed that whether Aife came back for us or not, we would be leaving in six days as planned. We started gathering supplies; two fur lined sleeping bags, water, extra clothes, matches, and a compass. Even though we had no idea where we were heading.

Katrina was convinced Aife would return for us, well, me specifically, but I had doubts.

I insulted and hurt her.

She may have said she was coming back when she left, but she owed me absolutely nothing. I had given her absolutely nothing; I was nothing to her but the last female she kissed. Or maybe I was not.

We had not heard from Gunnuti since Zelu's death but the last we discussed, she said the date was set and Aife would be here to meet us. But a large piece of me knew she would not be here. She would not escort us out of this Palace, and I feared I might never see her again.

Our bag was kept in my room behind the dresser where a hole sat within the wall, along with two black cloaks and an arsenal of weapons. Katrina and I had upped our training in preparation, and she was an absolute natural with an ax. Which was thrilling, but also made me slightly uneasy.

How did I feel about my best friend swinging an ax around like a sociopath? It left me unnerved, but strangely proud. I taught her hand-to-hand skills as well, and I am not ashamed to say she knocked me on my ass. It made me question if I was supposed to be the one who defeated Heptus and Gregorovich or if she and her dainty hands were. I like to think her taking a two-hour soak after our session meant that I was the toughest in our duo, but I am humble enough to admit I might not be the biggest bad ass.

The moon was a few days being full, but the grounds were quiet. Even the city seemed darker than usual. The trees surrounding the pond had bloomed; the leaves danced in the gentle breeze.

I remember the last time Aife and I sat here by the ponds, a few days before Indira died. Her legs folded together, she stared at her long fingers twirling them together.

She told me about her mother and father. How her mother, Kishan, had fallen in love with her father, Morhorn, who was not an elf. The elves were about protecting their bloodlines; they were supposed to marry and procreate with their own kind. Kishan had been promised to another elf within Matrador, who held power not just within their home but all over the Realm. A well respected and loved elf named Galadrial. He was good in general. He knew his new wife had spent her wedding night with Morhorn and in the end, created Aife. He knew she did not love Galadrial. They had been good friends for years. He never touched Kishan without her consent and eventually she learned to love him as more than just a friend. Aife was convinced that if her mother met Galadrial before Morhorn, everything would have been different.

Aife did not know much about her father, just that they looked so much alike, her mother sometimes cried looking at her. And her broodiness was a trait of him.

Goddess, I missed her.

I turned from the pond and headed to the Palace, keeping my head down and trying to stray away from thoughts of her. Katrina and I would escape through an abandoned railroad. The farm that sat on the border between the city and the railroad held a trail that many Revolucija sympathizers took. That was our way out, hopefully undetected. From there we would head towards Pearl City, where all the Revolucija went. Not very secretive, but I did not have any say when it came to their fight, not yet at least.

I avoided the crowded halls that led to Katrina's chamber and found myself in the royal hallway. The normally dim lighting seemed darker, and the halls were completely abandoned. There were always Guards sentry, never leaving the Royals side. Although this was the first time in a long while that Heptus and Alhma sought each other's company, and their sexual activity was not something anyone wanted to be around.

Quickening my steps, I headed to a pathway hidden behind a painting of Heptus depicted as a God when I noticed a bright light shining from one of the King's studies. Every vessel within me screamed to avoid it, but against my will, my body moved towards it. I pressed against the wall, asking the stone to suck me into it. Straining my ears, I listened through the open door and heard ragged breathing and what sounded like cooing.

A muffled cry and soft laughs.

Peering through a crack in the door, I was greeted with a red haze, heat pressed against my eyes as I blinked past the burn. I could nearly see the entire room from my vantage point, and I regretted it immediately. There were three people in the room. Javier, the Queen's lover, was tied to a chair with a red cloth stuffed in his mouth. He was screaming through the cloth and black tears leaked down his face like tar.

Lace and red drapes covered the room, seeming to breathe as they fluttered in a nonexistent breeze. In the center of the room, an eleven-pointed symbol was painted black on the ground. Within the symbol were Heptus and Alhma.

A naked Heptus and Alhma.

His face was buried between her thighs, her back arched. She quivered when he drew back. Heptus stood and moved beyond my line of sight and brought a pregnant woman to where Alhma lay moaning in ecstasy. The pregnant woman's mouth was open in a scream, but there were no sounds. I could tell she was human. They moved differently from us, less lithe.

Alhma stood and unbound Javier, leading him to the center where Heptus had the human. He did not fight, but those tar-like tears kept sliding down his face, his head high and defiant. Heptus and Alhma grabbed twin blades and their bodies moved in a fluid dance.

Together, they slit the throats of Javier and the woman.

Together, they licked the blood that poured from the wounds.

Bodies fell, but instead of the blood pooling around them, it formed thin lines into a symbol that lay within the star, and it started to glow. Heptus and Alhma surrounded it, an abnormal amount of blood covering their bodies. A buzzing started in my ears, and kept me from hearing the words they spoke as they cut their palms and clasped them.

A surge of power ripped through the air, the force blowing my hair back and Heptus' face shifted. Bouncing between sphinx and normal, the unnatural beauty of both merging into one mask of almost Godlike grace. He flipped Alhma around, bent her over the chair, and he thrust himself within her with an animalistic rage.

I ran. Out of the wing and pushed through the endless bodies that appeared. I slammed Katrina's door behind me and leaned against it, dropping my head into my palms, pushing my eyes until stars exploded. That was a ritual, and that image is forever embedded into my brain and scarred into my retinas.

My ears rang, a distant shuffle just reaching them when hands grabbed my wrists and pulled me to a cushioned surface. I sat and tried to breathe through the nausea twisting in my stomach and pounding head. As if sensing it, a bucket appeared in front of me, and I hurled. My eyes watered, throat burned, I got sick over and over as Katrina held my hair. When it subsided and there was nothing left, the bucket disappeared, and I leaned into the feel of Katrina.

"What's going on Ti?" I met her eyes.

"Heptus and Alhma, I think they did a Power Shifting Ceremony."

"How did they even find that kind of magic? I thought it disappeared with the Old Goddesses." Her lips pursed. "Must be what they went to the Empire for."

"We have to leave Katrina." Hysteria took over my words as I shook her shoulders. "Tonight. We have to go tonight."

About the Author

Long time writer and full-time bourbon connoisseur Adriana Sargent creates character driven, emotion inducing, fantasy novels that are guaranteed to transport you to another world. Her characters, while clever and cunning, will enthral you with raw reactions, desperate decisions, and foolish fearlessness.

Adriana aspires to fulfil three goals in life: travel LGBTQ+ safe countries spanning the globe, author best-selling romance fantasies full-time, and retire near a body of water with her wife Jennifer and dog Benson.

In her spare time, you can find Adriana curled up with a good book, practicing tarot, or judging wine while binge watching Supernatural.

Excellent LGBTQ+ fiction by unique, wonderful authors.
Thrillers
Mystery
Romance
Young Adult
& More

Join our mailing list here for news, offers and free books!

Visit our website for more Spectrum Books
www.spectrum-books.com

Or find us on Instagram
@spectrumbookpublisher